THE LAWS OF MURDER

Also by Charles Finch

The Last Enchantments

An Old Betrayal

A Death in the Small Hours

A Burial at Sea

A Stranger in Mayfair

The Fleet Street Murders

The September Society

A Beautiful Blue Death

THE LAWS OF MURDER

Charles Finch

Minotaur Books ✻ New York

THE LAWS OF MURDER. Copyright © 2014 by Charles Finch. All rights reserved. Printed in the United States of America. For information, address St. Martin's Press, 175 Fifth Avenue, New York, N.Y. 10010.

www.minotaurbooks.com

Library of Congress Cataloging-in-Publication Data

Finch, Charles (Charles B.)
    The laws of murder : a Charles Lenox mystery / Charles Finch.—First edition.
        pages cm. — (Charles Lenox mysteries; 8)
    ISBN 978-1-250-05130-1 (hardcover)
    ISBN 978-1-4668-5788-9 (e-book)
    1. Lenox, Charles (Fictitious character)—Fiction.   2. Private investigators—England—London—Fiction.   3. Murder—Investigation—Fiction.   I. Title.
    PS3606.I526L39 2014
    813'.6—dc23

                                                            2014019883

Minotaur books may be purchased for educational, business, or promotional use. For information on bulk purchases, please contact the Macmillan Corporate and Premium Sales Department at 1-800-221-7945, extension 5442, or write to special markets@macmillan.com.

First Edition: November 2014

10 9 8 7 6 5 4 3 2 1

This book is dedicated with very great love to my nephew, Jamie,
who knows how special he is.

Acknowledgments

My work begins and ends with my family, and I hope they know how dearly I love them: Emily, Lucy, Annabel, Mom, Dad, Rosie, Isabelle, John, Henry, Julia, Dennis, Linda.

Professionally, I keep thanking the same people only to find myself falling even deeper into their debt—yet again, I owe so much to April Osborn, Sarah Melnyk, Courtney Sanks, Melissa Hastings, Andy Martin, John Morrone, Paul Hochman, Esther Bochner, and everyone else in the irregularly shaped but warm confines of the Flatiron Building.

My agent, Elisabeth Weed, is fantastically intelligent and enterprising. I feel lucky to work with her. Many books to come!

Some of the best ideas for this story—character names, historical wrinkles—came from the funny and brilliant community of readers at facebook.com/charlesfinchauthor. If you ever want to get in touch, come join me there, or e-mail me at signedfinch@gmail.com. I can't promise to reply to every message, but I always try.

Most important: this book wouldn't be in your hands if it weren't for the kindness, grace, and patience that Charlie Spicer showed me in unique circumstances last winter. Charlie, thank you for being such a steadfast friend.

THE LAWS OF MURDER

CHAPTER ONE

A late winter's night in London: the city hushed; the last revelers half an hour in their beds; a new snow softening every dull shade of gray and brown into angelic whiteness. For a quarter of an hour nobody passed down the narrow street. Such emptiness in this great capital seemed impossible, uncanny, and after a few moments of deep stillness the regular row of houses, covered so evenly by the snowfall, began to lose their shape and identity, to look as if they had nothing at all to do with mankind, but instead belonged to the outer edge of some low, lightless canyon upon a plain, in a distant and lonely and less civilized time.

Watching from the window of his unlit second-story perch across the way, Charles Lenox began to feel like an intruder upon the scene. In his experience there was a ten-minute period like this lying beyond every London midnight, though its actual time was unpredictable—after the last day had ended, before the next day had begun.

Just as his pocket watch softly chimed for five o'clock, however, the human stir returned to Chiltern Street. Abruptly a hunched figure in a dark coat strode past, heading south, and not long afterward the first fire of the day appeared in a low window, a small stubborn orange glow in the darkness. Soon another followed it, three houses down. Lenox wondered who the man had been, whether he was out especially late or especially early, whether his errand was one of mischief or mercy. He had been dressed respectably. A doctor, perhaps. Then again, perhaps not, for he hadn't been carrying the handled leather bag of that breed. A priest? A burglar? Few other professions called for a man to be awake at such an hour.

Of course, Lenox's was one of them. He was a private detective—lying in wait, at this moment, for a murderer.

Across the street, the light of another fire in its hearth. Now the day was very near beginning. Lenox thought of all the maids of London—his own included—who woke during the brutal chill of this hour to begin their chores, to light the fires. Then he thought of his wife, Lady Jane Lenox, and their young daughter, Sophia, asleep six streets away, and with a shiver pulled his coat tighter around him. The room where he had waited all night didn't have a fire, since of course he didn't want the light of one to draw attention to his presence here. What a queer way to make a living it was, detection. He smiled. It did make him happy. Even in moments of discomfort.

Not long before, his life had been very different. It was early January of the year 1876 now; only in October had he finally, after seven years of toil, given up his seat in Parliament. During the last ten months of that period he had been a Junior Lord of the Treasury, drawing a salary of nearly two thousand pounds a year (to some men a very great fortune indeed, in a city where one could live opulently on a tenth of that sum), and it had even been dangled before him that he might, with continued industry and luck, hope one day to compete for a very high office—indeed so high an office that one could scarcely utter its name without a feeling of awe. Even on a humbler level he might have remained useful in Parliament indefinitely, he knew. He had both an interest in and a talent for politics, and the discipline that success in that House required.

But during every hour of those seven years he had missed—well, had missed this, the previous work of his life, his vocation, detection, and while the evenings in Parliament had been comfortable, with their beer and chops and amicable companions, they had given him nothing like the thrill of this cold, wearying night. He was where he belonged again: doing what he was most suited to do. It might puzzle the members of his caste (for Lenox was a gentleman, and nearing the age of fifty more rapidly than he would have preferred), but this disreputable line of work gave him greater pleasure than all the authorities and appanages of Parliament ever could. He did not regret going into politics, having long wished to try his hand at the game of it; still less though did he regret leaving the game behind.

The first carriage of the morning passed down Chiltern Street. Nearly every house had a fire lit below stairs now, in the servants' quarters, and in one there was a second bright flicker of heat a story up, where Lenox could see that the head of the family had risen and was taking his early breakfast. A stockbroker, perhaps. They often had to be in the City by seven.

Another fire, and another.

Only one house remained dark. It was directly across the street from Lenox's window, and his gaze was focused steadily upon it. Surely the time was coming, he thought. When another carriage rolled down the street he followed its progress intently, before observing that there was a coat of arms on its door. That lost the vehicle his interest. He doubted that his quarry would arrive in such a conspicuous conveyance.

Another fire. Another carriage. The sky was growing faintly lighter, the absolute darkness of the sky lessening into a black lavender. Soon enough it would be daytime. Perhaps he had been wrong, he felt with a first hint of unease. He was out of practice, after all.

But then it came: an anonymous gig, a pair of thick-glassed oil lamps swinging from its hood, pulled steadily through the snow by a youthful gray horse.

It stopped a few houses shy of the one Lenox was observing, and a man stepped down from it, passing a few coins to its driver, who received them with a hand to the brim of his cap and then whipped the horse hard, in haste to be on his way to another fare. Or home, perhaps, who knew. Lenox's eyes were fixed on the person who had dismounted. Certainly it was he. Hughes: Hughes the blackmailer, Hughes the thief, above all Hughes the murderer.

He was a very small fellow, not more than an inch or two higher than five foot. He was well made, however, with a handsome face and brilliantly shining dark hair. He carried a cloth case with a hard handle.

Lenox reached up above his right shoulder and gave the taut white string there one hard, decisive pull. He let it quiver for a moment and then stilled it with his hand. His heart was in his throat as he watched the criminal, to see if the man would fly—but Hughes continued without any hesitation toward the last dim house in Chiltern Street, the one Lenox had been watching. When he was at the door he peered at the handle for a moment, then opened his case and chose two or three items from it. He set to work on the lock. In what seemed a breathtakingly short time, not more than four or five seconds, he had the door open. It was the skill of a great criminal. He put his tools away quickly and walked inside with quiet steps, closing the door behind him. The house remained dark.

Lenox stood and smiled. He counted fifteen seconds and then walked toward the door of the room in which he had been sitting most of the night, careful to avoid moving past the windows, where his silhouette might be seen. His joints ached. His eyes felt at once tired and alive with alertness. It wouldn't be more than a moment now.

It was frigidly cold down on the street, and he was thankful, as he stepped into the snow on the pavement, for his rather odd-looking brown cork-soled boots, which he had ordered specially because they kept out the damp. The rest of his dress was more formal, his daytime attire: a dark suit, pale shirt, dark tie, dark hat, the only gleam of brightness on his person coming from the silver of the watch chain that extended across his slender midsection. He lit a small cigar, put a hand in his pocket, and stood to watch, his curious hazel eyes trained across the street.

"Come along, quickly," he said to himself under his breath. Chiltern Street was growing busier. Two carriages passed in quick succession.

Then suddenly the brick house opposite—the one into which Hughes had slipped so quietly—burst from stillness into commotion. A dozen lamps blazed to life, and a dozen voices to match them. When Lenox heard an aggrieved shout, he smiled. It was done. Hughes was captured. He dropped his cigar into the snow, stamped it out with his foot, and then, looking up and down the street to make sure no more carriages were coming, stepped briskly across to witness his victory at firsthand.

Thirty minutes later Hughes was secured in the back of one of the two wagons from Scotland Yard that stood on Chiltern Street. Enough people were awake and about that a small crowd had gathered nearby, their curiosity triumphing over the cold. Lenox was outside the house with Inspector Nicholson, a tall, bony, hook-nosed young man with a winning grin, which he wore now.

"He took the money in addition to the letters. Couldn't resist it, I suppose. Greedy chap." The dozen pound notes sitting alongside the letters in the desk had been Lenox's idea—their theft would make Hughes's crime easier to prosecute. "We'll need them for evidence, but you'll have them back in a month or two. Along with the rope and the bell."

Lenox looked up at the thin string toward which Nicholson gestured as he said this, hard to discern unless you were looking for it. It ran tightly overhead from one side of the street to the other; Lenox had used its bell to warn the constables waiting in the Dwyer house, the one that Hughes had entered, in case the thief was armed. Certainly he had shown time and again that he was not above violence. "There's no rush at all about the money," said Lenox, returning Nicholson's smile. "Though I'm afraid I must be off now."

"Of course. The agency?"

"Yes. Our official opening."

When Lenox had left Parliament, he had agreed to a proposal from his protégé, Lord John Dallington, to begin a detective agency—a venture that he had contemplated at first with reservations, but that filled him increasingly now with excitement. It would be the best in London. The founders were determined of that.

The young inspector extended a hand. He was one of the few men at the Yard who didn't look upon the new agency with territorial suspicion, or indeed outright disdain. "I wish you only the very best of luck. Though we'll miss the help you've given us over the last months, of course. Six of the seven names."

"Some scores to settle."

"And not bad publicity, I imagine."

Lenox smiled. "No."

It was true. Lenox had devoted the months of November and December to tracking down some of the old criminals whose freedom had rankled in his bosom, when Parliament had deprived him of the time to try to take it from them. Now the press that would gather in Chancery Lane an hour hence to take photographs and write articles about the agency's opening would have a ready-made angle: Lenox's return to detection prosecuted with single-minded determination over the past months, and resulting already in a safer London. It would bring in business, they hoped.

What a day of promise! Hughes in a cell, his partners waiting for him, the brass plate upon their door—which read LENOX, DALLING-TON, STRICKLAND, AND LEMAIRE—ready to be uncovered. Hopefully the broken window of yesterday had been mended; hopefully the office was tidied, ready for the eyes of the press. How right it had been to leave Parliament, he saw now! A new year. The energy one drew from embarking upon a new challenge, a new adventure. He walked briskly down the street, too happy with life to worry about the cold.

Had he known how miserable he would be in three months' time, he would have shaken his head bitterly at that misplaced enthusiasm.

CHAPTER TWO

Hughes is taken, then? I won't miss seeing him swan about at parties, as if butter wouldn't melt on his toast."

"In his mouth, you mean."

"In his mouth, then," repeated Lord John Dallington irritably. They were in the agency's office at Chancery Lane. It was a well-lit and well-appointed set of rooms, with a large, bright, central chamber full of clerks, and branching out in four directions from this a quartet of private offices in which each of the four detectives would work independently. "Neither way makes any sense. He took the letters?"

"And the money."

Now Dallington smiled. "Well done, Charles."

The house in Chiltern Street in which Hughes had been arrested belonged to Alfred Dwyer, patriarch of a cadet branch of a very grand ducal family. His beautiful eldest daughter, Eleanor, was betrothed to her cousin the Earl of Campdown, who would one day inherit the dukedom—a surpassingly eligible match, from the perspective of the Dwyers, and an acceptable one as far as the present duke was concerned.

It was known in certain circles, however, that as a sixteen-year-old Eleanor Dwyer had been desperately in love with her dancing instructor, a German named Stytze, and that there existed, in some dark corner of the world, letters between them of a compromising nature. These letters were the grail of every blackmailer in London. In fact they did not exist—Alfred Dwyer had bought and destroyed them years before—but Lenox had employed the rumor of their survival, with Dwyer's permission and the use of his house while the family were away for Christmas, to ensnare Hughes.

As Nicholson had said, Lenox had devoted much of November and December to a list of seven names. Each of them had, at some maddening moment, eluded Lenox's grasp. There was Anson the burglar, who had almost certainly slit the throat of a baker named Alcott in 1869; Lenox ran him to ground in Bath, where he was in the midst of planning a spectacular assault upon the Earl of Isham's row house. (Bath was known for having a police force so loose and disorganized, compared to London's, that many of the age's most intelligent criminals had now shifted their sights to its prizes.) There was Walton the housebreaker, who stole only rare wine. Chepham, the ugliest character of the lot, a rapist. The half-French Jacques Wilchere, who still played cricket quite admirably for Hambledon and for his home nation. Parson Williams, an impostor, owned a variety of clerical uniforms. Hughes was the only highborn member of this offensive coterie, which explained why Dallington had had the opportunity to grow weary of seeing his face in London society. All six were now in the care of Scotland Yard.

The seventh name—that, Lenox knew, would be more difficult. He couldn't think about it without brooding; anger; he saw no way to get at the fellow, but no way either that he could permit him to carry on in his designs. Anyhow, anyhow . . .

Aside from the satisfaction of seeing these men go to prison, Lenox had pursued them as a test to himself. He was out of practice, no doubt of that. There had been a time when he could have identified every significant criminal in London by the back of a neck, the motion of an arm, the cut of a frock coat, but time and inattention had rendered much of his knowledge obsolete, and certainly in that period his skills had dulled, too. The three stray cases he had solved as a Member of the House had demonstrated as much, even if each had ended in success.

In fact, Dallington was now probably the sharper of the two men. Certainly he was the better connected—to Scotland Yard, where he had the trust of several important men, as Lenox once had, and to the criminal underworld, where he had the contacts to, for instance, put into Hughes's ear the false word of the availability and location of the famous Dwyer letters.

It was a surprising reversal. Dallington was a young person just past thirty and for many years had had, in London, a very terrible reputation indeed—as a reprobate; a cad; a blackguard; a devil. Much of this reputation originated from his time at Cambridge, from which he was expelled, and in the two years following that expulsion in London, when he had seemed to inhabit every wine bar and gambling house in the city simultaneously. His parents, the Duke and Duchess of Marchmain—the latter was a very dear friend of Lenox's wife, Lady Jane—had nearly despaired of their youngest son, even contemplated cutting him from the family on a formal and permanent basis.

It was at the end of this two-year debauch that Dallington had, to Lenox's shock, approached him, asking to become his student. A detective. Lenox had taken Dallington on only with reluctance, in truth partly as a favor to Jane. It had been one of the great decisions of his life. It had led to a partnership, to Dallington's recovery, above all to friendship. Though much of London's upper class—slow to change its opinion of any man—still judged the young lord by his outdated infamies, he had changed. It was true that he relapsed, from time to time, into his old habits. Withal, it had not prevented him from becoming, in all likelihood, the best private detective in the city.

It was this fact that had driven Lenox after Anson, after Wilchere, after Hughes. Though he wouldn't have admitted it, he felt a sense of competition with his friend.

They were sitting now, each with a cup of tea in hand, by the window above Chancery Lane. On the sill were two inches of accumulated snow. In the street below, the busy day was running its loud, unthinking course, the noise of horses, hawkers, and hacksaws replacing the silence of the middle night. Lenox would be glad when the press had come and left, and he could rest.

Dallington, as ever, was dressed impeccably, a carnation in his buttonhole, his dark hair swept back, his face—which was unlined and very handsome still, his intermittent bouts of dissolution never telling upon it—wry, controlled, and with a hint of a smile. "Pretty casual of LeMaire and Polly, leaving it so late, I would have said."

These were their partners. Lenox glanced at his pocket watch. "They have twenty minutes."

"LeMaire has a case. He may be out upon business."

"And Polly is a woman."

"Well identified."

Lenox smiled. "I only meant that she may not be as—as punctual, perhaps, as a man."

"I call that rot. Very probably she was here earlier and grew tired of waiting for us. At any rate, what would Lady Jane say, hearing that slur? She is more punctual even than you are."

"You have my word that she is not," said Lenox seriously. "If I told you the amount of time she once took last spring to put a ribbon in her hair you wouldn't credit it, I promise you."

"Yes, and you're often early."

"I blame it on the school bells. I still have nightmares about being late for class and having a cane across my knuckles. Edmund does, too." This was Charles's older brother and in all the world his closest and most inseparable friend, Sir Edmund Lenox. He was also a powerful political figure—though perhaps the gentlest soul who could claim such a designation. "Still, at least it means that you and I are here to meet the journalists."

They wouldn't be alone, however—the door opened and Polly Buchanan came in. She was trailed by the massive seaman who served as her bodyguard and assistant, Alfred Anixter. Lenox and Dallington both stood, smiling.

These smiles vanished when they saw the concern upon her face. "Is everything all right?" asked Dallington, taking an involuntary step toward her and then checking himself. They were no more than professional colleagues still, after these many months when it had seemed as if they might become more.

Polly Buchanan was a widow of high birth, herself with a rather rakish reputation, though nowhere near as dark as Dallington's had once been; she said what she liked, one of the qualities guaranteed in London society to make a woman the target of malicious natter. She had founded a detective agency the year before, not under her own name but under the pseudonym of Miss Strickland, a ruse designed to keep her clear of the stain of trade. The agency had advertised in the papers and attracted a great deal of halfpenny clients, but Polly was better at her craft than those cases hinted she might be. More than even Dallington or Lenox she had a belief in science: on her freelance staff (now *their* freelance staff) were a sketch artist, a forensic specialist, a botanist, any number of experts whose knowledge might be drawn upon in a moment of need. As she was fond of saying, 1900 was on its way.

She shook her head. "Have you seen the *Telegraph* this morning?"

"What does it say?" asked Lenox.

She gestured toward Anixter, who was holding the newspaper. "The front page."

Anixter read it out loud in his London accent. "*Scotland Yard Urges Newly Founded Detective Agency to Cease Operation of Business.*"

"Good Lord!" said Lenox.

"Let me see that." Dallington took the paper and read the sub-headline out loud. "*Agency places public safety at risk, says Inspector Jenkins.* Oh dear, Thomas Jenkins. How sharper than a serpent's tooth is it when . . . when a chap you like says stuff to the *Telegraph.* As the Bible tells us."

Lenox shook his head. "I had a note from him yesterday, asking if he might see me. I'm sure he wished to explain."

Jenkins was a long-term ally of theirs. "I suppose his superiors might have forced him into it. His ambition is becoming inconvenient," said Dallington.

"Look at the eighth paragraph," said Polly. "You'll find the phrase 'dangers of amateurism' in there. Nicholson comments, too, albeit in less harsh terms."

"Nicholson! I was with him not half an hour ago. I almost believe he can't have known about this," said Lenox. "He was so very friendly."

Polly shook her head again. "Charles, you'll want to look at the second-to-last paragraph."

Lenox took the paper and scanned down it. This was bad, no doubt of that—much of their hopes for a successful beginning were pinned to positive publicity. He read, and soon found the line to which Polly had been referring. He read it out loud. "*One suspect falsely accused by Mr. Lenox, William Anson, has already been released with the apologies of Scotland Yard. Mr. Anson, a master carpenter—if he's a master carpenter I'm the Archbishop of Canterbury—has not ruled out a suit for unlawful imprisonment, and has informed friends that Mr. Lenox has long borne an irrational vendetta against him.*"

"Overplaying his hand there," murmured Dallington.

"*Inspector Jenkins warned that Mr. Lenox might find the transition from Parliament to the world of crime difficult, in particular. 'If he offers them no more than his name, Mr. Lenox will likely be more of a burden than an aid to his new colleagues.' As he may have been to his old ones,* a parliamentary reporter for the Telegraph, James Wilde, *confirms: 'He was scored off by Disraeli, and had to leave with his tail between his legs.'"*

The *Telegraph* was a conservative paper, and its owner, Lord Monomark, a fierce partisan and a great enemy of Charles's allies in Parliament, so that was scarcely surprising. The comment from Jenkins was more surprising—indeed, carried a sharp personal sting.

Dallington shook his head. "He'll regret saying that, if I know Thomas Jenkins. He'll come round and apologize, and we'll have a cup of tea."

"I suppose it's possible," said Lenox.

Polly seemed upset—not hurt, but angry. "Why would the Yard be so dead set against us? Hasn't Lenox above all proven that he can help them, in the last months? Haven't all three of us—all four of us—helped them in the past?"

Just then the fourth in their quartet came in the door, beaming, apparently unaware that anything was amiss. This was LeMaire, a Frenchman with an open, warm face, rather betrayed by the impatient intelligence of his eyes. He held his gloves in one hand and slapped them against his palm happily. "My friends!" he said. "Are we ready to open our doors?"

CHAPTER THREE

The next month was harder than any of them had expected. On the day of their grand debut none of the newspaper writers had been very interested in their brass nameplate, in the vivacious young Miss Strickland, or even in Lenox's quietly hoarded triumphs—the release of Anson told against those. The burst of positive publicity with which they had hoped to inaugurate the firm never materialized. Though for a while their names popped up in the newspapers, the slant was nearly always negative. Then they stopped receiving mention altogether; except, unfortunately, in the penny press, which adopted a gleeful gloating tone, celebrating the release of Anson in particular, one of their own, an East Ender.

Business, perhaps as a result, arrived much more slowly than they had hoped it would. Indeed, it arrived much more slowly than they could have imagined it might, even in their most pessimistic prognostications.

Despite this difficulty, for seven weeks the new office operated in a state of determined good cheer and hard work.

Then, finally, the stress told.

It was a sullen late-February morning, the sky a black-gray, as if night had never quite been persuaded to depart for day, a lingering suitor glowering after its lost prize; a freezing rain told a dull pattering tale upon the windows and the roofs, long minute after long minute, long hour after long hour. The four principals were at their customary Monday meeting, held each week to discuss new business. The head clerk, a bright young soul called Mr. Fletcher, took minutes.

"Any new business?" asked Dallington. He was tapping his small cigar against the table restlessly. In truth he wasn't suited to the administrative elements of the operation and spent less time in Chancery Lane than any of the others, impatient when he had to pass more than an hour or two in the office.

"Two new cases," said Polly, and described them. One was blackmail, one embezzlement.

Dallington also had a new case; LeMaire, two. The Frenchman was the leading detective within the expatriate community, among the diplomats and the foreign traders, French and German and Scandinavian. He spoke several languages, which helped. He was also popular among the fools of the English gentry, who believed only a Frenchman could make a detective, the Vidocq touch.

"And Mr. Lenox?" said Fletcher the clerk, in his springy Dorset accent.

"Nothing new," said Lenox, as evenly as he could.

"What a surprise," LeMaire murmured.

All five of them looked up, and Dallington started out of his chair, white-faced with anger. "What did you say?"

LeMaire looked as surprised as any of them, immediately abashed by this hint of dissatisfaction, and after a beat he stood and with great formality said, "You have my sincerest apologies for my unthinking utterance, sir," he said, "and I will be happy to place them in writing. I spoke without thinking."

"It's quite all right," said Lenox.

Dallington was nearly shaking. Polly, with a heavy sigh, interjected before he could speak. "Don't be foolish, please, fellows. I know that none of us would willingly insult another. It's an early morning. Sit down and we'll talk about billings."

The meeting resumed.

Lenox could scarcely pay attention, however, he felt so bitterly, miserably unhappy. For all four of them knew the truth: He had not brought a single case into the firm since its inception. The other three had seen their business decline, but not disappear; Polly had a reputation among the middle class and respectable lower middle class as an affordable, intelligent counsel, and still drew clients from her advertisements as Miss Strickland, which the firm had left in the papers as they had always appeared, altering only the address. Dallington had the faith of the members of his class—as Lenox once had. LeMaire's base of clients had eroded the least.

As for Lenox: nothing. All of the referrals he and Dallington had expected to receive from the Yard had evaporated, vanished. Even Nicholson would do no more than smile his friendly smile, and tell them that the Yard was ahead of its business at the moment, in need of no help at all. This when it was known that the coroner had a stack of corpses higher than he could ever hope to handle, each of them an unsolved death, the metropolis spared from their smell only by the glacial temperature of the season.

Meanwhile Lenox's parliamentary contacts had proved equally useless, even if they were friendlier, and whatever reputation he'd once had in London was gone, or had been distilled into Dallington's.

How hard they had been, these seven weeks that led up to Le-Maire's comment! In a way it was a relief to have the grievance in the open. Every morning Lenox had come into the office at eight, and every evening departed at six. How the hours passed between he was hard-pressed to recall, except that there was a mechanical smile upon his face the whole time, and in his words a constant false tone of optimism. He had spent some of this period organizing his old case files and amassing new profiles of the criminals of

London. He had also updated his archive of sensational literature, clipping notes on crime from newspapers that came to him from all across the world. Once or twice he had been able to add a valuable perspective on a colleague's case, but Polly was independent, Le-Maire jealous of his own work, and Dallington (who was most solicitous of his help) so rarely in the office.

All of this would have been tolerable to him were they not splitting their meager profits, and their increasing expenses, four ways.

The next Monday LeMaire was scrupulously polite when Lenox reported that he had no new cases, and the same the Monday following. But as March passed, the attitude within the office in Chancery Lane grew discernably less friendly. Soon LeMaire was stiffly polite, no more. Polly, though she was by nature a generous, warm-spirited person, and never changed in this respect to Lenox, did begin to seem downtrodden, as if she doubted that their new venture, which had begun so promisingly, had been wise. She had some small portion left over from her marriage, but she was very definitely in the business, as Lenox could not claim to be, for money, and by that measure the choice had been a bad one.

As for Dallington—it was not conceivable that Lenox could have had a stauncher ally than Dallington. At every meeting the young lord came in and swore to the heavens that Lenox had solved his cases for him, guaranteed the payment from their clients through his brilliance, single-handedly saved him from the embarrassment of an unsolved matter.

These were lies, and each week Lenox expected his friend's eyes to fall slightly, his support to falter in its vehemence, if not in its content. It never happened. An outsider would have sworn from Dallington's testimony in the meetings that only Lenox's grim determination and hard work kept the firm together.

The subject rarely arose between them. "Shall I put more money into the books myself?" Lenox asked in a moment of weakness one evening.

"Absolutely not," said Dallington shortly. "These others don't see how rich you're going to make us all."

Lenox had been so affected by this blind stubborn friendship that he had turned away, unable to respond.

Finally, after ten weeks, Lenox told Lady Jane about his troubles. Afterward he wished he had done it sooner.

It was over breakfast. Lenox's wife was the daughter of an earl and the sister of another, and therefore somewhat higher born than her husband, though they had been raised in and out of each other's houses, ancient friends. For many years they had lived side by side in London, each the other's closest confidant; then finally, with what seemed to them both in retrospect unforgivable slowness, they had realized how much they were in love. She was a pretty but plain woman, her dark hair in loose curls, more simply attired than the brocaded and upholstered women of her social sphere tended to be—a blue dress, a gray ribbon at the waist, that was her preference. Motherhood had rather softened her acute, forgiving eyes. Certainly it had added lines near their edges, lines Lenox loved for the thousand smiles they recalled to him: a life together, their love deepening as the unmarked days drew forward into each other.

Generally as they ate breakfast Lenox and Lady Jane read the newspapers, exchanging stories from them now and then when something struck one of them. That morning, as he stared at a plate of cooling eggs and kippers, Lenox couldn't bring himself to read. Right away she noticed.

"Are you all right, Charles?"

He looked up at her from his hands and smiled. "It's harder than I expected, the new firm."

She frowned. "How do you mean?"

"I haven't helped, you know. I'm the worst of the four of us."

She sat forward on her chair, engaged immediately, concerned. "At your work? That's impossible."

"Nobody has come in to hire me." It was hard for him even to say these words, or to look at his wife as he did. The truth was that he had never failed at anything in this way. "LeMaire is unhappy about it."

She crossed the table and came to his side, her hands taking up his own, her face consumed by sympathy. "I have wondered why you seemed unhappy. I had worried—worried that you missed Parliament."

"No, no," said Lenox. "Not that."

"You must give it time, Charles."

He shook his head. "I don't know."

Yet he felt better for telling her. He had long since forfeited that adolescent urge to seem perfect to other people, to show no outward flaw in himself—but it was hard to admit that he had tried his best at something and been unsuccessful, even to Jane, perhaps especially to Jane. Her own life was effortless, or so it seemed: She was one of the leading arbiters of London society, the writer of a small, mildly successful book for children that had been much treasured and feted by her friends, a mother of impeccable judgment. In the last months this perfection had worn on him, but when he saw her face now, he knew he had been wrong to keep his unhappiness to himself.

Or so he thought. That afternoon a client came in for Lenox, a young servant with a sister he wished traced into the colonies; and not much later another, the president of a society for the preservation of cats who was persuaded that her offices were being surveilled. Lenox thought of declining both cases, but he didn't have the heart to inform Jane that he had seen through her act of charity. Besides, each problem was real enough, by whatever obscure back channels she had located it, and by whatever means she had persuaded these clients to come to Lenox—and in truth, though it was likely his own money they brought him, the firm could use it. Neither matter took more than a day, and each brought in a few guineas. He thought the pity that they represented might kill him.

CHAPTER FOUR

One evening at the beginning of that April, Lenox and his friend Thomas McConnell, a physician at the Great Ormond Street Children's Hospital, sat in Lenox's study in Hampden Lane. They usually passed one or two evenings a week in each other's company, either at their houses or in one of the clubs on Pall Mall, drinking, smoking, and talking. McConnell was a tall, rangy Scotsman, rather weather-beaten but still handsome.

"I've been meaning to ask you," said Lenox at a lull in the conversation, "what do you think of a teaspoon of brandy for a child as its milk teeth are coming in, to help it sleep?"

"Is Sophia sleeping badly?" asked McConnell.

Lenox's daughter was two. "She is, the poor soul."

"You only need to freeze a ring of milk for her to suck on. That will numb her gums. As for brandy, I'm amazed at you, Charles!"

"Our own nurses did it for us, Jane's and mine—as they did for you, I don't doubt."

McConnell smiled. "Yes, but they lived in a dark age of physic."

"Dark, perhaps, but effective."

"Well, I cannot recommend alcohol for a child, I cannot, though I have seen chimney sweeps of eight and nine drink half-pints of gin to start the day. If you had studied the necrotic tissue of the liver of the average vagrant's cadaver as I have, you would hesitate to drink brandy yourself, a full-grown man."

"I consider it one of the achievements of my life that I have never studied the necrotic tissue of the liver of the average vagrant's cadaver."

"Has the child been keeping you up at night?"

"We hear her. Sometimes Jane goes to see her, though most often it falls to Mrs. Adamson." This was Sophia's nurse. "To be perfectly honest, it may be she that needs the brandy more than any of us, but she's a member of one of these temperance churches."

"They're doing wonderful things in the slums, some of them," said McConnell.

"I don't doubt it. Hers is called St. Luke's, as she's told me often enough."

"That's one of the ones I mean. Perhaps I ought to speak to her. She may have come across some case suitable for the hospital, and not realized there was any place to send them." Great Ormond Street took children to the age of thirteen, at no fee—all of them gravely ill. McConnell had only started working there recently, and Lenox had never known him happier. "In fact, is she here now?"

Lenox was about to suggest that they call for the nurse when a sixth sense, the kind that one develops after many years of inhabiting the same rooms, living within the same beams and bricks, told him that there was someone at the front door. Even as the thought came to him the bell sounded.

A moment later Kirk appeared. "Inspector Nicholson is in the hall, sir."

Lenox frowned and looked at McConnell, who raised his eyebrows. The doctor knew the Yard's generalized intolerance of the new agency. "You'd better tell him I'm not here," said Lenox.

"Yes, sir." Kirk hesitated. "Though I fear, sir, that he may have seen the light on in your study from the street. He might doubt my word."

"He will have to live with that doubt."

"Very good, sir," said Kirk, and withdrew.

"He's lived with his doubts as to me, the bugger," muttered Lenox.

"What if it's a case?" asked McConnell doubtfully.

"It's not."

The Yard was no closer to loving Lenox, Dallington, Strickland, and LeMaire than it had been in January. Nicholson had sent a note of cautious apology to Lenox; the more serious apostasy of Jenkins had produced a visit from their old friend to the office, a week after the publication of the article in the *Telegraph*.

It had been a stiff encounter, with never quite an apology from the inspector, nor an absolution from the other two men (for Dallington was also there to meet him). He had hinted that the opinions he expressed in the article had much more to do with his official capacities than his private feelings. That had not been explicit enough for Lenox, who was not in a mood for magnanimity. It was a painful break; they had worked closely together for many years now, and indeed two of the early cases that had made Jenkins a rising star in the department had been solved only through Lenox's direct intervention: that of the September Society and that of the murders in Fleet Street. In subsequent years Jenkins had repaid this debt by acting as an invaluable link to London's entire force of police. It was this amicable relationship—based on genuine mutual respect, Lenox had believed—that Dallington had gradually duplicated as parliamentary duties drew Lenox further and further from the world of crime.

In the past two years, however, Jenkins had seen the prospect of high office—commanding office—laid before him, and his ambition had been piqued. There had been a definite change in that time, according to Dallington. He was interfering now, less open, less secure in taking help. Then came the article in the *Telegraph*. If it had been Jenkins, not Nicholson, Lenox would have admitted the man to his study at this hour that evening, even though Nicholson's betrayal was less profound. The prospect of power could deform a man.

After less than a minute, Kirk returned. "Inspector Nicholson is most insistent that he be permitted to see you, sir."

"Tell him I'm not in, please."

Kirk lifted his eyebrows. "Sir?"

"Tell him I'm not in."

When Kirk had gone, McConnell said, "How are you sure it's not a case? Or are you overtaxed at work already?"

Lenox's sensitivity at this moment of his life made him wonder if McConnell knew about his lack of work—but he saw immediately that this was a mad level of assumption and said quickly, "No, no, I'm simply not in the mood."

Now Kirk appeared for a third time. He was a stubborn fellow, in his way. He had been Lady Jane Grey's butler for twenty years, which was long enough that he knew he wouldn't be expelled from Hampden Lane for a little perseverance. "Sir," he said, standing in the doorway.

"What on earth can it be now?"

"Before he leaves, Inspector Nicholson wishes you to know that he has a case upon which he hopes you might be willing to consult, sir."

"Fine, please tell him I know it, and don't care to consult for him."

"He instructed me expressly to inform you that it involves a murder, sir," said Kirk.

With this news, for the first time, Lenox hesitated. He stared at his brandy for a moment and then glanced up at McConnell, who was smiling faintly at him. "Would you mind, McConnell?"

"On the contrary."

Lenox paused again and then yielded at last. "Oh, hell, send him in."

"Very good sir," said Kirk. He shifted his considerable weight out of the room too rapidly for Lenox to reconsider the invitation.

McConnell stood. "I'll go, shall I?"

"No, stay."

Nicholson came in, his tall, bony frame filling the doorway. "Mr. Lenox. And Dr. McConnell," he said, inclining his head. He didn't seem surprised to see the doctor, who had often helped Lenox with his investigations in the past. Perhaps that was known at the Yard. "How do you do, gentlemen?"

"What brings you here?" asked Lenox.

"I say, it's a rotten night," said Nicholson, glancing toward the window. Outside a heavy wind was whipping around the house. "Could I have a glass of that, whatever it is? I'll pour it myself. I don't want to trouble you."

Lenox had been prepared to welcome his guest very coldly, but now he saw in the flicker of the lamp that the hollow-cheeked inspector seemed exhausted, absolutely worn, with worry, and despite himself Lenox's heart went out to Nicholson. "I'll fetch it."

The inspector waited silently and then took a gulp of the brandy Lenox handed him. "Thank you," he said. He paused, then went on, "There was a housebreak in Bath last week. The losses were substantial."

"So I saw in the newspapers."

"It was Anson, of course. Or so they think."

There was nothing Lenox could say to this.

"At least the other five are safely away in prison. Hughes. Six arrests, you know. Not bad."

"No," said Lenox.

Here Nicholson smiled rather tiredly. "What about that seventh fellow?" he asked.

"That may take longer," said Lenox, his voice short. "Is the break-in at Bath the case of which you told Kirk?"

"No, no," said Nicholson, waving a distracted hand in the air, his eyes down. He looked up at Lenox. "It's in London. Will you come out with me now and have a look?"

"You'll have to pay my fee," said Lenox.

Nicholson looked surprised. "Really?"

"Yes, of course."

"Well, that won't be a problem. I have a large enough budget now. Promoted last month. Most of the money goes to informants, of course." This was said somewhat slightingly, though it wasn't clear if Nicholson intended it as such. "Dr. McConnell, if you want to come along we could use a doctor. I don't suppose you have a fee?"

"No," said McConnell quietly.

"Does that mean there's a body?" asked Lenox.

"Oh yes, there's a body."

Suddenly something in Nicholson's bearing—a kind of reserved anguish, barely concealed—brought Lenox to the edge of the seat. "What's happened?" he asked. "Who is it?"

"Jenkins has been murdered this evening," said Nicholson. "Inspector Thomas Jenkins."

CHAPTER FIVE

When Lenox was twenty-two, pink-faced, new to London, and casting about for something to do with his life, one of the locally famous figures in the city had been Edward Oxlade. He was a police inspector who had recently retired. By the time of his retirement he had long graduated from his street corner to desk work, but after he left Scotland Yard he began to take one day each week to don his old bobby's uniform and walk his neighborhood, lantern and whistle rattling from his belt, a figure of white-haired amiability—kind to children, chatty to shopkeepers, helpful to anyone in straits. He had come to be very popular, an emblem of the new London, the one that had risen since the foundation of Scotland Yard, its safety, its security, a metropolis distancing itself from the nighttime garrotings and daylight coach robberies of the wilder previous century.

On one of the first cases upon which Lenox had consulted for the Yard, he'd had reason to call upon Oxlade very late one evening, past ten o'clock. Oxlade had greeted him sitting down, a book in hand, a blanket over his knees.

"How can I help you?" he had asked.

The case was a slippery one; Jonathan Charlton, a friend from

Oxford whose family owned a bank near the Savoy, had heard rumors that a ring of burglars was planning to strike against it. The
police were watching the bank, but Charlton had asked Lenox,
who as an undergraduate had been known for his idiosyncratic pas-
time of collecting information on crime, to look into the matter.

"I'm Charles Lenox," he had said in response to Oxlade's question. "I'm consulting on a case with Inspector Evans, and though I
know it's fearfully late, and cold outside—"

But before Lenox could even finish speaking, Oxlade had set his
book facedown on a table nearby. "I'm ready to go," he said.

It was that incidental act—setting his book down without
hesitation—that had always remained with Lenox. There was
something spirited and brilliant in it, something hearty, coura-
geous, perhaps especially because Oxlade at that time had been a
man closer to eighty than seventy. It was the act of a person with
character. The act of an Englishman, one might even say, embody-
ing the best qualities of the best Englishmen. In the end, as it happened, Oxlade hadn't even been able to help him; Lenox had hoped
he might be able to identify a man named Abraham Walters by
sight, but the identification had been a mistaken one. Nevertheless
Lenox had never forgotten Oxlade's readiness to leave, without
delay.

Thomas Jenkins could have published a hundred articles in
the *Telegraph* upon Lenox's imperfections of mind, manner, and
morals—could have stood at the Speakers' Corner of Hyde Park
reading them out loud each Wednesday—and Lenox would still,
upon hearing of the inspector's murder, have set his book facedown,
ready to go. Their history was too deep for anything else.

He felt himself trembling as he stood. "We must go at once," he
said. "Where is the body? Where did it happen? *What* has happened, for that matter?"

Nicholson was in less of a rush. He went and poured himself
another half-tumbler of brandy, an understandable liberty in the

situation. Jenkins had been his mentor. "It happened north of here," he said, "by Regent's Park."

"Kirk," Lenox called out loudly, "my carriage, immediately."

"I have one of the Yard's outside," said Nicholson.

"We'll follow you," said Lenox. He was patting his pockets, looking for a notebook. "It's useful to have an independent means of getting around the city."

McConnell, standing now, too, his face grave, said, "A medical examiner has been to see the body?"

"Yes," said Nicholson, "but you might as well come along. I told them to leave the scene as it was until I had fetched you."

For the first time Lenox paused to consider this. "Why?" he asked.

Nicholson smiled a bitter smile. "Last week I had supper with Jenkins—on our own time. He was quite secretive about it. He said that if he should be killed or go missing I was to come to you. He also said that I was to hand over all of his notes to you."

"He felt that he was in danger?" asked Lenox.

"He would say no more than I've told you, but he made me swear it. So it is that I am here, as you see. And that I asked them to keep the scene of the crime where it was."

Lenox went to his desk and picked up a small black grip that contained a few essentials of the profession—a stout knife, a calabash, and various more nuanced tools of detection, a magnifying glass, a kit to dust for fingerprints. He had found his notebook, too. "I'm ready to go. Where are the notes he wished me to see?"

"In his office, I would imagine."

"At home, or at the Yard?"

"Oh, at the Yard. I don't know that he ever took his work home."

Lenox nodded. "We must get them as quickly as possible."

"I can send a constable when we reach Regent Street."

"Perhaps just to watch his office, rather than to fetch anything," said Lenox. "I should like to look over his desk myself."

Kirk came in. "The carriage is ready, sir," he said.

"Thank you."

After Kirk had withdrawn there was a moment in which the three men, Lenox, McConnell, and Nicholson, stood in silence, looking at one another. It was hard to say what either of the other two was feeling, but for Lenox the shock of the news, which had galvanized him into action, was giving way to the realization that this terrible information was true. Thomas Jenkins was dead. A man he had known for twenty years. One of the other men in London who had known Edward Oxlade. His wife, his three children, left to themselves. His affections for organ music and a glass of strong beer. Vanished, forever.

Not much later, Lenox's carriage was jerking across the cobblestones of Oxford Street. "How did he die?" asked Lenox.

"A gunshot," said Nicholson. "A single wound in the temple."

"There is no evidence of an exiting wound?" asked McConnell.

"No."

"A small gun, then, something that could fit in a coat pocket," said Lenox. "A pocket revolver, or something of the sort. Would you agree, Thomas?"

"Likely a Bull Dog or some copy." The Bull Dog was a Webley revolver, immensely popular and oft-duplicated in the past five years, just two and a half inches long and therefore easy to conceal. "If you extract the bullet we shall be able to confirm it, I imagine."

Nicholson looked at him curiously. "Even on a bullet smashed all out of shape by the barrel of the gun—and all that it hit?"

"I've made something of a study of them," said McConnell.

Ahead of them the Yard's carriage, empty but for the driver, took a left-hand turn. Nicholson had ridden with them so that they might speak. "Were there any witnesses?" Lenox asked.

Nicholson shook his head. "It was on a dark corner of the park. We have two men who heard the shot and ran to the body. We're holding on to them this evening, giving them supper, in case they can help, but I don't think they saw much."

"What time did this happen?"

"Just after seven o'clock. We were there by half past the hour."

Lenox checked his pocket watch. It was nearly ten now. "It would have been dark by then. Too bad. Were there any wounds on Jenkins other than the bullet hole?"

Nicholson paused and then turned his head, face thoughtful. "You know, I'm not sure. I don't know that we checked."

"McConnell can look," said Lenox, writing in his notebook. There was a small lamp swinging on the outside of the carriage, casting just enough light that he could see what he wrote. "Was Jenkins out on police business?"

"I don't think so. He generally left the office at six o'clock, and today wasn't different."

"And went home?"

"Yes. He has three children. Lord, it's terrible to think of."

Lenox looked out of the window. "Scotland Yard is in Westminster, however, and Thomas Jenkins lives—lived—in Wandsworth Road, directly due south of his offices. We are driving north at the moment, into the north of London. In other words, when he left the Yard at six o'clock this evening, he traveled nearly two miles in the opposite direction of his home."

Nicholson raised his eyebrows and nodded. "Perhaps it was police business after all, then. If it was I wish he had told someone."

Lenox grimaced. "He may have, of course. His wife."

All three men were silent for a moment at the thought of this woman—of her evening. McConnell then said to Nicholson, "Has she been informed?"

"Henderson is going there now."

This was Edmund Yeamans Walcott Henderson, the Commissioner of Police of the Metropolis—the head of the Yard, a former officer in the army. He was an honest, unimaginative, duty-bound

fellow, with a bald head and mutton-chop mustaches. It was difficult to imagine him comforting a woman; he was the sort of fellow
more at ease in a mess hall than in a drawing room.

The carriage turned onto Portland Place, a broad thoroughfare
leading directly north into Regent's Park, lined with brick and
cream-colored houses. Some people considered it the most beautiful street in London.

"It's not far, just thirty or forty yards," said Nicholson. "You can
see the scene if you look."

Lenox and McConnell strained to look through the window.
Ahead there was a press of people, and above them, lofted onto handy
poles that the Yard had recently introduced for nighttime investigation, bright lamps to illuminate the area. Several large constables
kept people back from the pavement, crowding them into the street,
which made it difficult for the cabs and omnibuses along Portland
Place to pass. The shouting of their drivers added to the hellish din
and confusion. Lenox realized with a dreadful pang that the smallish body of his friend was at the center of all this; and dead.

As they stepped out of the carriage, Nicholson first, Lenox
looked up. The houses looked familiar to him, for some reason, not
just because they belonged to the rest of the very fine structures
along Portland Place, but these two or three houses specifically.

Had he been to a supper here recently, a ball?

Then he realized why he recognized the houses, and stopped,
chilled—for unless he was much mistaken, the body of Thomas
Jenkins was lying in front of the house of the Marquess of Wakefield. The seventh name on Lenox's list.

CHAPTER SIX

The person in charge of the crime scene in Nicholson's absence was a florid, overweight, and overwhelmed young sergeant named Armbruster. He met them on the pavement, a thick sheaf of papers clamped tightly under his arm. "The newspapers have arrived," he reported to Nicholson, "and I have sent out for hot soup."

"This is Sergeant Armbruster," said Nicholson, introducing Lenox. "He was in charge of the scene when I arrived, first man on the spot, which means he's been here for hours—stout fellow, Armbruster, well done. Hot soup, though?"

"All the men are cold and—and hungry, very hungry indeed." From its rather desperate tone, this latter assessment seemed as if it might apply more to Armbruster than any of his constables. "To lift the spirits, Inspector. We have been working past the clock for some time now. I myself am accustomed to having my supper very prompt."

"Yes, well, fine. Is the wagon ready to go?"

Armbruster looked unsettled—the wagon had absolutely nothing to do with soup—and took a moment to register the question before saying, "Yes, sir."

Nicholson turned to Lenox. "The scene is yours. Take the time you properly need, but work quickly, if you could. I would like to cause as little commotion here as possible, particularly with the journalists arriving, and the wagon is ready to take Jenkins's body to the morgue."

As Nicholson said this, Lenox and McConnell were gazing upon a roped-off section of the pavement, where a white sheet covered a low-lying lump. It was two or three feet from the house—not Wakefield's house, in fact, but the one directly next to it.

Lenox was still scarcely master of his emotions. "To whom does this house belong?" he asked.

Nicholson drew his own notebook out and flipped its pages. "John Clitheroe," he said. "Forty-two. A merchant from Northumberland. Unmarried."

"The house is dark and the lower windows barred, I observe."

"He is away for six months upon business, sir," said Armbruster. "In the Caribbean."

Nicholson looked at the sergeant. "The canvass has returned, then? Lenox, as you can imagine we sent out several constables to ask about the house."

"Yes, sir. No witnesses, sir, no, though we knocked on every door we could. Unfortunately we're so close to the park that there's not as much foot traffic here."

That might have been true on a normal evening, but now there were getting on for fifty people, perhaps even more, crowding in on them. "Disperse this crowd, Armbruster."

"But the soup will be arriving any moment, sir," said Armbruster.

"I don't give a damn about the soup."

"Very good, sir."

"Neither should you."

"No, sir, certainly not, sir," said Armbruster, though there was a hint of rebellion in his face. He did give a damn about the soup. Lenox wondered if Armbruster had known Jenkins, or if the inspector was only a name to him. The Yard was a large place, when one began to count all the constables and sergeants. There was no reason this fellow should know the kind of man—for Lenox still believed in Jenkins—that had been lost.

"Thomas, would you rather look at the body here or in the morgue?" asked Lenox.

"I might give it a cursory look here, and a more extensive one there," said McConnell. His hands were in his pockets. He shook his head. "I find it hard to believe Jenkins is under that sheet."

"Then let us inspect his body together first, after which I can look around the area for myself," said Lenox. "Nicholson, have you removed the effects from his person, his pockets?"

"Yes. They're in a box in my carriage. You're free to examine them at your leisure. For my own part I could not see very much in them—the normal things a man would carry."

"A notebook?"

"No, none."

Lenox and McConnell ducked under the rope—Nicholson having nodded them past the large constable manning it—and approached the body. Off to their left Armbruster was actually doing a fairly effective job of dispersing the crowd, though Lenox knew that at least a dozen of them would remain until every scrap of evidence had been carried off and the last black cloak of the Yard was gone.

"Do you know whose house this is?" Lenox murmured to McConnell as they came to stand near the body.

"John Clitheroe, forty-two, Northumberland merchant, unmarried. Or has that sergeant got it wrong?"

"No, the next one." Lenox jerked his chin. "There."

"Whose?"

"William Travers-George."

"Oh. Oh!" McConnell looked at Lenox in surprise. "Wakef—"

"Yes, but keep your voice down, please. We can discuss it later." Wakefield.

Lenox considered the name even as he moved about the scene. The blackmailer Hughes was of relatively gentle birth, while Parson Williams the impostor had been an orphan; both were of equally negligible origin, however, beside William Travers-George, the 15th Marquess of Wakefield. The title was among the highest in the land, outside of the royal family. Among nonroyals, only a duke was permitted to enter a room before him. On top of that the Wakefield marquessate was one of the oldest in England, bestowed first to a particularly loyal treasurer of Elizabeth the First in the 1580s, a lineage that meant that of the thirty-five marquesses in Great Britain (there were hundreds of earls, by contrast) Travers-George outranked all but two.

The family had extensive lands in Yorkshire, and of course Hatting Hall was theirs, which some people considered the most beautiful of all Hawksmoor's country houses. As if these credentials weren't enough to guarantee his respectability, William Travers-George's father had been a kindly, beloved old soul, rarely away from Hatting, and William Travers-George's son and heir, who per tradition borrowed the honorary title of the Earl of Calder, was a mild-mannered student at Cambridge. On either side of him, in other words, were decent men. There was no indication of madness or malice anywhere in the family line. Travers-George was biographically unimpeachable.

Yet Lenox doubted strongly that there was a man capable of greater evil currently alive in England.

McConnell bent down over the body, whispering to Lenox, "Should Nicholson arrest him?"

"No," murmured Lenox, bending down as well. "Not yet anyhow, certainly not."

They positioned their bodies so that they were as much between Jenkins's body and the crowd as they might be, and then McConnell pulled back the sheet.

Both men were silent at what they saw, for it was he; it was

Inspector Thomas Jenkins. There was a small round hole at his temple, but otherwise his face looked composed, almost Roman. He had been a handsome man.

"It is the pity of the world his life should have ended this way," said McConnell.

"I hope he didn't feel any pain."

McConnell shook his head. "He wouldn't have, no. It would have been instantaneous."

They had examined enough corpses in tandem that they were able to work in silence. McConnell studied first the head and then the neck of the body, loosening the tie Jenkins had been wearing and giving particular attention to the eyes, shining a light in them. "No response, the pupils constricted. It has been longer than ninety minutes. I suppose we knew that. Rigor mortis is setting in quickly."

"Is there ever a response after death?"

"For ninety minutes or so there is a reflex in the cornea."

Soon McConnell had moved on to the hands and forearms of the body, which again he studied with great care. Lenox meanwhile was checking to his own satisfaction Jenkins's suit pockets. They were empty, as he would have expected, even the small ticket-pocket in his waistcoat. Jenkins had carried his identification as a police inspector as a matter of course, but Lenox imagined that it must be in the box in Nicholson's carriage, together with the rest of the property that had been on Jenkins's person.

They spent ten minutes with the body. Finding little enough, at last they permitted Nicholson's constables to conduct it to the police wagon, where it would sit until the police were certain they were finished with the scene and it could be transported to the morgue.

"Did you find anything?" asked Nicholson.

McConnell answered. "Only a rather shallow cut on the left hand. It is about three days old."

"He didn't mention any kind of incident to me," said Nicholson, "and I saw him every day this week. Several times each day, in fact."

The doctor shrugged. "It could easily have happened with a letter opener, or a kitchen knife."

"Will you go to the morgue?" asked Nicholson.

"To see the bullet. Otherwise there isn't much point. I'll glance over the body again."

"Lenox? Did you find anything?"

"Did you or one of your men unlace one of his shoes?"

"No. I don't think so, anyhow."

Lenox frowned. "Peculiar."

"What?"

"One was laced, one nearly unlaced, that's all. It's probably not meaningful."

"It must simply have come undone," said McConnell.

"I don't think so. The right shoe was triple-knotted."

McConnell looked surprised. "That is odd."

"I thought so."

"What would you like to do now?" asked Nicholson.

"I want to see what Jenkins had on his person, then go look at these notes he wished me to see," said Lenox. "But tell me, first, has anyone asked at this house about the incident?"

"Yes," said Nicholson, flipping open his pad. "It belongs to someone called William Travers-George, a marquess, the lucky blighter. Only staff is present at the moment. They didn't see anything."

"Where is the owner?"

"They don't know. He left in haste two days ago, an unplanned trip, taking no servants, and hasn't returned. They couldn't tell us his whereabouts."

CHAPTER SEVEN

There was a great deal that Lenox hoped to accomplish that night, but he forced himself, now, to take a deep breath and survey the scene. Wakefield had vanished two days before, and now Jenkins was dead twenty feet from his house. It was a situation that required very great care.

"You've canvassed every house in the area?" he asked Nicholson.

"Yes, and spoken to the few remaining vendors in the park, too. The written report will be ready in the morning—you shall have it when I do—but the constables didn't learn anything of note, alas."

Lenox looked at the vast facade of Wakefield's house (the marquess's intimates called him by his surname, Travers-George; his acquaintances and his family called him Wakefield; all others, My Lord or Your Lordship or Lord Wakefield) and saw that on one of the alabaster columns in front of it was stenciled, in elegant black lettering, 73. Portland Place's addresses ended at 80, if he recalled correctly—there the park began, Regent's Park. Wakefield's was a particularly large house, but all of its neighbors were just as distinguished in their construction and maintenance.

Stylistically they were all the same except for 77, two doors down from where Jenkins's body had fallen; this was a low-slung brick edifice, rather of the last century. What caught Lenox's eye was that it looked almost dementedly protected, guarded. There was a wrought-iron fence that reached higher than the house's roof, its gaps far too small for even a child to squeeze between, and on its small gate were two heavy locks. All of the windows were barred. From the steps a figure, an older woman, was gazing at them. She would have had a good view of the crime, if she had been out there then.

"Who lives in 77?" asked Lenox.

Nicholson waved over Armbruster, whose task of managing the crowd had eased with the disappearance of Jenkins's body into the wagon. On the otherwise unbroken expanse of his white shirt there was a wet brown stain. Soup, Lenox would have wagered. "Armbruster, who was in 77?"

"It was a convent, sir," said the sergeant. "Or rather, it is a convent."

"Who answered the door?"

"A lady porter, sir. She said the sisters and the young novices and them were at prayers, sir, at the time Inspector Jenkins was killed. Nor did she see anything or hear anything, except when the commotion out here started. She said she wasn't a papist, for her part, she was quick to mention that. Only the porter of the place."

That explained the reinforcements on the house. Lenox wondered if they knew anything of Wakefield's history there. If they did the abbess might have contemplated moving away from the street.

"Did you look carefully around the body, to see if anything was thrown from it?" asked Lenox.

Nicholson smiled wearily. "We are not rank amateurs, you know. We looked at the entirety of the scene, in expanding concentric circles. Jenkins's own method."

In fact this was Lenox's method, though he said nothing. "And found?"

"Nothing out of the ordinary. There was the usual London mix. Discarded food and trash, cigar ends, bits of string."

"Nothing with writing on it?"

"No."

Lenox believed Nicholson but did his own methodical review. After ten minutes he, too, had found nothing.

He looked across to McConnell, who was standing by the van, speaking to its driver. This fellow was pressing a hand to his stomach and saying something with great animation, and the doctor felt the spot, palpated it for a moment, and then, speaking sternly, began to take out his prescription pad. At any rate some good might come of this night, Lenox thought. The living always do go on.

He went to Nicholson, who was consulting with his constables; two of them would remain near this spot overnight, observing. Lenox asked if he might see Jenkins's possessions now.

"Yes, come to my carriage. I ought to have shown you on the way." Nicholson's face was grim, gaunt. "But listen, Lenox, I'm afraid I can't stay with you all night. I've brought you in, as Jenkins wished, but I have superiors to whom I must answer, an investigation to begin building on my own. It's nothing personal."

"I understand. Perhaps you could leave Armbruster."

"Where do you want him to take you?"

"To the Yard—to Jenkins's office."

"I'll take you there. After that we can go off our separate ways."

"Understood."

"It's nothing personal at all," said Nicholson again. His face, always angular, looked very wan now, too, in the sallow light of the streetlamps. "For my part I would like to work together."

"We might meet tomorrow and compare notes."

"Yes, let's do just that," said Nicholson.

They went then to the inspector's carriage, its bored horse flicking its tail every so often, and Nicholson found the small black leather box into which he had put all of Jenkins's possessions. He opened the box. "Not much," said Lenox.

"Here's the list I asked Sergeant O'Brian to make."

Lenox took the list.

Taken from the person of Inspector Thomas Jenkins
4 April 1876
Scotland Yard Box 4224AJ

Keys on a ring, seven, none marked, none unusual
Billfold, twenty pounds in notes, three in coin
Pocket watch and chain, silver, embossed TJ
Pouch shag tobacco
Meerschaum pipe
Underground ticket, unpunched

"Nothing relevant to his work, then," said Lenox, sifting through the box to check its contents against the list. They matched.

"No, unfortunately. Perhaps the keys."

"And yet I wonder."

"Eh?"

"The ticket is unpunched. I imagine it was for his nightly trip home. Did he take a cab here, then? Was he meeting someone at seven? We can ask his sergeant at the Yard—Bryson, I believe was his name."

"Yes, Bryson."

"We can also ask his wife if she expected him later than usual. Then there's the money."

"What about it?" asked Nicholson.

"It seems like a great deal to me. I'm carrying four pounds at the moment and would have imagined that I was above the average even on Portland Place."

"True. I'm only carrying shrapnel." Nicholson drew a few coins out of his pocket, more of them copper than silver. "Enough to get home or have a meal in a pinch."

"I wonder if the three pounds was Jenkins's pocket money, and the twenty for some other purpose." Out of delicacy Lenox did not say it, but he couldn't imagine that the inspector earned more than two hundred fifty pounds a year. That meant he had been found with nearly a tenth of his annual wages upon his person—odder and odder. "Again we might ask Madeleine Jenkins, or Bryson."

Nicholson looked up at Lenox warily. "Perhaps you and I had better stick together after all."

Lenox smiled. "You want to make sure you're getting your fee's worth, I'm sure."

"Will you still take your fee, then?" asked Nicholson, rather surprised.

It pained Lenox to do it, but he nodded. For the first time he realized a strange truth: He was in trade. He had thought of the agency as a sort of clubhouse, but in fact he had broken the centuries-long sequence of Lenox sons who hadn't dirtied their hands with business. He felt himself flush, and then said, "I wouldn't for myself—because it's Jenkins—but I have partners to think of."

"Yes," said Nicholson. "I understand."

It was good for his self-regard, perhaps, thought Lenox. Humility. And then, it wasn't as if he were selling grain from a cart. Nevertheless it took him a moment to regain his concentration.

"Let's go to the Yard, in that case," said Lenox. "There's not much time to spare. I'll just speak to McConnell."

McConnell, having prescribed some medicine or other to his impromptu patient, was now standing by the police wagon with his arms crossed, smoking and patiently waiting. "There you are," he said when Lenox came to him. "It's getting rather late. Perhaps you could push us off now, and I could write you a note telling you what I find? Toto will be wondering where I am."

"Yes, by all means—or you can skip it altogether."

"No, no. I doubt I'll find anything, but because it is Jenkins—no, I will do as thorough a job as I know how, and hope it turns something up."

Nicholson had come out and waved to the driver and the constables nearby. The body could go. McConnell opened the back of the wagon and stepped inside. As he was about to swing the door shut, Lenox saw Jenkins's boots, protruding from under the sheet that covered him on the stretcher.

On an impulse he reached out as McConnell was closing the door. "Wait," he said.

The shoelaces still bothered him. Quickly he removed the unlaced shoe and examined it, turned it over. Nothing. Then, just to be safe, he unlaced the other boot and turned it upside down.

A very small envelope, smaller than a playing card, fluttered to the ground. Lenox bent down and picked it up. On it were written two words, which McConnell and Nicholson crowded around to read. All three of them looked at one another in surprise and consternation—for the envelope said, in Jenkins's crabbed hand, *Charles Lenox*.

CHAPTER EIGHT

The southward drive from Portland Place to Scotland Yard, which was situated not far from the river, was slow that evening, the streets clotted with theatergoers, with young men in spats and top hats on their way to late suppers, with vendors hawking fried onions and potatoes on one of the mildest nights of the year thus far.

"Would have been faster to take the underground," Nicholson observed angrily at one point, shooing away a man with a yoke slung around his neck, offering pint pots of ale from a large tray.

Of course they all would have been home faster still had Jenkins not been murdered, and Lenox, for his part, was ready to be patient. He stared out at the gaslight flicker of the city. First Baker Street, then Park Lane, the stylish hotels along it facing Hyde Park. There was too much to consider: on a human level, the death of his friend; on an investigative level, the nearness of it to Wakefield's house, and Jenkins's concealed missive to him. It had been unnerving to see his name upon that envelope.

More and more, his thoughts circled back to Wakefield.

The marquess was not one of these subtle madmen, showing a fine face in public and working from the shadows upon his designs.

He was simply malevolent, a wicked soul, one of those freak remainders that the mathematics of genealogy produces. Certainly there was nothing else in the Wakefield line, long stewarded by sensibly avaricious aristocrats, to have foreshadowed his existence.

Lenox had first heard of him more than a decade before, when the young heir had been forced to leave Hatting House for the Continent—for Spain, if Lenox recalled correctly—after whipping a stable hand into a coma. He had been angry because one of his hunting dogs, a fool puppy, had eaten cyclamen and died. The stable hand had lived, though he had lost one of his eyes. Nor had this been a first incident. There had been some violence toward a housemaster at Winchester, and later Wakefield's wife had left him two months into their marriage amid reports of intolerable cruelty, a young woman named Effie Maher, though not before conceiving the child who would become his son and heir. Much of the blame had attached to her, however, as she left; it always did to the woman, until the man was proved beyond doubt to be at fault.

That didn't take long. At this time Travers-George was still only the heir to the marquessate, and therefore under some control by his family. When his father had died he had come into the full allocation of rights and perquisites belonging to his rank, however, and nobody had been alive any longer to check his behavior. If he had been born Jack Smith in Whitechapel he would have been hanged half a dozen times. He had thrashed a bobby; killed one of his own racehorses with a rifle out upon the turf at Goodwood; harassed a young woman who did not return his affections into retreating to Shropshire, terrified for her safety. Yorkshire was certainly too hot to hold him, and now he lived on the fringes of respectable society in London: His companions were men of the turf, or aristocrats drummed out of the military, or those striving families who lived on the edges of good neighborhoods and to whom the title of marquess inspired such awe that no imaginable behavior short of murder on their doorsteps could have barred him from their dinners and dances. And possibly not even murder on their doorsteps.

All of this would have been enough to draw Lenox's attention—but what had made him so set upon seeing Wakefield in prison (he would have to be tried in the House of Lords, of course, which was what made his prosecution a trickier matter than that of Hughes, or Anson, or Wilchere, or any of the other six names on his list) was something else altogether.

At around the time that Lenox had first stood for Parliament, a servant in Wakefield's household had died. Her name was Charity Boyd. By all accounts she had been a quiet, dull girl, with few references and entirely without connections, which explained why she had taken a position in a household that held a poor reputation among those in service.

She had died by falling from the roof of Wakefield's house. The afternoon upon which this had happened had been a wet, windy one, and the girl's duties did take her to the roof from time to time, if the fireplace inside was smoking.

But a man who lived across the street had sworn up and down that two people had been upon the roof, not five minutes before Charity Boyd's body fell to the ground. The second had been a man with close-cropped black hair. This was a description that fitted the butler and the second footman, and for that matter any number of men in London—but also Wakefield himself, the owner of the house.

Jenkins had been on the point of arresting the marquess when suddenly the witness came into Scotland Yard, voluntarily, to re-tract his story. There was a great weal upon his cheek.

"Has the marquess intimidated you?" asked Jenkins.

Lenox had been sitting there. "No," said the fellow stoutly. He was a bachelor who owned a string of jewelry shops in London.

"We can protect you."

A smile ghosted to the surface of the man's face, then disappeared. "I was mistaken. I think I must have been in shock, hearing this poor girl died. At any rate I know she was alone upon the roof."

The case had fallen apart after that. There had been no violence on Charity Boyd's body other than that which had been caused by the fall, but according to the coroner she had been active sexually. Lenox had seen her in the morgue. She had an ugly, angelic face, very pale. The fall had broken her neck.

A few weeks after the inquest upon her death, Wakefield had gone on a tour of the colonies with just two servants, leaving London for six months. While he was away he had made investments that had increased his already substantial fortune; by the time of his return, London had forgotten many of the whispers against him.

Lenox hadn't.

One of his regrets during the years he had spent in Parliament was how little time he was able to devote to the lingering cases that had once been always half on his mind, a night or two every few months if he were lucky. Of the seven he had selected, Wakefield was the one he most despised. Perhaps it was because he could not forget Charity Boyd's lifeless face. Perhaps it was because they belonged to the same sphere of social life, he and Wakefield. So much had been given to the marquess; and he had taken more. Jenkins hated him, too, and they long ago had formed an alliance of two to keep their eyes on the aristocrat.

As the carriage drove down Dacre Street, Lenox could picture Wakefield in his mind's eye, short, immensely strong, with a permanently sunburned face, jet black hair, and blue, sparkling, mad eyes. He must have been the man to murder Thomas Jenkins—must have been, lurking near his home even if his servants hadn't seen him for a few days. But why? Why now? What had Jenkins known?

They would learn the truth soon enough; Jenkins's notes would tell it.

Lenox felt the tiny square envelope in his jacket pocket. It had contained two things, when they opened it on Portland Place: a red claim ticket without any identification as to its source, blank other than the usual overelaborate printed sequence of letters and numbers that luggage counters used, in this case SRKCLC#AFT119, and a scrap of paper, which said, *See my notes. TJ.*

"What do you think it is?" asked Nicholson.

Lenox shrugged. "We'd better look at his notes. Is the carriage ready?"

"I suppose he might have been carrying it for months."

"No. It's not worn enough to have lived in a shoe for that long."

"Then we don't know anything."

"We know that somebody tried to look in his shoe, after he was dead," said Lenox. "Did you know he kept things there?"

"No."

"Nor did I. And yet you and I knew him pretty well."

Nicholson took this in, considering it. "True," he said.

"Were his pockets turned out when you found him?"

"No." Nicholson opened the door of the carriage, inviting Lenox to step in ahead of him. "In fact, we were surprised to find so much money."

"Whoever it was went straight for his shoe, then." Lenox held the square notecard up in the air. "This was what they wanted. But they had to flee before they could find it."

Now, driving through London, he wondered what they might discover in Jenkins's notes. An entire case built against Wakefield, tidily written out? A few random thoughts? Another letter?

As they pulled into the horse enclosure of Scotland Yard, Lenox suddenly remembered something that had vanished from his mind completely until now: Two or three weeks before, when he had returned to the office from a midafternoon meeting with his solicitor, one of the clerks had informed him that Inspector Thomas Jenkins had called and left his card. At the time Lenox had assumed it was another gesture of reconciliation.

What if it had concerned the marquess?

Lenox was inclined to dismiss the thought. If it had been anything urgent, Jenkins would have called again, surely.

Or would he have? Perhaps the course of the investigation had
become rapid, consuming, or perhaps he had decided that Lenox
was best left out of it—the final vestige of friendship on Jenkins's
side discarded at last.

That was an ungenerous thought toward the dead man. And almost certainly wrong. There was the note in his shoe, after all, and
Thomas Jenkins had told Nicholson to get Lenox if anything should
happen to him.

McConnell went with Jenkins's body toward the morgue; Nicholson and Lenox climbed the empty stairwells and walked the
empty corridors of the building, nodding at the few people who remained there on late duty. Jenkins's office had been on a corner,
with a view of the Thames. A sign of his status.

When they reached it, Nicholson turned on a lamp, which
flooded the room with yellow light. The desk was crowded but tidy.
An aquatint of the Queen was the only framed picture upon the
walls.

Nicholson walked in, and Lenox followed him, determined to
discover what was in his notes that had made it worth murdering
an inspector of Scotland Yard.

CHAPTER NINE

To take at least a superficial glance at every paper in Jenkins's office took twenty minutes. Lenox and Nicholson did this together, impatient at first to find his cache of notes—they started with the drawers of the desk—and then with increasing puzzlement when it did not appear.

Nothing on or in his desk seemed to be related to Jenkins's work at the Yard. There was a cabinet nearby with two drawers, one for open cases, one for closed. They looked at the former carefully, the latter more quickly. Most of Jenkins's half-dozen open cases were no-hopers. There was a string of burglaries in Bayswater, which had ended in the death of a shopkeeper there. Two cases were from the East End, bad debts in all likelihood, or perhaps drink. In Lenox's experience one or the other was behind most of the murders one saw in the London slums.

Nothing referring to Portland Place—and nothing in the office at all that looked particularly marked out for immediate attention, to Lenox.

"Might his notes be at his home after all?" asked Nicholson.

"We had better hope so. That's our next destination."

Nicholson consulted a brass pocket watch. "It's passing eleven.

Henderson will have told her the news, Mrs. Jenkins, some time ago. I wouldn't be surprised if she had gone to bed after a glass of brandy. For the shock, you know."

"We must go tonight nevertheless, I fear," said Lenox. He hesitated, looking around the office, his hands in his pockets. This felt wrong to him. "Has somebody woken up Jenkins's sergeant? His constables?"

An officer of Jenkins's rank would have had as an immediate subordinate a subinspector, with the rank of sergeant; below these two would have been a pool of revolving constables, generally two at a time. The four men would attack each case in concert, drawing more constables from the Yard when Jenkins judged that they might require greater manpower.

"I don't think so," said Nicholson. "I suppose word might have reached them, but it happened too late for the evening papers, and all of them will live some way out on the underground. I imagine they all went to their homes at six o'clock. I wish Inspector Jenkins had done the same."

A terrible thought struck Lenox. "I hope they have not come to any harm themselves."

Nicholson's eyes widened. "Good heavens. You don't think they've been murdered, too?"

"I don't know. I hope not. It depends whether they were involved in whatever case brought Jenkins to his end, at least as long as we do not believe this was a random act of violence."

Nicholson put two fingers between his teeth and whistled down the hallways sharply. A constable, in his high bobby's hat, came striding briskly down to Jenkins's office. He was short and pimply, and couldn't have been more than eighteen, working the less desirable evening shifts during his first year or two on the job, junior to everyone. "Sir?" he said nervously.

"Send word that Sergeant Bryson and Jenkins's constables—whoever they are now—are to report for duty this evening."

"Sir."

"Send telegrams. I expect them here within the hour. You have their names and addresses?"

"They will be on the rotation list posted out front, sir."

"Good, see to it immediately."

"Sir."

As the young man walked away, Lenox looked once more around the office. It was surprisingly free of personal affect, but even so it seemed intensely sad: the room waiting for Jenkins as he had left it, its few objects gathered together into the shape of his absence, the ashtray, the small silver cup given him once by the government of Belgium, the aquatint of Victoria. One of his daughters bore that name, if Lenox recalled correctly.

Next to the silver cup, he noticed, was an empty rectangular space. He frowned. There was a kind of organized chaos of objects everywhere else on the desk—a pouch of tobacco, a stack of newspapers, some correspondence (including, rather embarrassingly, two notes from creditors to whom Jenkins owed money), a small ship in a bottle—but there, toward the back left, was this empty area. Ringed with objects, it looked suddenly as noticeable to Lenox as a pale rectangle on a wall from which a painting has been removed.

"Look," he said to Nicholson. "This space. You don't suppose someone's taken papers from it, do you?"

Nicholson, who had been studying one of Jenkins's open case files for a second time, shrugged. "It might be. Perhaps he took them home with him. More likely it's nothing at all."

Lenox felt uneasy, however. Jenkins had been a careful investigator. "Did his door lock?" he asked Nicholson.

"They all do, yes."

"And yet we didn't have to unlock it when we came in. It was open."

"Perhaps he left it open."

"Perhaps."

Still, it was hard to imagine Jenkins taking the care to write a note to Lenox and triple-tie it in his shoe, then leaving the crucial file on Wakefield—for Lenox thought it must be about Wakefield, all of this, the coincidence too great to imagine otherwise—in plain sight upon his desk, door open. That would have been stupidly careless. Jenkins had not been a careless fellow.

There were footsteps in the hall, more than one pair. The young constable reappeared in the doorway. "They've been sent for," he said. "And you have a visitor—visitors. Lord John Dallington and Mrs. Polly Buchanan."

Dallington and Polly rounded the door now, crowding past the constable. "There you are, at last," said Dallington, his generally imperturbable face flushed with anxiety. "Is it true?"

Lenox nodded. "I'm afraid it is."

"What can I do?" asked the young lord. "I'm here. Put me to work, Nicholson, if you like."

"And me," said Polly, who was half a step behind him. Her face was full of concern, too—but her eyes were cast toward Dallington, not Lenox.

"For the moment, anyhow, one of you might wait here," said Lenox. "Or indeed both of you. Nicholson and I mean to go see Jenkins's wife."

"Why does one of us need to wait here, then?" asked Dallington.

Lenox explained that they had called in Jenkins's subordinates. "They'll know where he kept his current paperwork, and what he was working on," said Lenox. "They may also know if Jenkins was meeting anyone tonight."

"I'll stay," said Dallington. "Polly, you've already had your evening disrupted—shall I put you in a carriage home first?"

"No," she said. "I'll stay with you here. I may be able to help."

Dallington didn't object. "Very well, thank you." He turned back to Lenox. "Do you have any sense of what might have happened, Charles?"

Lenox hesitated. It wasn't the moment just yet to disclose to Nicholson his thoughts on the Marquess of Wakefield. He felt he needed more information first. The Yard would find it difficult enough to pursue an aristocrat if they had substantial reason for suspicion. In this instance they didn't, not yet. "Only that it relates to a current case of his," said Lenox.

They knew each other well enough that Dallington had observed his fraction of a moment's pause, Lenox was sure. "How do you know?" was all that the young lord said.

In response to this question, Nicholson and Lenox described the sequence of events that the course of the night had unfolded: the circumstances of the murder, Jenkins's insistence that Lenox be called in (Polly looked surprised at this but said nothing), the twenty pounds in the inspector's billfold, and finally the note in his shoe.

"May we see the claim ticket?" asked Polly at the end of this account.

Lenox produced it, and Dallington and Polly inspected it. "Presumably it is important enough that he didn't want to leave it with his notes. They may offer some explanation."

"Or he didn't know what it was himself, and hoped you might make the link if he . . . if he was murdered," said Dallington.

"It doesn't belong to the luggage counters at Paddington, Liverpool Street, or Charing Cross," said Polly.

Lenox looked at her curiously, smiling. "Yes, I drew the same conclusion. And it's not from any of the better hotels. They print their tickets on finer paper. But how did you know?" he asked.

"I make a point of remembering them when I see them," she said. "In my old firm I dealt with a great number of lost property cases."

Nicholson and Dallington looked impressed. As for Lenox— there had been moments, in the past few months, when he had come to suspect that Polly had the brightest future in this field of any of them. Dallington had a great deal of talent, LeMaire a methodical mind; Polly had both. She was capable of insight and of deep organization. She saw structures—like the claim tickets—in a way that Dallington did not, in a way that was invaluable to anyone looking for patterns within the flurrying indiscriminate totality of London's crime.

So did Lenox. "Funny you say that. I keep these every time I receive one. The book I keep of them is at the office. I was going to check it before I went home this evening."

Now Polly looked at him curiously, and nodded slightly. He wondered how much the past months had depreciated her opinion of him, and whether he might raise it up again. He hoped he might. "Good," she said.

They spoke for a few more minutes, and then Nicholson looked at his watch again and said that he and Lenox had better be going; they agreed to separate, and Lenox and Dallington, at any rate, said they would rendezvous again the next morning in Chancery Lane.

CHAPTER TEN

Each of the four principals of the detective agency—Lenox, Dallington, Polly, LeMaire—had dragged some of his or her old workplace into this new association. For Dallington that meant erratic hours and an aversion to paperwork; for Lenox the occasional use in his (now scarce) work of supernumeraries, chief among them McConnell. Polly had Anixter always fixed to her side, the burly ex-seaman whose brawn complemented her quick wit. Moreover, from the start of her career she'd had the idea to employ, as the need arose, a well-organized array of forensic experts, of whom all four partners now made intelligent use. It was an innovation that was valuable nearly every day for one or the other of them—the sketch artist, the chemist, the gunsmith, the botanist.

As for LeMaire, he had brought two people along with him. The first was his nephew Pointilleux, a handsome young fellow of seventeen who served as apprentice and clerk to the office; the other was an Irish woman of fifty named Mrs. O'Neill, who had been LeMaire's first landlady in the English capital and was now his permanent charge.

When Lenox arrived in Chancery Lane the next morning just

before eight, Mrs. O'Neill was the only person there. She was on her knees in front of the fireplace, "How d'you do, Mr. Lenox?" she said.

"Fine, thanks, Mrs. O'Neill. Could you have the Coach and Horses send up breakfast, please? And we'd like a pot of coffee, too. I can make up the fire while you arrange it."

"You and Mr. LeMaire, sir?"

"No, Dallington's coming in."

"Oh!" Her eyes widened. She was generally a practical woman, but a title set her heart a-flutter. "I'll go straight away."

She beat Dallington back to the office—he came in five minutes after she did, wet from the rain. "Sorry to be late," he said, glancing at a clock on the wall. "What a storm there is outside. I should have paid attention during the swimming lessons at school, for as it stands I'm liable to drown if I go back out."

Lenox smiled tiredly. He had been up late. "I asked Mrs. O'Neill to get some food. I think she's in the pantry, putting it on plates."

"That was sporting of you," said Dallington, brushing the water off his charcoal-colored suit. "I'm starved."

"I take it you spoke to Jenkins's team at the Yard, after we left?"

"We did, we—"

Just then the Irishwoman pushed her way into the room, a tray in hand—which made her attempted curtsy for Dallington a uniquely awkward one. "M'lud," she said.

"Let me help you," said Dallington. "I don't think I've ever wanted a cup of coffee more."

"I've brought you extra bacon," she said.

"Thank you," said Dallington. "Marvelous."

She looked at him critically as he poured himself coffee and ignored the bacon. Whenever he was in the office she pushed food on him, seeming to imagine that, as a bachelor, he was always more or less upon the precipice of starvation. "Are you going to eat the bacon?" she asked after a moment.

"There's not much else to do with it." Dallington picked up a piece with two fingers. "Look, excellent. Lenox, shall we talk?"

Mrs. O'Neill was deaf to this hint, however; she went to the sideboard and tidied needlessly. "The poor, brave dear," Lenox heard her whispering to herself as she spooned extra sugar into Dallington's coffee.

"That's all," said Lenox sharply. "Thank you."

She hesitated in the door—but eventually departed. Lenox shifted some eggs onto his plate. There was something oddly comforting about this meeting room to him, for the first time, after Jenkins's death. It was certainly handsome: painted a light blue, with a long oval table that had been shined to a high brightness with beeswax, and big windows overlooking Chancery Lane. Dozens of raindrops were dawdling down them, moving infinitesimally until one would decide to fall all at once in a split second, as if dashing for a forgotten appointment. A melancholy day outside. But the office, the eggs, the coffee, Mrs. O'Neill, even the rain, conspired to make things seem faintly less desolate.

Now to capture the killer. Lenox set his mind firmly forward. "So. The sergeant," he said.

Dallington nodded. "Yes. Polly and I waited. The two constables arrived first, about fifteen minutes after you left. The sergeant, Bryson, followed them by another ten minutes. He lives farthest out."

"Where do they all live?"

"All of them far south." Dallington smiled. "I had the same idea."

"That one of them might have been involved?" said Lenox.

"Yes, precisely. So I did some checking. All three of them were on their usual trains at six o'clock, going in the opposite direction of Regent's Park and therefore, of course, of the scene of Jenkins's murder. None of them—according to Nicholson, who checked the records—had filed any type of grievance against him. And certainly all three seemed distraught."

"What information did they have?"

Dallington grimaced. "Not much, unfortunately."

"No?"

"The two constables hadn't seen Jenkins all week." It was Friday now. "And Bryson barely had either. Apparently on Monday Jenkins called all of them into the office and divided up his open cases among them. Bryson had the Bayside burglaries, and did say that Jenkins came with him to Bayswater on Wednesday morning. Otherwise he was away from the desk."

"And the constables?"

"They were working on the less serious crimes individually. Taking names, gathering information. One of them's very nearly solved a robbery in Mayfair, as he was only too pleased to tell me. I think he knew Polly and me—perhaps even wanted a job."

"Was it usual for Jenkins to delegate this way?"

"I was coming to that—no. Not at all. Customarily these four work very closely together. They're all very chummy." Dallington lifted a corner of toast and took a bite, staring down at his notes as he chewed. "In general they go to the scene of any major crime together, and then Jenkins and Bryson conduct the case in concert, while the constables do . . . well, constable work."

"Canvassing, questioning."

"Yes, exactly."

"To what did they attribute the change?"

"None of them is a fool. They all imagine that whatever made him go on his solitary way is also what killed him. They're all raring to investigate, too. They've joined Nicholson's team. Have you seen the papers this morning? Maybe out for blood."

Lenox nodded. "Yes."

The London newspapers were full of the murder, each one calling more loudly than the next for its immediate solution. Nicholson, with his amiable face and gangly frame, looked unequal, in the pictures published of him by the cheaper papers, to the task.

"If it comes to it, so am I, I'm afraid." The young lord shook his head. "It's the saddest damned thing I ever saw. He was a fine fellow at bottom, I always thought. Never mind that bother he gave us in January."

"Did any of the three remember a file upon the desk, in the spot I showed you?"

Dallington shook his head. "No, though they couldn't remember the papers *not* being there, either. But it may be worth mentioning that Bryson, who's been with Jenkins for two years now, said that he almost always carried his notes about London with him."

"His note to me makes him think he was keeping them separate on purpose—out of caution. It didn't work, unfortunately."

Dallington's eyes narrowed with concern. "Wait—why do you say that? Was the file not at his home? I assumed that you had re-trieved it from his house. You should have told me straight off."

"It wasn't in his study at home. No papers were, from the Yard. And Madeleine Jenkins didn't recall him bringing any papers home. Said he never did."

Dallington's face was grave. "I'd like to know where those notes are, then."

Lenox nodded. "So would I. I mean to go back to his office at the Yard and check again there. For the moment, however, I think we must assume that they've been stolen."

"Who would have done that?"

Lenox sighed and took a draught of his coffee. "The man I'd like you to find, actually. William Travers-George."

"Oh hell, Wakefield?" said Dallington.

"Wakefield."

CHAPTER ELEVEN

Mrs. O'Neill came to clear their plates soon—not quite daring to tut at the fullness of Dallington's, for she could sense the sobriety of the mood in the room—and filled their cups of coffee again before she left. She had interrupted Lenox's account of visiting Jenkins's wife, or rather now his widow.

"She was not hysterical, then?" asked Dallington.

"No. The other way, lifeless, dull. Very polite."

It had been a small, attractive, clean house in the leafy southern precincts of London, with a row of five uncommonly lovely gray alder trees giving it privacy from the street. Perhaps because of these the small plaque on the brick walkway to the front door named the house TREESHADOW. Lenox, who had grown up among houses with names bestowed upon them by the length of years, rather than the aspirations of their owners, had paused and stared at this as they entered, feeling intrusive. Who could now know what Jenkins's private dreams of stateliness had been. Certainly it was a fine house.

"And she was no help at all?" asked Dallington.

"Not for lack of effort. She showed us Jenkins's study, unlocked all of the drawers in his desk, let us go through the pockets of his suits. We were very, very thorough. Thank goodness for Nicholson—he has a gentle touch, and they know each other socially, I believe."

"How many children? Two?"

"Three, the third very young."

Dallington sighed. "I suppose the Yard will do something for them."

"Yes, I suppose. We might donate—the office."

"Or you and I, since we knew him. That might make more sense."

Lenox perceived underneath these words that his friend thought it might be wiser not to ask LeMaire, and even Polly, to part with any more money, which he ought to have considered himself. Briefly the frustrations of his position here returned to him, but he dismissed them. "Just so, you and I. Absolutely."

Dallington rapped the table with his knuckles. "Right," he said. "What are we to do today, then, you and I?"

"You're free to work?"

"Polly has agreed to take on all of my little cases."

"In that case I think you might try to find Wakefield. The timing of his departure is suggestive, obviously. I wish we knew where the scoundrel had taken himself."

Dallington nodded. He had heard all about the location of Jenkins's death, and knew from the past years about the marquess's reputation. "And what will you do?"

Lenox took the small envelope Jenkins had left for him from his pocket. "I stayed up late, trying to match this ticket to the left luggage counter of a hotel or a train station. Without luck. I have seventy-odd samples, all quite distinct, but none of them match this one."

"How will you find it, then?"

"I don't know, to be perfectly honest. We need Jenkins's notes. I might try to speak to his subordinates at the Yard. In the meanwhile someone ought to assemble a précis of the crime that has occurred around Portland Place in the last month, as well as any mentions of Wakefield that have been in the press. Something took Jenkins up to Wakefield's neck of the woods—something attracted his notice."

"We can have Marseille do it." Marseille was what Dallington called LeMaire's nephew Pointilleux.

"He doesn't like that nickname, you know."

"He should have been born English and not French, in that case. The initial error was his."

"He's from Paris anyhow."

Dallington smiled. "I know, it's only a joke. I'll try to call him by his name. Only he gets so superbly annoyed."

There was a knock at the door then. "Come in," called out Lenox.

It was LeMaire, leading McConnell, who smiled and lifted a hand. LeMaire nodded, stiffly, and said, "You have a visitor. We entered the building at the same moment."

"Thank you," said Lenox. Both he and Dallington had risen.

"I am sorry to hear about Inspector Jenkins," said LeMaire. "If there is any way in which I might help—please, do not hesitate to ask me."

"Thank you," said Lenox again. This formal civility was awkward. The worst of it was that LeMaire wasn't at all a bad fellow. Only a pragmatic one.

When LeMaire was gone McConnell came in and poured himself a coffee, after asking if he might take some. "I'm due at the hospital," he said, stirring in some sugar, "but wanted to come by. It was the bullet that killed Jenkins, I thought you ought to know. He was as healthy as an ox until the moment he died. No poison in his system, nor any alcohol, nothing unusual in his stomach. Sometimes the body throws up a surprise, but not in this case. It was a .442 Webley that shot him. Disappointingly common gun."

Lenox was still holding the claim ticket, and he stared surreptitiously at it as McConnell spoke, willing some idea of its origin to come to him. Nothing did, but he could feel the back of his brain working on the problem. "What about the wound on the hand?" he asked, looking up.

"Ah. That was slightly more interesting."

"What wound?" asked Dallington.

Lenox explained that there had been a cut, two or three days old, on Jenkins's left hand. "I asked his wife, and she said she didn't know about it, but that he had been much out of the house, not sitting to supper with his family, this week."

"I am all but certain that it was made by a short serrated knife," said McConnell. "The sort carried by a sailor to cut rope and sailcloth or a cook to chop vegetables."

"Or a police officer, perhaps?" asked Dallington.

McConnell thought for a moment. "I cannot see why. Of course the most likely thing is that he cut himself."

"We can ask his men if Jenkins carried a knife," said Lenox. "I don't ever remember him doing so."

As Dallington was about to reply, LeMaire came to the door. "Gentlemen," he said, "may I ask if this room will be free in fifteen minutes?"

"Do you need it?"

"If the trouble would not be too great."

Dallington, whose casual faith that the world would be well sometimes made him blind to awkwardness—or perhaps merely made him seem that way—said, "LeMaire, come and have a look at this claim ticket. We can't make anything out of it."

"A claim ticket?"

"Yes, and who knows, there may be a bag of money sitting out there that only this particular ticket can fetch. All hands on deck, you know."

LeMaire stepped forward; Lenox handed him the ticket unwillingly, and he took it and studied it for a moment. He was a handsome fellow, with dark hair that fell in a shag down below his collar, a gallant small pointed beard upon his chin, and a liveliness in his eye that bespoke quick intelligence. In many regards he was the Englishman's idea of a canny Frenchman. Certainly it was this veneer upon which he had built his business.

"I'm sorry, gentlemen," he said. "I cannot make anything of it."

"Call in Pointilleux," said Dallington. "Perhaps he can exercise his brain upon it. We're supposed to be teaching him something anyhow."

LeMaire raised his eyebrows but turned his head around the door. His young nephew appeared, a tall, straight-backed, superior young man with light brown hair. They gave him the claim ticket and like his uncle he studied it, though perhaps more thoroughly, turning it over, holding it up to the light. He was a very particular young fellow, who spoke dreadful English; Lenox rather liked him.

"I cannot make sensible of it," the boy said at last, in his heavy Parisian accent, handing it back to Lenox. "*SRKCLC#AFT119*. No. I am mystify."

"Mystified," LeMaire corrected him.

"Well, don't feel so bad," said Dallington. "None of us—"

But as he took it back from Pointilleux, Lenox, looking at it with fresh eyes, suddenly saw something new on the claim ticket. "Wait," he said. "I think I've got it."

The four other men in the room looked at him. "What?" said McConnell.

It had perhaps been the mention of sailcloth, or the phrase *all hands on deck,* or perhaps just the ceaseless invisible mechanics of his brain, but it seemed so obvious now. "SRKCLC," he said, repeating the letters on the ticket. "Southwark to Calcutta. AFT119. A ship has berths fore, starboard, port, and aft."

"It's a ticket for passage on a ship," said LeMaire.

Dallington whistled. "To India. My God."

Lenox nodded. "I don't know whether it's a ticket for a person or for cargo."

Dallington had already stood and was putting on his jacket. "It's for Wakefield, it must be."

"Damn it, you may be right," said Lenox. "He's probably leaving the country even as we speak."

LeMaire looked impassive, but his nephew seemed impressed. "It is done very handsome," said Pointilleux, in a grave voice. "Southwark to Calcutta. I see it now, of course."

"It took long enough," Lenox said, and then to Dallington, "Let's get along to the docks. Thank you, LeMaire."

CHAPTER TWELVE

As the cab drove to Southwark, Lenox stared out at the wet streets of the city and brooded upon the death of Jenkins, of his friend Thomas Jenkins of Scotland Yard. There were more points of oddity in this murder than most: the twenty pounds, the missing papers, the claim ticket, the unlaced boot, the wound on Jenkins's left hand, and above all the proximity of the body to the house of William Travers-George, Lord Wakefield.

Where had Wakefield fled? And why?

The Southwark docks were immensely busy. Eighty or ninety large ships were crowded along the banks of the Thames there, some of them with barely room to turn, their complex riggings latticing the sky with shifting shapes. Lenox could smell a strong odor of fish, wood, and especially tobacco—the Tobacco Dock, lined with immense warehouses where merchants with ships that went to America could store the stuff, was nearby.

They alighted at one of the docklands' many entrances. "There's a half-crown if you hold the cab," said Lenox.

The cabman touched his cap.

As they came nearer the water, Lenox and Dallington could feel its sharp breeze. Down in the water, though it was so cold still at this time of year, were the mudlarks, as everyone called them—very poor young boys, some only six or seven years old, who waded near the banks of the river, searching for coal, iron, rope, even bones, anything whatsoever that might be sold. Slightly more prosperous were the wherries that floated between the ships, tiny boats that offered quick passage to the docks for a coin or two, or ran errands for harried ships' stewards trying to put to sea on time.

This was also the location of the *Dreadnought*, instantly recognizable because it loomed higher on the horizon than any other ship. She was ancient by now: In 1805, she had been one of twenty-seven ships commanded by Horatio Nelson in the Battle of Trafalgar, part of a fleet that was outgunned by French and Spanish ships, of which there were thirty-three. But Nelson had been a genius. When the day was over the French and Spanish had lost twenty-two ships—the British, none. It was the greatest naval victory in the history of the world, as all English schoolboys learned. *Dreadnought* had been there.

Now she served a humbler purpose. She was a floating seaman's hospital, a place where any current or former seaman could find medical care for free, if he didn't mind close quarters and irregular doctor's visits. It was one of the most popular charities in London.

In sight of *Dreadnought*, Lenox and Dallington found a small stall with a sign that said CARGO AND SHIPPING. It looked as promising as anything else. They went in.

Behind the counter was an old white-haired man with scruffy white stubble on his face, dressed in a pea coat and poring over a ledger. He looked up. "Help you?"

Lenox held up the ticket. "We were hoping to claim some luggage. For the ship to Calcutta."

"You've gone three dockyards too far west, in that case," said the man, smirking. "Not regulars in these parts, are you, chaps?"

"Lenox here sailed with the *Lucy*," said Dallington indignantly. "All the way to Egypt and back."

"Oh, begging your pardon," said the man, with wildly exaggerated deference. "To Egypt *and* back you say? Has he written his memoirs? Has he visited with the Queen?"

Dallington frowned. "Yes, you're very funny."

"The world must know his story! Egypt and back!"

They left this derision behind with as much self-possession as they could muster and hopped in the cab again, which they directed to drive west as they counted off the docks. In the first yard had been more passenger ships, and while this looked to be full of cargo ships, there was another small stall with a similar sign. This one had a bit more enterprise; it said HELMER's CARGO, SHIPPING, WOODWORKING.

As soon as they went in it was apparent that Mr. Helmer was also engaged in a different kind of business—five women, very plainly prostitutes, were sitting at a table playing cards. They were genial in their greetings. Helmer, apparently, was at the moment aboard a ship called the *Amelia*. No, it wasn't bound for Calcutta; that was the *Gunner*, in slip eleven. But they wouldn't be permitted on board either ship without Helmer. Even the ticket, which Lenox held up to show them, wouldn't allow them that.

"Cheap buggers on the *Gunner*, if you were hoping to make any money on your backs," one of them added, by way of good-bye, and for the second time in the docklands Lenox and Dallington left with gales of laughter in their wake.

The information had been good, however. Helmer was just leaving the *Amelia* when they arrived at it, dashing down the taut diagonal rigging between the ship and the dock, though he must have been sixty and was certainly overweight. He looked up to answer to his name.

"Yes?" he said.

Lenox held up his ticket, and for the first time there was recognition in someone's eyes. "I'd like to claim my property." He had decided that it was more likely the ticket was for a piece of cargo than for a berth upon a ship. "If it's not too much trouble."

"That ship is leaving in ninety minutes," said Helmer, his eyes hooded and suspicious. "Why on earth would you take something out of it when you'd paid handsomely to ship it, a hold in the aft?"

"Do I need to provide my reasons?"

"Well—no," said Helmer. "But it's unusual, you know."

"Then you'll have a story for the pub," said Dallington. "Here, you can buy everyone a drink to tell it."

Helmer cheered up considerably when he saw the half-crown Dallington was offering, and led them to slip eleven. "Captain won't be happy, you know. But I suppose it's within your rights."

"What kind of ship is it?" asked Dallington.

Helmer stopped and turned toward him with frank astonishment as they walked side by side. "Isn't it your cargo?"

"No—my friend's. I just happened to see him and come along."

"Which it's a cargo ship, mostly." He started walking again. There was a thick plug of tobacco in this entrepreneur's cheek and a tattoo upon his forearm. Obviously he had once been a seaman, and perhaps after his ship had taken a prize he had used his portion of it to open his business. He seemed successful enough, to gauge by the prostitutes he employed. There must have been immense demand for them, ships full of men isolated for months at a time. "The *Gunner* takes mail, parcels, and of course goods from England. A great deal of sugar and flour and cloth. For the lads in India, you know. A few passengers, if need be. Sometimes the navy lets a few berths for its men, or the marines, if they're chasing their ships, is what it is."

The *Gunner* was a slovenly ship, Lenox could tell at an instant, with none of the trim efficiency he had come to know on the *Lucy* (upon which he had, indeed, spent several diverting weeks in transit). Its ropes were slack, its paint was chipping. Men idled fore and aft. It also didn't look as if it could move very quickly, which made it surprising when Helmer said it was reckoned the fastest mailboat to India.

"They look out for her in Calcutta, you know. Most recent newspapers and such. If you're lucky the *Gunner* might bring you a copy of the *Times* that's only eight weeks out of date, if you're one of them great sahibs sitting on a balcony with ten darkie servants. Admiral Fanshawe never sends his mail by any other vessel."

"You'd think he owned the bloody ship," muttered Dallington, falling a step behind.

"Or that someone wanted to ship their cargo with very great haste."

Dallington considered this. "Yes, true."

As they walked up the gangway a great number of eyes turned toward them, none friendly. Lenox had heard of mailboats whose officers and crew committed acts of piracy when chance threw a weaker foreign vessel in their path. There was a blood oath among all those on board—punishable by death for its transgression—that the secret of these crimes was to stay among them. If it weren't for the ship's renowned speed, Lenox would have believed it of the *Gunner* in an instant. She had no very great appearance of rectitude.

At the top of the gangway they were stopped by a sour-looking lieutenant, irretrievably sun- and wind-burned, past forty. "Who's these?" he said.

"Two paying customers, what's let a hold on this ship," said Helmer. He had some pugnacity in his voice. "Where's Dyer?"

"Indisposed."

"Dispose him prompt."

The lieutenant's eyes grew dark, but then he saw that Helmer was patting the little pocket of his waistcoat, and understood there was money to be made. "This way."

The appropriate, extortionate number of coins changed hands, first with the lieutenant and then with Captain Dyer, a rat-faced but well-spoken man—a gentleman's son, at any rate, probably ex-navy, with no chance of promotion within those ranks because of lack of interest—who took the claim ticket.

"You can have it back, whatever you put in there," he said, "but not your money. We ship in eighty-four minutes, you know."

"Just so," said Lenox.

They descended into the hold by a series of short ladders, the smell worsening the farther they went from daylight. Hammocks were bundled up into the rafters on the lowest level; on every side were small doors with numbers stenciled on them. Dyer and Helmer led the way toward the aft, the rear, of the ship. Numbers 119 and 120 sat on top of each other, their door divided halfway. They were two of the larger storage doors.

"Do we need a key?" said Lenox.

"Only mine."

Dyer opened the door. Lenox hadn't been sure what he was expecting, but something more interesting than what he saw—first, an old and very large sea trunk of wood and brass, its lock flapping open, and second, a stack of old hammocks, extras, presumably. "Dallington, help me pull the trunk out, would you."

With the help of Helmer—who was clearly anticipating further remuneration at the end of this adventure, a hope in which Lenox looked forward to disappointing him—they maneuvered the trunk into the cabin. "Not overly heavy," said Dallington. "Though it will be some work to get it aloft. Shall I open it?"

The young lord pulled back the lid and frowned. "What's that?" he asked.

There was something grayish filling the large trunk to its very top edge. "Salt," said Lenox, and felt his heart begin to race. He dropped to his knees and began to push it aside.

It took a second, two seconds, to brush away the top layer of coarse salt. At the same instant all three standing men gasped. Helmer yelped. "Is that a body?"

"It is," said Lenox.

Helmer shook his head. "Christ, Dyer, you've copped it now."

Lenox uncovered the face. "Who is it?" asked the ship's captain.

Dallington had seen, and his eyes widened. He turned to Lenox for confirmation, and Lenox nodded. "Yes, it's him."

"It's who?" said Helmer.

"Eighty-four minutes may be an overoptimistic estimate of your departure time, Captain Dyer," said Lenox. "This is the body of the Marquess of Wakefield."

CHAPTER THIRTEEN

Unsurprisingly, Lenox returned home that evening much later than he had planned, later than supper, past eight o'clock. Despite the hour he heard children's voices when he opened the door, and smiled. He guessed Toto—McConnell's wife, and one of Jane's intimate friends—would be visiting.

His confirmation came almost immediately; as he walked up the long, softly lit central corridor of the house he saw a young person shoot from the drawing room with unladylike verve: little Georgianna McConnell. This was Thomas and Toto's only daughter, a beautiful child with light brown curls and wide striking dark eyes.

"Hello, George," he said.

"Hello, Uncle, give me a candy please," she cried as she hurtled toward his legs.

Lenox braced for the impact, and after it came patted her head as she held him at the knee. "I haven't got any. Though I do owe you a birthday present. Five years old, was it? I wish I could have been at the party."

"It was my birthday," she informed him.

"Yes, I know, I just mentioned it."

"I'm five."

"I never, were you?"

They discussed the party for a moment in serious tones. Charles took care not to refer to her unmet wish—to ride above the city of London in a hot air balloon, something that McConnell, a worrier, would no more have permitted than a donkey in the dining room—because he knew it was still a point of sore disappointment to her. "Did you have a cake?" he asked.

"Of course I had a cake," she said pityingly, as if he were soft-headed even to ask.

He led her by the hand into the drawing room. It was where Lady Jane spent much of her time, a light space with rose-colored sofas and pale blue wallpaper. Jane and Toto, a young woman of high spirits and high humor, were sitting close together. Both looked up and smiled, then said hello. Near them on the floor was Sophia, Lenox's own daughter. With a feeling of deep love, almost as if he had forgotten, he perceived that she was tired, perhaps fussy, though at the moment she was absorbed in some kind of wooden toy made up of a ball and a dowel.

He picked her up and kissed the top of her head, ignoring her cry of displeasure when he pulled her away from her toy, and then set her down again. "I've just been with your husband," he said to Toto.

"Have you? About poor Mr. Jenkins?"

"Poor Mr. Jenkins and more, unfortunately. But why are these girls up?" he asked. "It's very late, you know."

Toto looked at the gold clock on the mantel. "So it is. But I cannot hold with putting a child to bed when there's still light in the sky. We aren't Russian peasants. There must be some joy in life, Charles."

"It's been dark for two hours."

"It's also unattractive to be so literal." She sighed. "Still, I do need to take George home. Jane, thank you for the glass of sherry, and the biscuits she ate. George, step to, time to go home and go to bed."

George was standing by Lenox. "Shan't," she said.

Around her father—of whom she stood in awe—George was saintly. She was more comfortable around her mother, and correspondingly far more willful, possibly one of the most willful children in London, Lenox sometimes thought. Beside her parents, the rest of her loyalty in life was given over to one of Lenox's dogs, Bear, whom she worshipped with uncritical adoration. She begged every day to be allowed to visit him. Now she walked over and lay down on top of him. He was a docile dog and didn't mind, and neither did Lenox or Lady Jane, though these were unorthodox manners in a child. An aristocrat's child could perhaps make her own rules, to some degree.

Toto frowned at her daughter. "You shall too, or your father will know about it."

She was holding Bear's ear with her small fist. "Shan't and won't."

Lady Jane smiled mildly and said, "Charles, tell us about Jenkins while George rests."

This was a clever stratagem. The child already looked tired, as if Lenox's arrival had reminded her that it was late, and after only a moment or two of adult conversation she was half-asleep on top of the dog. Lenox lifted her carefully up and carried her out to Toto's carriage, where Toto waved a silent but cheerful good-bye. Back inside, Sophia's nurse was taking her up to bed.

"You know how to end a party," said Jane as they walked back up the steps. "You must have been terribly unpopular as a bachelor."

Lenox smiled and took her hand as they reentered the house. In the front hall he stopped at the table and looked through the calling cards on the silver rack—left by their visitors for the day, cleared at midnight—and at the stack of post next to it. Nothing very interesting. Jane, next to him, put a hand on his shoulder and kissed his rough cheek.

"Are you hungry?" she asked.

"Just a bit."

"I'll have Kirk fetch something. Will you tell me what's happened about Jenkins?"

What had happened about Jenkins—it was a story that could fill many inches of column space. "I will. Have the evening newspapers arrived?"

"They're on your desk."

"I just want to glance at them. I'll be along to the dining room shortly."

"Let's eat in the drawing room, it's more comfortable. Will roast pheasant do?"

"Handsomely," he told her, and then went to look at the papers.

A glance was enough to tell him that they had been fortunate for a second straight day—Wakefield's body had been discovered just too late, probably by half an hour or so, to make the presses. The morning papers, broadsheets and rags alike, would be full of the matter, of course—the death of one of the highest peers in the land—but the papers of this evening contained only news of Jenkins.

When Dallington and Lenox had uncovered Wakefield's body aboard the *Gunner*, the whole apparatus of Scotland Yard had churned once again into motion. First there was the constable who patrolled the dockyards (Helmer made himself scarce, perhaps wishing to avoid the nuisance of any questions about his semilegal brothel), and soon a fleet of his kind followed. After only fifteen or twenty minutes Nicholson had arrived.

"Is it true it's Lord Wakefield?" he'd said. "That's what I was told."

"Yes, it's true."

"Heavens. This will mean a great deal of attention."

"I should imagine," said Lenox. "We would like to consult upon this murder, too, if you don't mind."

"Mind! I'll pay both of you, but for pity's sake, help me, help me."

Nicholson smiled faintly as he said this, looking gray and washed-away, as if he had barely slept, and Lenox was reminded how much he had enjoyed working with the inspector that winter, before the opening of the agency. He was refreshingly without pridefulness, but sharp, too, and competent.

"The three of us together will crack it," said Lenox. "At any rate let us hope this is the end of the deaths."

"One a day might be reckoned too many by some, yes," said Nicholson, shaking his head.

Lenox had sent for McConnell. The Yard's medical examiner hadn't been long in arriving, but he was a harassed and overworked fellow, and would admit himself that he didn't have the training McConnell did. The body showed no obvious signs of violence, which was odd.

"Poisoning, do you think?" asked Lenox as a swarm of constables lifted the trunk up to the topdeck.

"I don't think it was natural causes," answered Dallington, staring behind them with his hands in his pockets.

"The salt to preserve his body, I suppose. The voyage to India is long and hot."

Dallington nodded. "Enough so that I doubt the salt would have done the job."

Lenox had shrugged. "It would have kept the smell down long enough that the ship was unlikely to turn back to London. Forty miles would have been enough, from what I'm guessing of the economic interests of the ship. Perhaps four."

"True."

"And very likely when they discovered the body, in two or three weeks, they would have buried it overboard. Sailors are madly superstitious about a dead body on board. They're a breed of people that can find an omen in every seahawk, of course. A corpse is almost too ominous to conceive for them."

"Then the body would have been gone, with a cannonball at its feet, to the bottom of the ocean," said Dallington, "and no evidence that it was Wakefield at all. We might still have been chasing him, thinking he had absconded in the middle of the night after killing Jenkins."

"Yes," said Lenox. "Word to the Continent, police officers everywhere looking for him, hundreds and thousands of hours wasted. Now only one thing remains to be discovered."

"What's that?"

"Who paid to ship him to India?"

CHAPTER FOURTEEN

Helmer hadn't been able to tell them the answer to this question.

They went almost straightaway to his little stall, which was now, predictably, empty, the women who had occupied it before evidently not caring to make the acquaintance of the members of the Metropolitan Police force. Helmer, perhaps aware of his uneasy position, was now eager to help, though the prospect of a payout had gone. To Lenox's surprise, he kept excellent records. Unfortunately even his precise ledger didn't tell him who had let storage space AFT119.

"That's one of the captain's spaces," he said.

"The captain rented it?" asked Dallington.

"No, no. It only means that it's a standing order—that the same person ships out in that space every time the *Gunner* goes to India. We call those the captain's spaces, always have. See, look here. I have a list of spaces available for the next run right here." There was a little diagram of the ship's hold. "The squares that are cross-hatched are the ones I've rented. The ones that are blacked out altogether—those are the *Gunner's* standing orders, the captain's spaces. Four dozen, say. One of them belongs to Admiral Benson, I happen to know, because I stow it up for him."

"What does he ship?"

"Scotch whisky, crates of the stuff. Don't know if he's selling it or drinking it."

"I'm sure he would appreciate your discretion," said Dallington.

Helmer looked indignant. "Which you're the police, ain't you?"

Lenox didn't answer the question, since it put him rather in a false position. "Who stows up the spaces if not you?"

"The owners."

Dallington and Lenox exchanged looks. "We'd better ask Captain Dyer, then," said Lenox.

"I think it's a capital idea," said Helmer. He was at constant pains to prove he had nothing to hide, was even willing to let them take his ledger away with them, as long as he could make a copy first. Who knew where the ledgers for his secondary, less salutary business were kept. One problem at a time. "Though he'll be wanting to set sail. The *Gunner's* nothing without she's on schedule."

Lenox and Dallington went back out from Helmer's stall into the open air of the docklands. Dyer was standing on the forecastle of his ship, arms crossed, observing the constables on their business. He looked out of countenance. This was a severe disruption to his plans, of course. Lenox knew from his time on the *Lucy* that the forecastle was the preserve of the common sailor, but the quarterdeck of the *Gunner*, which the officers alone were permitted to use, was at the moment dominated by the trunk with Wakefield's body. Its lid was open, the ivory relief of the corpse just visible above its edge.

They crossed the gangway and went to him. "You've brought me a pretty peck of trouble, gentlemen," he said, smiling grimly. "Though I'm glad the responsibility is out of my hands before we ship."

"Captain Dyer, I understand that the hold space with the trunk in it, 119 aft, is a captain's space? Held by the same person for all of your trips."

"Yes, that's right."

"Who?" asked Lenox.

Dyer looked surprised. "Why, Wakefield!"

Dallington and Lenox glanced at each other. "You mean to say that Wakefield let that space from you?" asked Lenox.

"From the ship's owner, yes."

"Is that you?"

"I wish it were. No, the *Gunner* belongs to the Asiatic Limited Corporation. They have nineteen ships in all."

"I've heard of them," said Dallington.

"How long has Lord Wakefield had that space?" asked Lenox.

"Six or seven voyages, so it must be a couple of years," said Dyer. "He once or twice came aboard the ship himself to stow his cargo."

"What did he ship?"

"I never would have presumed to ask him."

"You didn't feel obliged to check the contents of the trunk?" asked Dallington. "For the sake of the ship's safety? What if it had been . . . I don't know, explosives?"

Dyer looked at him oddly. "The thought never occurred to me. Anyway, I imagine he usually sent liquor, European liquor. Nine-tenths of our hold is filled with it, either for sale or use."

"Aren't the men tempted to steal it?" asked Lenox.

"I know the drunkenness of the our navy is a national joke, but I have a crew I can trust—a crack crew. I turn hands away. They'd drop any man who tried overboard before I could do it myself. We share out the earnings, you see. All of us are here for the money. Anything that gets in the way of it is a nuisance. Like this, for instance, with all respect to the lord."

"The trunk came aboard this morning?" asked Lenox.

"Yes," said Dyer.

"At what time?"

"I wasn't here." He spotted a passing officer. "Lieutenant Lawton, what time did AFT119 come aboard this morning?"

Lawton thought for a moment. "Fairly early, not after eight o'clock."

"I take it Wakefield didn't bring aboard the trunk himself," said Lenox.

"No," said Dyer dryly.

"Who did?"

"Lieutenant, who brought the trunk aboard?"

"Two dockhands, sir."

"Did you know them?"

"Not by sight, sir. The usual sort."

"There are a thousand stevedores on these docks," said Dyer, turning back to Lenox and Dallington. "Any of them would have brought the trunk on board for a few coins. They had the correct tickets?"

"Oh, yes," said Lawton. "We always check twice, as you know, Captain."

How had Jenkins come by Wakefield's claim ticket, Lenox wondered? And had he known what it was? Of course, it might have been a ticket from a past voyage, too.

"Who took the contents of Wakefield's hold from you in Calcutta?" asked Lenox.

Dyer shook his head. "I haven't the faintest idea. We're often many leagues homeward by the time anyone collects what we've left, of course."

Dallington frowned. "What do you mean? Don't they have to come on the ship and gather their things?"

"In the Asiatic warehouse at Calcutta there's a room the exact dimensions of our hold, and with all the same markings, too. The men simply transfer every box's contents into its replica, and we set sail. India is a slow-moving country. They have several months— until we're back again, in fact—before their things must be out."

"But who would have been permitted to take away the contents of Wakefield's box?" asked Lenox, puzzled.

"He would have had an arrangement with one of the local companies, almost certainly. The Asiatic office can likely tell you. I'd be happy to give you their address." His eyes scanned the decks of the ship critically. "Perhaps it might persuade the Yard to let our ship leave port sooner."

Lenox made a note on his pad to consult with them. It was slightly maddening, this whole thing—they knew more than they could have hoped when they came to the docks and also less. Was Wakefield still a suspect in Jenkins's murder? Or had the same person killed both men? It was critical in cases like this, Lenox had learned, not to let the second murder seem more important than the first.

After they had finished speaking to Dyer and getting descriptions from Lieutenant Lawton of the two stevedores who had brought the trunk on board—which were singularly unhelpful, since nearly every man on the dock wore the same navy or black woolen jersey, and most were also "dark-haired, I think"—Dallington and Lenox went back down to the docks, where Nicholson was ordering people about.

"Are you going to hold the *Gunner* in London?" asked Dallington.

"For a day or two at least. This is a disaster, you know. Parliament will scream bloody murder. They don't think the Yard monitors the shipyards well enough as it is."

Dallington looked around at the dozens of ships nearby. "It would take more men than are in London to monitor every hold of every ship."

"You and I know that," said Nicholson. "This Wakefield—you know he owned a house on the street where Jenkins died?"

Lenox nodded. "Yes."

"Did you suspect him?"

Lenox decided that it was time to tell Nicholson what he knew, and he relayed it now: Charity Boyd, what Dyer had just told them, the mystery of Jenkins holding Wakefield's claim ticket. "I think they must be linked," he said.

"Certainly it would seem so," said Nicholson. He didn't look pleased to be hearing of Lenox's suspicions a day late. "What now?"

"I think before the city gets hold of the news, Dallington and I had better go speak to the people at Wakefield's house. Will you come with us?"

Nicholson looked around. "Yes, why not," he said.

"Please tell whomever you leave in charge that McConnell is coming shortly. He can tell us at any rate how Wakefield died, if not why."

CHAPTER FIFTEEN

As the carriage horses pulled the three men toward Portland Place, Lenox glanced at his watch. It was still shy of noon. They neared Wakefield's house, and almost as if on time for their arrival Lenox saw the high black gate of the convent two doors down open. After a moment two columns of girls emerged in a somber procession. Their eyes were trained on the ground. They looked rather old to be in school—seventeen or eighteen. Novices, perhaps. Behind them an old woman in a habit shut the gate behind them and locked it. Were they going on a walk to Regent's Park? They turned in that direction, anyhow. Lenox sighed. It looked a grim life—orphans, most of them, he imagined, mixed in with a girl or two who had gotten into trouble very young. Still, they had better lives than many of the orphans in the East End. During the winter especially.

When Nicholson knocked on the door of Wakefield's house it opened immediately, as if someone had been standing near it and waiting. "Sirs?" said a young man.

"Are you the butler?"

"May I inquire as to your business?" he said.

Nicholson showed his identification. "Scotland Yard."

"Ah. I'm not the butler, no, I'm the footman, sir. Just a moment, if you don't mind, and I'll fetch him. Please, come in and wait here."

He led them into a hallway with a black-and-white checkerboard floor, the walls painted a stark white. It had the kind of bloodless beauty one occasionally saw in the houses of aristocrats with very little sense of domesticity; there was a beautiful secretary against the wall, a small portrait of a lady and her King Charles spaniel that must have been painted the century before, and underneath it a complex carriage clock with rubies to mark the hours. There was no sign here of inhabitation. No umbrella stand, no letter rack. It was very clean, very finely appointed, and very cold.

Soon a butler came, a pale man in middle age with a slight limp and dark hair. "Gentlemen?" he said. He had returned alone. "You asked for me?"

"Lord Wakefield is out?" asked Dallington quickly, getting in ahead of Nicholson.

"Yes, sir."

"Where is he?"

"Perhaps if I had some idea why you sought him out, sir."

Nicholson glanced at Dallington and then shook his head. "You might as well know—Lord Wakefield's dead."

The butler, though trained his whole life to suppress the instinct, couldn't help but react. His eyes grew wide, and his breath seemed to catch. "Dead, you say? Lord Wakefield? Are you quite sure?"

"Yes. And I know from one of my constables that he'd been gone for a day beforehand."

The butler hesitated. "I suppose you had better come in," he said. "Dead, my goodness. I suppose I shall have to look out for a new place. Not that . . . in the circumstances . . ."

"How long have you worked for His Lordship?" asked Nicholson.

"A little more than one year, sir."

"And how many staff does he keep?"

"Five of us full-time, sir."

"All living in?"

"Yes, sir. A butler, a footman, a cook, and two maids. To be honest there is barely work for each of us to fill our time, sir. Lord Wakefield's needs are few. He lives—lived—largely in two rooms upstairs. This was his father's house, and he has left it as he found it when he inherited it."

"Are all five of you here this morning?" asked Lenox.

"Yes, sir."

Lenox looked at Dallington and Nicholson. "I think we had better see all of them now."

The interviews took not more than half an hour. All the servants told the same tale: a master they didn't know well, though if he ever paid them attention it was because something had angered him, not pleased him. The cook in particular, a pretty, timid young woman from Lancashire, seemed intimidated by the marquess. She was just as ignorant as the rest of them about Wakefield's movements around London.

"What about visitors?" said Lenox to the butler—his name was Smith—after the interviews were concluded. They were sitting in a room with high vaulting windows and a view of a serene and exquisite back garden, with manicured hedges and thickset rosebushes. "Did Lord Wakefield often entertain?"

"Not often, sir. Private dinners now and again—but even those were rare. He was most often at his clubs."

"Was there any difference to him in recent weeks?" asked Dallington.

Smith looked up, thinking. He had refreshingly little of the reticence one found in most household retainers; it was clear that he bore Wakefield neither much loyalty nor much malice, and that his professional scruples were sincere but not limitless. "Now that you mention it, sir, Lord Wakefield has entertained more often than was usual with him, this month or so. He had four or five different visitors. Though only a single visitor came more than once."

"Who was that?"

"We addressed him as Mr. Francis, sir."

"Addressed him—was that not his name?"

"I don't know, sir. I phrase it that way only because I recall that Lord Wakefield called him Hartley, when they spoke one to one."

Nicholson said, "So his name might be Hartley Francis, or Francis Hartley."

Lenox frowned. "How often did he visit?"

"Three or four times a week in the last month, sir, often for several hours in the evening."

"Was he someone who might have been in Lord Wakefield's employ? Or was he a friend—a gentleman?"

"Oh, no, sir, he was a gentleman. He and Lord Wakefield met on quite equal terms. Mr. Francis even chaffed His Lordship, now and then."

"When was the last time Francis was here?"

"He was here just last night, sir, very late, after midnight. He asked to see Lord Wakefield, but as you know His Lordship had been gone by then for some time. He left a parcel."

"Mr. Francis did? Or Lord Wakefield?"

"Mr. Francis, sir, last night."

"Do you have it still?" asked Lenox.

"Yes, sir, in the front hall."

"Could we please see it?" said Nicholson.

For the first time Smith looked doubtful. "I think I had better return it to Mr. Francis—or perhaps to Lord Wakefield's heir."

"Your master was mixed up in some very bad business, Mr. Smith," said Lenox. "Your interests no longer lie with his. We really must see that parcel, if you don't mind."

Smith hesitated, and then acquiesced. "Very well, sir. If you wait a moment I'll fetch it."

As they waited, Lenox, Dallington, and Nicholson sipped at cups of tea, which the footman had brought in and the butler had silently poured for them as they asked their questions. They conferred in low tones about their interviews with the other four staff members—nothing particularly pertinent, they concurred, though all five servants had agreed that Wakefield had seemed preoccupied in recent weeks. According to the footman he had thrown a plate of turtle soup across the room and stormed out three nights before. That was the worst tale any of them could tell of him. Perhaps, however, that was because all were relatively new to his employ. Smith had been at Portland Place the longest—only a year.

The butler returned with a parcel bound in brown paper and tied with string. It was covered all over with stamps. "I thought you said he delivered it by hand?" asked Lenox.

"He did, sir," said Smith. He looked at the package. "Oh, the stamps, sir. No, I cannot explain those."

"They aren't canceled," said Dallington, running his eyes over the parcel as he took it.

"Perhaps he intended to send it by post and changed his mind, sir?"

"Hold it with this, if you don't mind," said Lenox to Dallington, drawing out a handkerchief. "McConnell may be able to make something of the fingerprints."

Dallington passed the parcel over, and Lenox studied it. He could remember the stamps of his childhood so vividly: fourpence for the first fifteen miles a letter was to travel, eightpence the next eighty, seventeen the next even hundred. In those days, of course, the recipient had paid. Poor people had often sent each other empty envelopes, which the addressee rejected, simply as a message to let each other know all was still well. Then Rowland Hill had invented the postage stamp, and it had all changed . . .

"Shall I open it?" asked Lenox.

"Carry on," said Nicholson.

Lenox had a small pair of silver-handled scissors in his breast pocket and took them out to cut the sturdy string. He tried, on principle, not to untie knots in his detective work, since they were occasionally as distinctive as fingerprints.

Within the package was another small wrapped parcel, in a box, and a note. Lenox opened the note first and read it aloud.

Travers-George—here it is back for you. Tomorrow just before midnight at York's. Urgent that we tie up loose ends. Hartley.

"Tomorrow—that means today," observed Nicholson.

"What's in the box?" said Dallington.

Lenox was busy opening it—a small box, not quite large enough to hold a quarto. Despite experience inuring him to surprises, he gasped when he saw what it held.

"What is it?" asked Nicholson, leaning over to get a look.

Lenox lifted the object with his handkerchief. "A pistol," he said.

Nicholson paled. "A .422 Webley. The kind of gun that killed Jenkins," he said.

CHAPTER SIXTEEN

The three investigators and the butler sat there in silence for a moment, and then Nicholson said, very pointedly, "What else can you tell us about this person—Francis, Hartley, whatever the hell he's called?"

Unfortunately Smith knew very little. He was more than happy to recapitulate the few small details of dress he recalled—a crimson dinner jacket one evening, for instance, as if he had come from or was going to attend some fashionable event—but he couldn't offer a great deal else. To Lenox the most interesting thing the butler told them was of the variable nature of Hartley's visits. He sometimes came for ten minutes, sometimes three hours. It suggested either close friendship—or business.

It was an odd feeling to hold in his hand the gun that might have killed Jenkins, with its very slight heft, its small size a kind of final insult.

"We must go and meet this fellow tonight," said Dallington at last, glancing up at the wall clock. "I suppose York must be a friend of theirs."

"Yes. It's not all that common a last name, either. The first thing to do is check the rolls of his clubs," said Lenox. "Smith, what clubs was Lord Wakefield a member of?"

"Too numerous to mention, sir—many lifetime memberships came down to him from his father—but the two he regularly visited were the Cardplayers and the Beargarden. He almost always took his luncheon at the Beargarden and his supper at the Cardplayers, and then stayed on after supper for his cigar and his glass of port, playing whist."

That made sense. Both were clubs devoted to drinking and gambling, dominated in their membership by young men. Wakefield wouldn't have found the clubs along Pall Mall congenial, in all probability, with their staid dining rooms and older members snoozing above the *Times*. "We'll start there," said Nicholson.

"But if I might suggest—" said Smith.

"Yes?"

"One of the entrances to Regent's Park is called the York Gate, sirs. Might the reference in the letter be to that?"

They exchanged a look. "That's rather helpful," said Dallington. "Why did that pop into your mind?"

"I must pass it half a dozen times a day."

"You aren't very secretive, Mr. Smith, I suppose, on Lord Wakefield's behalf?"

The butler shrugged very slightly. "Lord Wakefield has not been what I wished he might as an employer, sir. You may ask my former master—Jarvis Norman, of Turk's Crescent—and he will tell you that I have recently asked for a reference, hoping to find a new position. I was deceived by a title, I suppose, sirs. It does not surprise me that Lord Wakefield came to a bad end. Private habits are often the truest sign of a man's morals." Smith hesitated. "And my father was a constable with Sir Robert's first peelers, sir. I have always felt very great loyalty to the Yard."

"Was he never!" said Nicholson, brightening. "What was his name?"

"Obadiah Smith, sir."

"Obadiah Smith," said Nicholson, thinking.

"He died in the year '71, sir. Born dead on the stroke of the new century, January 1 of 1800, so he was seventy-one himself when he went. His area of patrol was near the Inns of Court."

"I think I recall the name. Bless him, anyhow. There are few enough of that old guard left."

"Indeed, sir."

"If you ever want a change of career, your father's service could help you find a place on the force. You spotted York's Gate quickly enough. It might be a line of work that suits you."

"I'm very obliged, sir, but it was my father who pushed me into service. One too many knives he'd seen, he always said. 'Better polish 'em than dodge 'em,' he'd say. And I must admit that by and large I've been happy."

"You mentioned private habits," said Lenox. "Wakefield's were bad?"

Smith hesitated again. "I wouldn't wish to speak ill of my master, nor of the dead, sir," he said. "So I am doubly compelled to keep my thoughts to myself, you see."

"Anything you say will remain very strictly within our confidence," Nicholson said. "And it may help us stop a very dangerous man."

Smith looked doubtful. His resistance before had seemed pro forma, but now he looked disinclined to speak. "I really feel I must wait until Lord Wakefield's son—someone from the family, that is, anyone . . . in short, it is not my place, sir."

Lenox had half-forgotten Wakefield's son, the Earl of Calder. Somewhere in a room at Downing College, in Cambridge, without knowing it, the lad had inherited a marquessate and Hatting Hall and this London house and who-could-say what else. His own title, at the very least—his current one being borrowed from his father, as was customary among the old aristocrats, because they had so many titles that they could give the lesser ones to their children; it was by this method, in fact, that the Prince of Wales was so called, borrowing the honorific from the monarch, his mother or father. Lenox wondered how young Calder would hear the news. He hoped not from the papers. Would the perfunctory relationship the father and son had had make this death harder to bear, or easier?

"Mr. Smith," said Lenox.

"Sir?"

An underrated quality in a detective was charm. You might also call it charisma. Charm could persuade a witness to speak more openly; it could redress the imbalance that was inevitable when one person had all the information and the other none. It could make a witness want to speak, want to go on speaking, when otherwise he or she might not have. Jenkins had had it. Nicholson didn't, quite, though he was affable, which was a different kind of strength—a more comforting one.

Lenox didn't have inherent charm, either, but over the years he had cultivated a certain tone of voice for use on recalcitrant witnesses. It contained a mixture of superiority, amicability, and confidentiality. It was a performance.

He spoke in this voice now. Wakefield had been a bad man, he explained—that was the unfortunate truth. By contrast their friend Inspector Jenkins had been a good one, indeed a very good one. If it had just been Wakefield's death they were investigating, they might well have been happy to wait for Smith to speak with the marquess's family, to take his time. But there was Jenkins. Lenox described Madeleine Jenkins and her three children. His voice grew more urgent as he spoke. In all it took only a minute or so to make his case, but by the end of that time Smith was nodding. His face was serious.

"I see, sir, I do. I hadn't realized the death of Mr. Jenkins—the one in the papers—well, I didn't know, sir, that it was related."

"May be related," said Nicholson. "We—"

But Smith, whose manners throughout the conversation had been very deferential, was now impatient to speak, and cut in. "I hadn't put it together, you see, sir, but Inspector Jenkins was here. He called upon Lord Wakefield, sir."

The three investigators exchanged glances, all interest in Wakefield's private habits set momentarily to the side. "Jenkins was here?" asked Lenox. "When?"

"He called twice, sir. I hadn't even linked his visit in my mind with the fellow in the headlines, oddly enough. But it was him—or at any rate it was an inspector from the Yard named Jenkins."

"There was only one," said Nicholson.

Dallington had a folded newspaper in the inner pocket of his jacket. He pulled it out and unfolded it. "Is that him? The picture there?"

"Yes!" said Smith eagerly. "That was the man who visited—I'm sure of it."

"When?" asked Lenox again, more urgently.

The butler's eyes were raised to the ceiling in concentration. "The first time was two weeks ago," he said. "He called when Lord Wakefield was out. He waited here for fifteen minutes."

"He gave a name? A card?" asked Lenox.

"No, sir, and I thought it was odd at the time. I would never have known his name if he hadn't called again, four or five days ago."

"How did he introduce himself, on his second visit?" asked Lenox.

"He didn't. But Lord Wakefield said to me, 'Smith, have some tea sent up for Inspector Jenkins. It's not every day we receive the very great honor of a visitor from Scotland Yard.' He was being ironical, I mean to say, sir. And it was the very *profound* honor, now I recall, sir. 'It's not every day we receive the very *profound* honor of a visitor from Scotland Yard.'"

"How long did they sit together?" asked Dallington.

"An hour, perhaps longer."

"Did you overhear anything they discussed?"

Smith shook his head. "No, sir. They were silent whenever I came into the room."

"Did they seem agitated? Angry?" asked Lenox.

"Only silent, waiting for me to be gone I'm sure."

"There weren't any raised voices?"

"No, sir."

"What did Wakefield do after Jenkins had gone?"

"He immediately called for his coach and went out."

"How long was he out?"

"An hour or so, sir."

"And he returned alone?"

"No, sir. He returned with Mr. Francis. They were closeted together for several hours, late into the night, that evening."

Dallington looked at Lenox. Neither man needed to speak to understand the other's thought: that they were now getting very close to the truth indeed.

CHAPTER SEVENTEEN

After they had finished interviewing Smith, the detectives split apart. Nicholson had a fleet of constables arriving to help him, ready to comb the house for clues about Wakefield's activities in the past few weeks. Another group of constables were investigating the Asiatic Limited's offices, to see if they might learn anything further about aft hold 119 on the *Gunner*. An inspector and now a marquess: the full mechanism of the Metropolitan Police had been triggered into motion. No case could conceivably have a higher priority.

That left Lenox and Dallington with a job that Nicholson agreed they might do more quickly than the Yard could—to find out what they might of Mr. Francis, preferably well before he was waiting by the Duke of York's Gate at Regent's Park that evening at midnight to meet Lord Wakefield.

"That's if he even comes," said Dallington.

"Why wouldn't he?" asked Nicholson.

"I can think of two reasons. First—he's heard of Wakefield's death somehow. Second—he killed Wakefield himself."

Lenox nodded. "Very fair. Nevertheless I think we had better be there, watching."

"Damned right we better had," said Nicholson. "I also want to know if Bryson or either of Jenkins's constables knows that he met with Wakefield last week. Though I doubt it."

"So do I."

Lenox and Dallington walked out into Portland Place. It was warm now, the middle of the day. Lenox looked left and right and saw that there was a line of cabs by Regent's Park, to their right. He had sent his own carriage home when they arrived here, because his driver hadn't liked the look of one of the horse's forelegs. "Shall we go see York's Gate for ourselves, quickly?" suggested Lenox. "Then we can find a cab."

"To where?"

"I'm not altogether sure. Are you a member of either the Beargarden or the Cardplayers?"

"The Beargarden," Dallington said, with an abashed smile. "I scarcely go."

"You can go all you like, of course," said Lenox. He thought of Polly. "At any rate we can begin the search for Francis there. According to Smith he was a gentleman, which makes it seem at least possible that he and Wakefield shared a club, if they were so close. I take it you don't know the name?"

Dallington shook his head. "Not from the Beargarden. My mother once had a maid called Mrs. Francis. I think she's dead. And of course she was a woman. So I doubt it's the same person."

Lenox laughed. "Don't jump to conclusions too swiftly, I've always told you that."

As they walked toward Regent's Park, with its high line of trees just coming back into leaf above the nearer houses, they passed the convent, the one with the towering black gates. There was an old woman in a nun's habit standing behind them, staring out, a rather fattish person, puffed out by age, her skin gleamingly healthy given that she must have been seventy-five or so. She was the same woman who had been gazing at them as they stood near Jenkins's body.

On impulse, Lenox stopped. She looked at him quizzically. "Do you spend much time here, in front of the convent?" he asked through the narrowly spaced black bars.

The woman shook her head, not to answer the question but to signal her incomprehension. Then she took a card from a fold of her habit and passed it to Lenox, who read it.

The nuns of St. Anselm's operate under a vow of silence.
Additionally, if the box below is checked,
the bearer of this card does not speak English.

The box was checked, and next to it someone had written *Sister Grethe, Germany.* Lenox nodded, showed it quickly to Dallington, then passed it back, holding up his palm toward Sister Grethe to indicate that he understood and to thank her. She nodded. She didn't seem perturbed by the interaction.

"Were you hoping she had seen something?" asked Dallington.

"I imagine the Yard's canvass would have made certain that each sister saw nothing. They were at their prayers anyhow, according to the porter. We can ask Nicholson later if he has any more information in the actual written report. I just found it interesting to see her again, for a second time now, in perfect view of where Jenkins died. If only she had been standing there when he was shot. I suppose it's not impossible."

"Hadn't we better go and ask Nicholson now?" asked Dallington, stopping to turn back toward Wakefield's house behind them.

Lenox shook his head. "I doubt he'll know. Armbruster is the one we ought to ask, or another of the sergeants. It will keep. I can't imagine they came away from the convent without a thorough account from the sisters. Whatever the nuns' vows might be, the average bobby isn't very fond of either obstruction or silence."

"Or Germans," Dallington pointed out.

Lenox smiled. "Or Germans."

"A rum sort of life it seems to me, sitting in the middle of London, never saying a word, longing all the time for the pastures of Bavaria, or whatever they have over there. Standing in the cold behind some bars and handing out a card that says you can't talk. It's not what I call cheerful."

"No wonder she watches the traffic," said Lenox.

"Well, quite."

They spent a few minutes then looking at the spot where Francis and Wakefield were meant to meet each other that evening, a tall gilded black gate with the Queen's arms worked into its wrought-iron. There were refreshment stands nearby, and after these closed at nightfall it would be easy to conceal themselves behind one and watch the gate.

As they gazed upon the stands, discussing how they ought to hide, the peculiar rich smell of the London Zoo, situated within the park, floated toward them on the air, some mixture of hay and manure and animal. It wasn't unpleasant. For Lenox it recalled a trip he and Lady Jane had made there with Sophia the fall before, the child happily babbling for a very long time at the only orangutan ever to be seen in London, her favorite animal. She had also dragged them again and again back toward the quagga, a strange beast whose forward half resembled a zebra but whose back half resembled a horse. Lenox smiled to remember her amazement at the creature. It was an excellent zoo, very likely the best in the world. Two aristocrats had founded it in 1827, for the purposes of scientific study; only in the past few decades had it opened to the public as well, but they loved it beyond anything, coming in their multitudes to look at the oddities of Africa, of Asia, of the Continent.

When Lenox and Dallington were quite satisfied with their survey of York's Gate, they hailed a cab and made their way to the Beargarden Club. It was only a short drive. Dallington signed Lenox into the guest book, and then they went to look at the rolls of membership, which were listed in a book hanging from a string near the bar. On a blackboard nearby were chalked the debts that members owed each other—only the bartender could reach it, Lenox saw. Dallington was owed six shillings by someone called Roland Raleigh. The wager was over a year old. Lenox didn't ask what it had been, and Dallington, absorbed in the membership book, didn't offer any explanation.

After riffling through it, Dallington dropped the book, which swung back and forth on its string in a lessening arc. "Nothing," he said. "No Francis, no Hartley. That's unlucky."

"Would they have the peerages here?"

Dallington brightened. "Yes, that's not a bad shout. Let's have a look. Shall I order us some tea first? We could come back here and read."

"That sounds marvelous, now that you say it. Ask if they have toast, too, would you?"

Dallington spoke to the barman and then led Lenox through a dim hallway back to the snooker room, which was lined with cartoons from *Punch*. Above the snooker table was a complex system of pulleys and cords by which one could manipulate a scoreboard at the far end of the room. Two very well-dressed young men, one with a monocle screwed in tightly, were playing balls across the vast green felt.

"Hullo, Dallington," said one of them. "Here for a game?"

"Not unless you've improved."

"I have done, I'll have you know," said the fellow indignantly.

"Keep practicing anyhow. I'm only here for these."

Debrett's and *Burke's*, the two great lists of aristocracy in England, were on the end table, much thumbed. Lenox and Dallington took them back to the bar. Their tea was waiting on a table, with several stacks of golden-brown toast, glistening with butter.

"I'll take *Debrett's*, shall I?" asked Dallington.

"I'll take the toast."

Soon they were reading and sipping their tea in companionable silence, the pale midday light flooding the empty room. Bars were always most pleasant in daytime, Lenox thought. The tea was wonderful, dark and sweet. He had been hungrier than he realized. He helped himself to another piece of toast, folding it in half and crunching it between his teeth, then following it with a sip of the warm tea.

After half an hour they'd found nothing. There were plenty of people named Francis, and a few named Hartley, but none seemed to match the man they were looking for: a man of under forty, living in London. Most of the Francis clan seemed to be based far in the west, and none of the men were below fifty. Lenox copied out a few addresses anyhow, just to be sure. There might be second sons, cousins. Nevertheless it was dispiriting.

Dallington signaled to the bartender for more hot water, then turned back to Lenox, rotating his cup ruminatively in his hand. "What the hell do you think is happening, then?" he asked. "First Jenkins, and then Wakefield?"

Lenox considered the question for a moment. He took a wedge of toast and ate it. At last, he said, "The thing that worries me most is the third mystery."

"Which is that?"

"Not Jenkins's death, nor Wakefield's—but the fact that Jenkins's papers, the ones he felt were important enough that he left a note for me about them in case he should be killed, seem to have vanished completely."

CHAPTER EIGHTEEN

For the rest of that afternoon, as Lenox and Dallington contin-ued their search for Wakefield's friend and compatriot Francis (or was it Hartley?), this was the subject they discussed: the missing pa-pers, a mystery that was easy to overlook because it was bookended by two murders. Were they merely hidden somewhere by the inspector, who had evidently been in a mood to take precautions? Or had they been stolen? If they had, was it from Jenkins's office or from his per-son? In fact, was it possible that he had been murdered *for* the papers?

"They might have contained the information that would send Wakefield to prison," said Dallington. "Or to trial, at any rate."

"I'm not sure," said Lenox. "We'll have to see what McConnell says."

"About what?"

"Wakefield's body. I'll be very curious to learn how long he's been dead. Whether, for instance, he was dead at seven o'clock last night, when Jenkins was shot—or whether he might have killed Jenkins himself and then been murdered."

Dallington considered this. "A marquess," he said. "I cannot imagine he would commit such a crime himself, and so close to his own house."

"He would if he were desperate," said Lenox.

Dallington nodded. "Yes. If he were desperate. Which he might have been, after all."

"Who do you think killed these two men?" asked Lenox.

Dallington smiled. "It was you who taught me the principle of parsimony, Lenox, I believe six or seven years ago now. That the simplest path between events is the most likely."

"And what is the simplest path between these events?"

"I think it was this Francis fellow, whoever in damnation he might be. That's why I wish we could find him."

Unfortunately the afternoon saw this wish go unmet. The two men checked in at the Cardplayers Club in Old Burlington Street, where several exceedingly drunk young men in the front hallways were boasting to each other about old darts victories, but there was no member called Francis or Hartley there. (The porter knew Dallington by sight, though he wasn't a member.) After that they checked several of the clubs along Pall Mall. They weren't quite sure how else to proceed. *Who's Who* had nothing to offer them, but all that really told them was that Francis wasn't a Member of Parliament or a bishop, neither of which scenarios had ever seemed particularly likely. It would be a boon to detectives all across England if *Who's Who* began to expand its scope, as rumor had it doing. There was also no Francis or Hartley who was contemporary with Wakefield at school or at university, according to a quick scan of the old directories at the Oxford and Cambridge Club in Pall Mall. The business directories of London contained several men named Francis, but none of them were under the age of fifty.

At six, thoroughly frustrated, Lenox and Dallington split apart. Dallington was going to continue the search; Lenox wanted to speak to McConnell. They were due to meet Nicholson at eleven thirty at York's Gate but wanted to talk over their evening's work first, and so they agreed to meet again at eleven o'clock at Mitchell's. This was a restaurant near Regent's Park, which Lady Jane was fond of saying served the worst food in London. Still, it was handy, staying open until midnight to accommodate the post-theater crowd.

Lenox ran McConnell to ground at the enormous house where he and Toto lived in Grosvenor Square. He was red-eyed, as if he had been squinting, and his tie was off. He answered the door himself.

"I thought it might be you," he said. "Come in. I've been working on Wakefield since you sent word for me."

"You can't have his body here?"

McConnell led Lenox up the fine light-filled front staircase, in the direction of his lab. "No, no. I went and consulted on the autopsy. The Yard isn't usually so rapid with its autopsies, but this time they brought in Dr. Sarver—from Harley Street, you know, very eminent fellow—and it was done in a proper operating theater. They were kind enough to give me some of the stomach tissue."

"A profound kindness indeed," said Lenox, though the wryness in his voice was lost on the doctor, who merely agreed. When he was working his absorption was such that he sometimes lost his sense of humor. "Did they decide what killed him?"

"It was certainly poisoning. We all concurred upon that point. After that it is less clear, though I have a theory of which I feel pretty confident."

"What is it?"

"Come in, and I'll tell you."

McConnell conducted his scientific studies in a beautiful two-story library on the east side of the house. Toward the far end of the lower story were several long and wide tables full of faultlessly organized bottles of chemicals, alkalis, acids, rare poisons, the dried leaves of exotic plants. The middle of the room was dominated by a set of armchairs, which were always scattered, when McConnell was working, with leather volumes randomly pulled down from the bookcases.

These bookcases were in the gallery on the second level, which contained row upon row of scientific texts. One reached them by a very narrow winding staircase made of marble, with cherubim cut into its sides.

McConnell's career had been proof, in its way, of the limits of money. It was Toto's family's enormous fortune that had allowed him to stock this laboratory, this library, but for all the years he'd had it, the pleasure he got from his work there had never equaled the pleasure he derived from his work as a practicing physician. This had been his vocation before his marriage, but her family had been too great to welcome a doctor into its midst and had been adamant that he give up his position. In the decade between that forfeiture of his career and the last year, when he had started working at the Great Ormond Street Hospital for Children, McConnell had never seemed quite himself—no matter the luxury of his laboratory. It gave Lenox a sense of relief to know that his friend, who was inclined to drink in low times, was once again content; as for Toto's family, McConnell now quite sensibly ignored their protests. Toto herself was a willful person but more significantly a loving one. She had come to accept the new job for what it was: the best of outcomes for her husband's happiness.

McConnell led Lenox to the tables, where a glass bowl was full of a dark red liquid. "This is wine," he said.

"While you're working?" asked Lenox.

McConnell smiled. "When I boarded the *Gunner* and saw that there were no markings on Wakefield's body, no wounds, the first thing I looked at was—"

"His hands," said Lenox, who had known the doctor's methods for a long time.

"A good guess, but no—his gums. They can often tell us something about a poisoning. As they did this time, though not in the way I had expected. On both his upper and lower gums, very near the teeth, there were thin, steel gray lines. It was a textbook example of the Burton line."

"What is the Burton line? What poison does it mean?"

"That's what's so interesting—I would never have expected to find the Burton line on the gums of an aristocrat. It indicates an exposure to lead."

Lenox frowned. Lead. "Is that so unlikely?"

"Yes, it is. He was not a painter—they will go on using lead in their paints, no matter how they are warned—and he was not a metalworker. Fortunately they gave me this tissue sample."

"What did you find?"

"Something called litharge of gold. It's very definite confirmation that Lord Wakefield ingested lead. And I would be surprised if it hadn't caused his death."

"Why would he have ingested lead? Doesn't it taste awful?"

"I told you before that lead poisoning is no longer very common. It is nevertheless famous enough that I'm sure you've heard of it. The reason is that for twenty centuries or so, since the Romans began the practice, human beings, idiots that we are, adulterated our wine with lead. More specifically, with this litharge of gold, which is in fact not gold but a brickred color. It sweetens sour wine and makes the flavor of it more even, or at least that's the conventional belief. Unfortunately it also kills you. Though I should say that first it drives you insane. Nearly every mad Roman emperor was probably suffering in some measure from lead poisoning. It's only been in the last seventy years or so that we've persuaded people to stop using lead in their wine and port. The benefit to the public health has been dramatic, genuinely significant."

"So he was poisoned by wine?"

"I believe so, based on his stomach tissue. And for the first time in two millennia you can feel fairly sure that it can't have been accidental."

"Wouldn't it have tasted bitter, this wine, if it were full enough of lead to kill him just like that?" asked Lenox.

"Ah, I should have been more clear. The line I described on Wakefield's gums doesn't indicate simply that he was exposed to lead. It indicates that he's suffered from *chronic* exposure to lead. I believe someone had been poisoning him slowly for many weeks, perhaps even for months."

CHAPTER NINETEEN

It was following this illuminating discussion with McConnell that Lenox finally returned to Hampden Lane after his long day, to find Lady Jane and Toto together with their daughters. When Toto had gone he ate a quick bite and then sat in his study, thinking. Lady Jane stayed with him there to keep him company, reading next to the fire at the end of the room, occasionally closing her eyes to drowse. Lenox, for his part, was wide awake. His mind was working, working. Eventually he pulled a sheet of paper from his desk and began to write up his notes from his day's activity.

A slow, methodical poisoning—it stood in stark contrast to the brutal and instantaneous method of Jenkins's murder. Lenox wondered what Wakefield's habits of drinking had been. According to his butler he had generally eaten lunch at the Beargarden and supper at the Cardplayers. It would be necessary to inquire there about his drinking habits—indeed, they might even have his bills, showing what he drank and when. Lenox jotted down a word to remind himself to check this.

"Why would the lead have suddenly killed him just now, so soon after Jenkins's death?" Lenox had asked McConnell in the laboratory. "I mean to say, if the poisoning had gone on for weeks, mightn't he have died at any moment?"

McConnell shook his head. "By the time he died, he would have been inured to the taste of the lead in his wine, I expect, and whoever was poisoning him could have increased the dosage enough to kill him outright. His body would have been so toxic at that stage that any little extra amount would have pushed him over the edge."

"A brilliant method if you have the time," said Lenox. "I'm surprised I've never come across it. An ideal means for a wife to kill a husband, I would have thought."

Replaying this conversation in his mind, Lenox looked across at his own wife and smiled. "Jane, if you had to kill me, how would you do it?"

Without opening her eyes, she said, "I'd have elephants stomp you. That's how they do it in India."

"It seems unnecessarily harsh."

"You shouldn't ask questions if you don't want the answers." She opened her eyes and looked across at him pointedly, but couldn't keep a straight face, and laughed. "I could never kill you. What on earth do you mean by asking, Charles?"

"If I weren't me and you weren't you, I suppose I mean."

"Thank goodness that's not the case."

"But if it were? Would you poison me?"

"I don't want to think about it. This sort of thing never came up when you were in Parliament." She looked up at the clock on his mantel. "It's late, too."

He stood up from his desk and went across the room to give her a kiss on the forehead. "You ought to go up to bed."

"Aren't you coming?"

"I have to go out again."

"Do be safe."

"I will, I will. You have my word."

She squeezed his hand and stood up from the chair, her copy of *Middlemarch* under her arm. She kissed his cheek. "I love you."

"I love you, too."

After Jane had gone to bed Lenox sat at his desk again, ruminating about the case. He felt as if there were too much to do. He mustn't lose track of Jenkins. That was crucial.

At ten forty, tired, he departed Hampden Lane in the carriage, his horses apparently again in full health. He stopped in front of Mitchell's, where he saw Dallington just about to enter. "John," he called from the carriage.

Dallington turned. "Ah, there you are."

"Let's go to Wakefield's instead. I'll explain on the way what McConnell has told me."

"Right-o."

It was too late to expect Wakefield's servants still to be awake, and the house was mostly dim, so when Lenox rang the bell it was with the expectation that there would be a wait of some time. Instead the door opened almost immediately. Wakefield's butler, Smith, was still dressed for his job.

He bowed slightly. "Your Lordship, Mr. Lenox, how do you do. Can I help you?"

"We had a few more questions we wanted to ask you, and perhaps the other servants."

"By all means, sir—though I should say at the moment Lord Wakefield's cousin is here, Mr. Theodore Murray. I have been attending to him."

"What is he doing here?"

"I am given to understand that he is arranging Lord Wakefield's business matters," said Smith quietly. They were standing in the front hallway. "In preparation for the new Lord Wakefield's arrival tomorrow—my employer's son. He has been informed of his father's death and is coming to London by an early train."

This was the Earl of Calder, at Cambridge, Lenox recalled. "We needn't come all the way in," said Lenox. "We are primarily curious about His Lordship's daily habits, and you might just answer our questions about those."

"His daily habits, sir?"

"His meals, for instance. You mentioned that he often ate out."

"Not breakfast, sir."

"He ate breakfast here every morning?"

"Yes, sir, in his rooms. He took two pots of tea and four eggs, poached on toast. It was a very regular thing with him, sir."

"And his lunch? His supper?"

"I don't think His Lordship ate either meal here more than a dozen times in the year I've been working for him, sir. He was very constant at the Beargarden and the Cardplayers."

"Did he return home in between? Did he have a glass of wine before he went out?"

"He sometimes returned home between lunch and supper, sometimes not, sir. As for a glass of wine—no, his preference before supper was for ale. We always keep a great supply of it from Hatting Hall, where they make it themselves. It's very strong."

"Do you know if he drank wine at supper, at his club?" asked Lenox.

"I couldn't say, sir. He didn't generally drink wine, though I know that he was fond of port, Lord Wakefield. He had it by the case from Berry Brothers. He kept it in his rooms."

Lenox looked at Dallington. Port—that could be it. "Could we see the bottles of port he drank?"

"Yes, sir. Would you like me to fetch it, or would you like to come up to his rooms for yourselves?"

"If you wouldn't mind, I'd rather we went up."

Wakefield's rooms were tidy and as impersonal as the rest of the house, with the exception of his desk, which was covered with loose snuff, chits of paper, all manner of debris. Smith, observing them take in the state of the desk, said, "We were under orders not to disturb it."

"Did Nicholson and his men look through the desk?" asked Dallington.

"Oh, yes, sir, very thoroughly."

Near the fireplace in the second of the two rooms Wakefield used for himself was a stand of liquor, and there on top of it was a bottle of ruby port. Lenox opened it and sniffed it. "Could I take this?" he asked.

Smith looked doubtful. "Perhaps if you could ask Mr. Murray?" he said. "Only I know that port is very expensive, sometimes, sir."

Lenox had a small glass phial in his valise. "Here's a bargain for you—I'll take a thimbleful and leave the bottle."

"Oh, in that case—yes, that should be fine, sir." As Lenox shook the bottle hard (McConnell had told him the litharge of gold might sift down to the bottom) and then took his sample, Smith went on, saying, "You can see, under here, sirs, where he kept the rest of the case."

He opened the cabinet to reveal a wooden crate with an open top, which must have held six bottles once. Now it held two. Dallington pulled it out and inspected it. "It's stamped with Berry Brothers' seal on the side, right here," he said.

Lenox closed the phial, put it in his valise, and took the crate from Dallington. He held it under the lamp to look more closely. "Look," he said to Dallington, "an invoice."

Glued to the underside of the box was a sheet of paper. Lenox pulled it off and read it. His eyes widened, and he looked at Dallington. "What?" asked the young lord.

"Look at the order."

Dallington took the sheet of paper. After a moment his eyes, too, widened. "We need to take this as well," he said to Smith.

"As you please, sir," said the butler. "It was only that I didn't want anything that the heirs . . . that might be of value."

Not much later Dallington and Lenox walked out along the street, passing the convent as they strolled toward Regent's Park. It was not quite eleven thirty. "I'm disappointed in Nicholson and his men that they missed the invoice," Lenox said.

"It was glued to the underside of the box, in fairness."

Soon they met the inspector at the gate, where he was waiting, and together they took up their chilly post. They stayed until twelve thirty, but there was never any sign of Francis.

Softening the disappointment of this, however, was that invoice, which they showed Nicholson before they went their separate ways—for it gave the address of the person who had bought the potentially fatal port that Lord Wakefield had spent his last weeks of life drinking: one Andrew H. Francis, of Mornington Crescent.

CHAPTER TWENTY

The next morning at the offices of Lenox, Dallington, Strickland, and LeMaire, the four principals of the agency gathered for their weekly meeting. Though they had been awake late, Lenox and Dallington were the first two to arrive, as if in accidental obeisance to the order of their names upon the brass plate outside the office's door. They sat and were halfway through a cup of tea by the time Polly and LeMaire entered the room, each with a polite hello.

It was the loveliest day yet of 1876—the sweet o' the year, as Shakespeare had called this time in April. The sun shone a mild gold through the lightly shifting trees, and the streets below, still wet from a cleaning, sparkled brightly. The mood of the city on mornings like this one was somehow brotherly, amiable, ineffably unified. Through the windows of their second-story offices it was possible to see the small conversations that took place on every city street— the cabman calling down a joke to the fruit seller, the banter between a nurse pushing a pram and a constable swinging his whistle. Sometimes Lenox loved London very much indeed.

Polly seemed tired. Anixter was speaking to Pointilleux in the next room, loudly enough to be overheard, and as she poured herself a cup of tea from the pot Mrs. O'Neill had made she looked testily toward the door. Lenox watched concern fall across Dallington's face.

LeMaire, meanwhile, had a large sheaf of papers. He set these down on the table in front of himself.

"New business first, then?" said Dallington, when Polly sat down. "Charles has a case that we're working on together, as you both know. Polly, I hope you've been able to manage without me?"

"Somehow," she said, though she smiled to reduce the bite in this reply.

"I have a piece of firm business first, if you would not mind," said LeMaire.

"You do?" asked Dallington. "What about the order of the meeting?"

It was usually LeMaire who was most conscientious about sticking to the schedule by which these meetings always ran. "My patience is not long at the moment," said LeMaire. From his sheaf of papers he pulled a newspaper. "I wonder if you have seen the *Telegraph* this morning."

"No," said Dallington.

From her eyes, Lenox could tell that Polly had. It wasn't fatigue in her eyes, it was worry. He hadn't—he'd woken late and quickly absorbed the main headlines of the *Times* on the way here, but the other papers were arranged in a neat half-moon on his desk, awaiting him. "We are mentioned," said LeMaire. "Not as favorably as might be wished."

Lenox's heart fell. LeMaire had slid the paper across the table in the general direction of the other three, and Lenox took it.

Former MP Takes Hand in Jenkins Investigation
Hon. Charles Lenox making personal search for murderer
Interference feared detrimental to inquiry

Quickly he ran his eyes over the text of the article. One paragraph stung particularly:

> *Ironically, it was Jenkins himself who warned the* Telegraph, *in an on-the-record interview shortly before his death, that "London criminals have more than enough to fear from Scotland Yard already, and London citizens more than enough protection. The firm is a reckless venture."*

It was a new quote, one that hadn't appeared in the previous article. Lenox passed over it as best he could and finished reading. "There is no mention at all that I'm a member of a firm," he said when he was done. "Nor that our services have been retained by the Yard."

"That's not fair," said Dallington.

LeMaire's eyes widened slightly, as if Dallington's incredulity at this unfairness did him no very great credit. "Did you expect it would be?" he asked.

Dallington took the paper and looked at it for fifteen or twenty seconds, then offered it to Polly. She declined it. "There's no mention of all of Charles's past successes," said the young lord. "Nor ours, for that matter. We must write a letter."

LeMaire sighed heavily. "If the three of you choose to write a letter, of course you must."

Now, for the first time, Polly looked alert. "What do you mean?" she asked.

"Oh!" said Lenox. She had gotten there more rapidly than he had. "LeMaire, surely not."

Dallington looked up and down the table. "What?"

LeMaire nodded, his face set with forbidding determination. "I must leave the firm at the end of April," he said. "That will give me time to conclude my open business here. I will pay my quarter of the rent through the end of May, which should be ample time to let this space and find a new one, should the three of you wish to move into smaller premises, but I must ask that my name be taken off the firm's letterhead at the end of the month."

"This is hasty," said Lenox. "It's only been three months. All businesses struggle at the start."

LeMaire shook his head. "I have very great respect for all three of you, but I do not believe the business is viable. The idea was good—but, if I may speak frankly, three cannot support four, and when, in addition, the fourth brings only negative attention to the firm . . . no, it is not sustainable, Mr. Lenox, I am sorry. I have the greatest respect for your achievements of the past, as I say."

There was silence in the room. LeMaire lifted his cup of tea and took a sip from it, meeting their gazes levelly, awaiting their replies.

It was Dallington who spoke first. He stood up. "Good riddance, then," he said. "Best of luck, and all that, of course. For my part, I think we'll be better off without you."

"Since I account for thirty-eight percent of the firm's receipts I cannot agree," said LeMaire. "Mrs. Buchanan accounts for twenty-nine percent. You for twenty-two percent, Lord John. Nearly a quarter, I will grant you."

LeMaire had the politeness to stop there, but nobody needed to do the math for Lenox. Eleven percent, and that included the cases that somehow Lady Jane had arranged for him. He felt his face get red. What a mistake it was to have left Parliament. He wished the earth would open up and swallow him.

"I really do think we just need a little bit more time," said Polly now. "And I think the first thing we need to do, by hook or by crook, is to arrange some kind of favorable press. I don't care if we have to pay someone for it."

"I cannot see it helping, unfortunately," said LeMaire.

Polly persisted. "Why not agree to reconvene this meeting in two months' time, at the start of June? If you feel as you did, you can leave with immediate effect, and with no hard feelings."

"With immediate effect, anyway," said Dallington shortly.

"I really do think things will look up," said Polly, ignoring Dallington and focusing on LeMaire.

LeMaire opened the door and called out something in brisk French. After a moment his nephew came in. LeMaire invited him into the room and closed the door behind him. "Pointilleux, what are they saying about us, the people in our profession that you've met in London since you came to live with me? My nephew attends a great many professional luncheons, you see, as part of his training."

Pointilleux thought for a moment, raising his eyes, and kept them there as he said, in his methodical way, "They say the firm is run very bad. They say the firm is four chickens without even one head. They say it is all some jokes, they say it is . . . I don't search the word in my brain . . . *incompetentente*."

"'Incompetent' is the word in English," said Lenox.

"Incompetent," Pointilleux repeated brightly, pleased to have learned something new.

LeMaire raised his hands, as if his case were made, and then stood. "I will speak with Mrs. Buchanan about the financial arrangements of my departure, since she has the business head among the remaining partners—no offense to either of you, rather take it as a compliment, please, Mrs. Buchanan. Otherwise, I hope when we meet it will be as friends, despite this unpleasant conclusion to our professional association. Do any of you wish to ask me anything?"

There was silence, and after a beat the Frenchman bowed and left the room. None of the three remaining partners looked at each other.

There was still one surprise left in the meeting, however. Pointilleux, who had been sitting in a chair near the door, placed some feet back from the table where the principals always sat, rose. "For my part, I would like to stay," he said. "I have observe you all very closely, and though I respect my uncle, I think the firm will be nevertheless a"—here he groped for the correct phrase in his brain, and apparently found one from the West End stage posters he must have seen—"a marvelous hit for the ages."

Now they did exchange glances, and then Dallington said, speaking for all of them, "We'd love to have you, of course."

Pointilleux smiled and said, "Excellent," then left the room.

CHAPTER TWENTY-ONE

When Nicholson's team had examined Wakefield's house the day before, they had also interviewed each of the members of the marquess's staff more extensively. As Lenox and Dallington rode across London in a hansom, on their way toward Mornington Crescent, they looked over the notes.

All five servants agreed on Francis's appearance, albeit with some minor points of variation. The cook—who likely would have had the least opportunity to see him, as Dallington pointed out—felt passionately sure that the scattering of moles on his face was on his forehead, though the other four placed them on his cheek. (No one was sure whether it was left or right.) This was the most significant physical marker of their suspect. He was of average height and build. All five servants said he had dark hair, and the three women called him "not bad-looking," "dead handsome," and "a right Billy boy" in their respective interviews.

"What is a Billy boy?" asked Lenox.

"I'm dismayed that you think I would know," said Dallington.

Lenox asked one of the servants, for clarification: "a man prettier than a woman" was the elliptical answer, and left him contemplating what it might mean.

Francis was also, apparently, an unusual dresser. It was Smith, the butler, who was best able to articulate this in his interview, perhaps because he had been responsible for dressing Wakefield and therefore understood clothes better than the other four. According to Smith, Francis never wore a tie, but had some sort of bright scarf at his neck generally, and his pants were cut very loose, almost as if for summer lightness, even in the winter. All five servants mentioned that his clothing was odd. The footman used the word "poncey," which was new to Lenox. It meant effeminate, according to Dallington, and then Lenox recalled that prostitutes sometimes called the idle men they kept with their earnings, their beaux, "ponces."

The final detail of interest to Lenox was that Francis had, apparently, been a generous tipper. Both maids and the footman recalled as much, and Smith, after an embarrassed refusal to answer at first, had eventually admitted that he received a pound from Francis at Christmas. It indicated money; also exceptional closeness to Wakefield. Lenox occasionally tipped the servants at houses where he spent a great deal of time, but only if they were the employees of very intimate friends. It would have been inappropriate otherwise.

They had arranged to rendezvous with Nicholson at 11:00 A.M. in Carlow Street, just around the corner from Mornington Crescent, thinking it was less conspicuous if two carriages didn't pull up precisely in front of Francis's house.

Nicholson was waiting for them in front of the Crowndale Arms. "Gentlemen," he said, an agreeable look on his thin face. "Shall we make an arrest?"

"Thank you for letting us come along."

"Of course. You have the order form from the box of port?"

Dallington did. In the addressee box had been Wakefield's name; in the billing box, however, it had read *Andrew H. Francis, 31 Mornington Crescent, London NW1.* The H must stand for Hartley, all three men agreed. Perhaps it was the nickname by which Francis went among his friends.

Mornington Crescent, a long curve of houses named for the brother of the Duke of Wellington, was in a nice, quiet part of London, just east of Regent's Park. It probably wasn't more than a fifteen-minute walk to Portland Place and Lord Wakefield's house, though that walk marked the gap between affluence and genuine wealth; this was merely a fine part of the city, not a grand one. Dickens had once lived here, Lenox recalled.

The three men walked down Carlow Street. "I've sent men back to confiscate the rest of the port," said Nicholson. "From what I understand Wakefield's son is there. I imagine he'll be eager to assist us."

"I have a sample, at any rate. It's off with McConnell right now, though he may not be able to look at it until the evening, since he's at the hospital."

"Mm."

As they emerged onto the crescent itself, a natural silence fell over their small group. It gave Lenox a moment to think about Le-Maire.

What was clear to him now was that, above all else, Polly and Dallington must not be punished for their loyalty to him. Or more specifically, that Polly must not be. Dallington would never be worried for money. Polly was a widow, however, and her position was uncertain. By whatever means he had to do it, Lenox would make sure she did not depart the business—should it disband, should she wish to leave—with less money than she had when she arrived. At least he could be sure of that.

The other thought that had been going through his mind was harder to bear: It was that LeMaire was perhaps correct.

The three of them had talked very little after the Frenchman left, and fortunately the fillip of Pointilleux's loyalty had made the conversation less strained than it might otherwise have been. Polly had acted as if nothing were changed, at least among the three of them. Dallington, meanwhile, had mentioned in the carriage how sorry LeMaire would be when he was drummed out of the business by their success.

Lenox, for his part, wasn't as optimistic. "Three cannot carry four," LeMaire had said, or words to that effect, and it was true. The newspapers were the worst of it. His notability, which he had hoped would be an asset to the firm, had instead proven a disadvantage. Many of the newspapers had scores to settle with him; apparently so did the Yard. It surprised him, he had to admit to himself. He had made more friends than enemies in politics. There was something puzzling in the attacks, something troublingly out of balance with reality. Was some force behind them, some invisible mover? Or was that an unreasonably suspicious thought?

They arrived at 31 Mornington Crescent. Nicholson led the way up the steps and knocked sharply at the door; it was a single-family house, not, like some others along the crescent, divided up into apartments.

"Freshly painted," Dallington murmured to Lenox, nodding toward the house's front, and indeed, now that he looked more closely this house did seem to shine more brightly than its neighbors.

"Money again," said Lenox.

"Yes, indeed."

There were footsteps audible behind the door. It swung open, and a housemaid appeared, dressed very formally. "May I help you?" she asked.

Nicholson had his identification ready. "I'm Inspector Nicholson of Scotland Yard," he said. "We would like a word with Andrew Francis, if you don't mind."

"Andrew Francis?" she said.

"Yes. Is he in?"

The housemaid shook her head. "You've the wrong house, I'm afraid. Did you check the number? This is 31."

"That's the house we want. You're telling me that Andrew Francis doesn't live here?"

She shook her head again. "No. This house belongs to Mr. and Mrs. David McCaskey."

"How long have they been here?" asked Lenox.

"Ten years," she said. "I've been here seven of those myself."

"Does anyone else live here?"

"Three other servants, and Mr. and Mrs. McCaskey's child, Laurel. She's six."

"Nobody by the name of Francis has lived here in the seven years you have?" asked Nicholson, skeptical.

"No," she said very firmly.

"I hate to be rude, but would you mind if we confirmed that with your mistress?"

On the contrary, the housemaid didn't mind at all—she seemed eager to prove to them that they were wrong, and led them straight to Mrs. David McCaskey, who was sitting with several friends sipping tea. Nicholson introduced himself, Dallington, and Lenox, and then said he would be happy to speak to Mrs. McCaskey in private. But she was just as happy to have it out in front of her friends. No, she didn't know anyone named Francis; not Hartley either; her husband's business address was 141 East India Dock Road, near the wharf—he was an importer—and he would be more than happy to speak to them whenever they pleased.

This was all distressingly convincing. Nicholson apologized for their intrusion, both to Mrs. McCaskey and the now-triumphant housemaid, and bade the women good day.

"You're not related to Lady Jane Lenox, are you, Mr. Lenox?" asked one of them as the three investigators turned to leave the room.

Lenox turned back. "I have the honor of being married to her, madam," he said.

The faces of all four women seemed to light up. "Could you possibly pass my card to her?" asked Mrs. McCaskey, which earned her a deathly stare from the person who had first inquired whether

Lenox knew his wife. "I feel very sure that she would be interested in my work with the West African Trust—she could come to tea any morning, could name her time."

Lenox accepted the card as politely as he could, and three more followed it instantly, though he assured them that Jane's schedule was full, most unfortunately full, with barely room to breathe.

"At least you've made Lady Jane some new friends," said Dallington as they left. "I can only imagine how gratified she'll be."

They came out onto the steps. "It's all very well to joke," said Lenox. "But if this house is brimming with McCaskeys, where on earth then is Andrew H. Francis?"

CHAPTER TWENTY-TWO

The three men drove to Berry Brothers and Rudd, the venerable wine shop that had delivered the port to Wakefield. The clerk there, an older gentleman, was unable to help; he did consult the ledger, an immense leather-bound volume three feet across, and found the order for the case. But the bill had been paid in person and in cash, and the order then picked up by hand, so the shop had never run into the problem of finding Francis to charge him for the port—which was very fine, he noted, if that was helpful, among their most expensive.

"Would you have a record of Mr. Francis's account?" asked Lenox.

"Not unless he's ordered very often," said the man, a Berry or a Rudd, presumably, as he flipped through a drawer full of customer cards. "No, no Andrew Francis. There's Lord Francis, who was in India for forty years and now lives in Devon. We deliver wine to him every month."

"Not our chap," said Nicholson. "Here's my card—please see me if Francis comes in again, would you. Immediately. And don't let drop to him that anyone asked about him."

"Certainly."

Lenox paused. "When you said earlier that the order was picked up by hand—does that mean you didn't deliver it?"

"Correct. The customer picked it up. In this case either Lord Wakefield or Mr. Francis."

"Then why glue an order form to the bottom of the crate?"

"Standard practice."

Dallington and Lenox and Nicholson exchanged glances. If Francis had picked up the port, it meant he had delivered it himself, which would have given him time to tamper with it. Of course, they would have to see what McConnell said about the sample Lenox had taken.

He'd had enough of Wakefield just for the moment, however; it was time, he thought, to go back to Jenkins and the missing papers.

First, though, he was scheduled to have lunch with an old friend.

He left Nicholson and Dallington together, promising to come by the Yard at three o'clock to see them, and then directed his carriage to Parliament, a place from which, he felt with a sharp pang of regret, he might easily wish it had never strayed.

In the year 1854, Lenox had been a student at Balliol College, Oxford. His scout—that is, the person who kept his rooms in order, lit his fires, brought his tea, pressed his clothes—had been a slightly younger local man named Graham, quiet and efficient, tactful, intelligent. Their distant friendliness had changed very suddenly one night, when a trauma in Graham's family, which Lenox witnessed, had brought them closer. After that experience they understood each other; certainly they trusted each other, implicitly on each side. When Lenox graduated from Oxford and decided to move to London, he had invited Graham to come along as his butler. Graham had agreed.

Since then, twenty-one years had passed. In that time the butler's roles had been various, ranging between the traditional and the unusual. Up until the moment of Lenox's marriage to Lady Jane

Grey and for some time beyond, he had run Lenox's household with seamless efficiency; he had also, as the moment demanded it, acted many times as a helpful assistant in Lenox's cases. Later, when Lenox entered politics, Graham had been a particularly effectual representative on his behalf, cajoling voters and planning political strategy.

When Lenox had actually gone to Parliament, he had taken the highly unusual step of promoting Graham from butler to the position of political secretary—a job that most men handed to a young promising person from the upper classes—and when Lenox had left Parliament, he had eyed another promotion, very nearly an unimaginable one, for his old friend.

Lenox's carriage left him near Westminster Abbey, and he crossed the road toward the Guests' Entrance of Parliament. (It was strange not to use the Members' Entrance.) There he saw Graham, standing under a portico. Lenox could have recognized him from a thousand paces, even with his head turned away, as it was now. Graham had a particular stillness—a kind of readiness, his intelligence patient, never restless, but always prepared. He was a compact, sandy-haired man. He stood holding a pair of leather gloves in one hand and scanning the crowds.

When he saw Lenox, he smiled and walked out to meet him halfway.

"Good afternoon," he said, and they shook hands.

"How do you do," said Lenox. "I'm glad at any rate that you haven't grown too grand to have lunch with me."

"Never, of course," said Graham. There were fewer "sirs" in his address now, though they seemed to lurk invisibly behind his words, a residual sense of formality. Yet there were probably not four people in the world who knew Lenox better, or for whom he cared more. It was one of the deep and true friendships of his life. Few enough are given to each of us. "Shall we go inside and sit down to lunch?"

"Yes, by all means."

It was one of the peculiarities of the British political system that a man need never set foot in a district in order to represent it in Parliament. In other countries—America, for instance—one had to have some geographical connection to a place, however tenuous, to be its senator or congressman. Not so in England, where a rich Londoner could stand for a seat five hundred miles to the north without visiting it. Money and interest were the presiding factors.

It was this strange fact that several years before had led Lenox to win the seat for Stirrington, a small constituency near Durham with which he otherwise had no connection. The leaders of his party had deemed him a worthy candidate to stand for some seat, and Stirrington had simply been the first to come open, on a by-election.

When Lenox had left his seat in Stirrington, a brewer called Roodle wanted it; Lenox, for his part, had the rather mad idea that Graham might try to win it. It weighed against Graham that he was of low birth, and not connected to Stirrington other than by Lenox. On the other hand, his talent for politics had grown famous in parliamentary circles, where he had fought fiercely with the other secretaries. In the end it was just reckoned, in the absence of a viable alternative candidate, that Graham might run.

But Roodle had won. After losing three times to Lenox, he had mounted a final assault, claiming that it was an insult that Lenox could leave office and simply expect to hand off his position to—of all people!—his former butler. It was an effrontery; it was a folly; it was an arrogance. Such was Roodle's argument, and enough of Stirrington's citizens agreed to send him, finally, to Parliament.

In the aftermath of this disappointing loss, Lenox had felt terribly responsible for Graham's failure, until, thank goodness, something unexpected had happened. It had been in early December, now four months ago. A man named Oswald Hart, the Member for a small constituency in Oxfordshire, had risen, upon his father's death, to the House of Lords, leaving a seat suddenly vacant. Many men might have competed for it, but Hart had come to know Graham in the past, from his time as Lenox's political secretary; indeed, they had always had a cordial bond, because they hailed from the same patch of earth, in between Oxford and the Cotswolds.

He invited Graham to run for his seat, promising his full support if Graham still had Lenox's financial backing; and Graham had won.

So that now, not six months after his own departure from the Commons, Lenox could visit the House as the guest of his former butler. On its face it was one of the oddest transitions British politics had yet known, but anyone who had worked with Graham, who understood his qualities, knew that he had ended up in the position best suited to his abilities. In fact, Lenox knew from his brother that Graham had already begun to make his mark on the House, in a multitude of subtle, significant ways.

The two men walked into the House together and toward Mr. Bellamy's restaurant, where they sat and ordered. Then for forty minutes they simply exchanged news, their conversation easy and free-flowing. They still saw each other often, though for the first time in a long while they lived under different roofs, and so there was more to tell. Graham nowadays consulted with Lenox about the minutiae of Parliament at least every two or three nights, for he was finding that the stratagems and alliances he had deployed while working as a secretary were very different than those a Member could. A Member had to be softer at the edges, had to make friends, and there were many men in Parliament who didn't care to make friends with someone who had come from service.

Partly just to be seen with Graham, then, Lenox came here to lunch at least every fortnight. Then, too, he liked to discuss his cases with his old friend; Graham had always been insightful about these, a first auditor. Now, over lamb pie and redcurrant jelly, they discussed Jenkins's death—Graham was very solemn in mourning their old friend—and then Wakefield's, teasing out ideas about the possible connection, going over clues.

"Have you spoken with Inspector Jenkins's wife about his movements in the last week of his life?" asked Graham.

Lenox considered this. "Not directly, you know. Nicholson spoke to her. I really ought to call upon her anyhow, to offer my respects. Perhaps I might see if she's receiving visitors after I leave here."

"She may know something significant without realizing it."

"You're quite right."

Their plates had been cleared away by now, and the waiter came with a small list of desserts. Lenox asked for trifle, and both men for coffee. When it came some moments later, the conversation had shifted again toward Parliament. There was a small bill up for vote that would add "Empress of India" to Queen Victoria's long train of titles. Many members of the Liberal party were opposed to this act, which they called a kind of backdoor annexation, but Graham wondered whether it might be pragmatic to lend it his support. It wouldn't make a difference to the ultimate outcome of the bill, and it might prove to some of the House's most traditional Members that he was not a progressive firebrand, eager to deprive them of their inheritances, but someone with whom they could reasonably deal. Lenox was forced to admit the savvy of the idea, though India made him uneasy. It was a large country, a long way from home. Who knew how long it would submit to the control of Queen Victoria—or how bloody the revolt might be when it came. They sipped their coffees and discussed the positives and negatives of such a vote at great length.

After ninety minutes, Graham said he had to return to the floor for a vote. Before he left, however, he asked if they might quickly go up to his office together.

"Of course," said Lenox. "Why?"

Graham had a valise, which he opened now. He took a folder from it. "There's one last piece of business I've been intending to conduct as your secretary," he said. "They've asked me more than once if you could fill out this form. You can do it at my desk, if you like—it shouldn't take more than fifteen minutes. As you know, there was never such a place for record-keeping."

Indeed, the form was bizarrely thorough. It ran to eight pages, and asked Lenox questions about all of the places he had once lived, about his sources of income, about his close and his extended family, about his personal habits (*Do you take port or brandy in excess after supper?*), and about his staff, including Graham.

Graham read a blue book as Lenox filled in the pages, and when the form was done, congratulated him—he had rounded off the circle, at last, and concluded his final act as a Member of Parliament.

"Unless you mean to stand again one day," said Graham, smiling. "We could use you, of course."

Lenox returned the smile, and the sheaf of papers, with a feeling of lightness. "No," he said. "I think I'm best off leaving it to you. And now you'd better hurry, if you mean to get to that vote."

CHAPTER TWENTY-THREE

Between the end of this midday meal with Graham and his scheduled meeting with Dallington and Nicholson at Scotland Yard, Lenox only had about an hour and ten minutes; it was perhaps just enough time to squeeze in a visit to Madeleine Jenkins. At any rate, he could be fifteen minutes late to the Yard without very much guilt, were it necessary.

His carriage trundled across the river, and as he looked back at the lovely golden stretch of Parliament, at the high clock face of Big Ben, he realized that he didn't regret driving away from it. Good to know, he thought. He'd meant what he said to Graham. He had no desire to stand for Parliament again. Whatever LeMaire might decide, whatever a newspaper might write, he was a detective once more. That was reward enough on its own.

Time, now, to find out who had shot his friend Thomas Jenkins.

Fifteen minutes later he stepped out of his carriage into a bright, leafy street, and paused for a moment to study the Jenkins house, which signified, everywhere, its recent grief: Its windows were closed, even on this lovely day, there was a black velvet knot on the door, and each of the five gray alder trees on the lawn had a cross at its foot. All of this was at odds with the first spring beauty of the green grass upon the small lawn, and the tiny buds on the flowering bushes near the house's broad porch. Lenox glanced up at the windows of the second floor. Behind one of them, he knew, was the body, which by tradition would be kept in the home until the funeral. That was scheduled for tomorrow. With a heavy heart, he went and knocked on the door.

A housekeeper answered, and behind her, crisp and businesslike, was a woman of about fifty, with gray hair in a tight knot and a manner that suggested visitors were unwelcome. She admitted to being Madeleine Jenkins's sister before asking Lenox rather shortly what business brought him here.

Just as Lenox was about to answer, Madeleine herself floated into view, her face distracted, distant. She just barely made eye contact with Lenox. "Oh, hello, Mr. Lenox," she said. "Please, come into the sitting room. How kind of you to visit."

"Mrs. Jenkins," he said, approaching her quickly, "I cannot adequately express my sorrow at your loss."

"Thank you," she said. "Please, sit. Clarissa, would you ask if the maid could fetch Mr. Lenox some tea? He was a colleague of . . . of my husband's."

Lenox sat down upon a hard small couch. It was stiflingly warm in the room. All of the mirrors were covered, all the clocks stopped, further traditions to honor the dead. He hated them all, for some reason, though he understood that others might find them comforting.

Madeleine was dressed in the habiliment that was called deep mourning, a black weeping veil, a house cap, a long black dress. It would be a year and a day before she could enter second mourning, the stage at which she might add small bits of color to her person, even a piece of jewelry, though black would still predominate. That might last another six months, and then it would be half mourning—gray dresses, or lavender, though still always with some black added at the waist or the shoulders.

These were the forms. In truth Lenox doubted, from her broken face, whether Madeleine would ever come out of deep mourning, at least in the sense of deep anguish. She was still a pretty woman, with long dark hair and soft eyes, and by rights she might marry again within two years. But he couldn't imagine she would. He had rarely seen a widow who looked more surprised, or more hurt. Their children were very young.

They spoke gently to each other for a few minutes. Finally, Lenox said, "As you may know, I am helping to investigate Thomas's death."

She glanced up at him. "I saw that in the newspaper this morning."

"I hope you don't believe that I would ever compromise the—"

"No, no. He trusted you completely, too, you know. He would have chosen you himself."

Lenox had believed this, and the letter in Jenkins's shoe indicated as much—but it was still meaningful to hear it from her, a relief. Saddening, too, because their breach had been so pointless. "Thank you for saying so," he said.

"Not at all."

"As you may know from Inspector Nicholson, the difficulty we've had is that we cannot find your husband's case files. He was working on something substantial, I believe. He left me a note—"

"Yes, saying that you ought to consult his papers."

"You have no idea where they are?" Lenox asked gently.

"I wish I did. They wouldn't be here—that's the only thing I know."

"Did he have a safe?" asked Lenox.

"Yes, but we've looked in it twice now. It has a few certificates, locks of the children's hair, and my jewelry, along with a few oddments. Nothing professional."

"He never brought his papers home, in your recollection?"

"No."

"Did he work from home?"

She shook her head. "Very rarely. Once in a while he sat up late in the kitchen thinking over a problem. He liked to be alone. I would make him a pot of tea and he would take his pipe and his tobacco. The kitchen fire is warm all night, and he would sit in a soft chair I keep there."

"Did he write while he did this?"

To Lenox's surprise, she said that he had. "Sometimes he asked me for pen and paper. But he always burned his notes. It was an aid to thought for my husband, writing."

"I take it you haven't seen any papers he left lying in the kitchen?"

She smiled faintly. "No. Believe me, Mr. Lenox, I am conditioned to be on the lookout for papers, for any piece of paper Thomas might have left behind. You cannot imagine how dearly I wish I could find one for you. The moment I see any kind of paper at all it is yours. It's only that it hasn't happened yet."

"You have been in and out of the kitchen recently?"

Her smile widened, wanly. "Only two or three hundred times."

It made sense that she would spend a good deal of time in the kitchen, even at a time like this. The Jenkinses would have kept a single maid, Lenox imagined, and perhaps hired another in special circumstances. Madeleine would have been in the kitchen a great deal—a working wife, not a sitting room wife. "Did Jenkins stay up late any night this week or last?" he asked.

For the first time she looked slightly surprised by a question. "Well, yes, I suppose he did. I think Tuesday. I heard him come to bed after midnight."

Tuesday, two days before his death. "Could I see the kitchen?" he asked.

They walked down the narrow staircase in single file, but the kitchen itself was slightly less overheated than the sitting room; near the ceiling was a row of small windows, one of which was open to let in the breeze. Something was cooking slowly on the stovetop in a closed pot. Rabbit stew, perhaps? It smelled wonderful.

"This is the chair?" asked Lenox.

"Yes," said Madeleine. She raised a hand to her mouth and for a moment looked as if she might break down, but composed herself. "That's where he sat."

"Can I ask—without wishing to seem a narcissist—whether he had mentioned me recently? I wouldn't, usually, except for the note he left me."

She shook her head. "I'm afraid not," she said.

Lenox stood up and looked under the cushion of the chair, then shook out its pillows. No piece of paper fluttered away from them, alas. He stood, trying to think of what would have preoccupied Jenkins down here. "Your fire's gone out," he said, gesturing toward the gray ashes.

"Yes," she said. "We've been distracted."

Then he saw something. He bent down; the fire was in a small cradling grate, much smaller than the hearth itself, with brick all around it to catch any sparks. "There's a piece of paper back behind the grate," he said. "It's in a ball."

"Is there? No, there can't be." She bent down to look, too, and saw the balled-up paper. "Can you reach it?"

He could. It was charred but mostly intact. He unfolded it and read for a moment before he realized, with disappointment, that it was a recipe. "Is this your handwriting?" he asked.

"Yes," she said. He started to ball the page back up, but then she said, hesitantly, "But on the back—might that be Thomas's? I think it might, you know."

Lenox turned the page over and saw, with a thrill, the heading of a list.

Wakefield
PP 73-_77_; New Cav 80-86; Harley 90-99; Wey 26-40

"This is Thomas's handwriting?" he asked.

"Yes, do you know what, it is," she said. Her face was eager. "Could it help?"

"I don't know yet," he said. "It could, perhaps. I hope."

"What do you think this code means?"

"It's not a code." Lenox had seen immediately what the short-hand meant. "Portland Place, New Cavendish Street, Harley Street, Weymouth Street. These are addresses, all within a few blocks of each other."

And all within a few blocks of where your husband was killed, he almost added, but thought better of it.

CHAPTER TWENTY-FOUR

On the ground floor of Scotland Yard was a long room of democratic usage. There were desks at which men could work; there was a corner dominated by armchairs and newspapers, which looked almost like the nook of some rather down-at-heel gentleman's club; up toward the opposite end was a great urn full of tea with a tottering stack of cups next to it.

Within the Yard everyone called it the Great Room, and it was here that Lenox met Dallington and Nicholson twenty minutes after the hour. He apologized for his lateness, though perhaps with a note of self-forgiveness in his voice—since after all he had something to offer them, the list of addresses he'd found behind Jenkins's kitchen grate.

Nicholson took the list and looked at it for a moment, then expressed his irritation that his men had missed it. "I'll have a word with Armbruster. Not to mention Jenkins's own sergeant and constables, who have been around there for a second look."

"What do the addresses mean?" asked Dallington.

Nicholson shook his head, staring at the paper. "I've no idea, except that Wakefield himself lived in 73 Portland Place, obviously."

"They could be witnesses Jenkins wanted to call on," said Dallington.

"To what?" asked Lenox. "It's such an unusual assortment. Why not 71 Portland Place, right next door? And what could anyone have seen at 99 Weymouth, two streets away?"

"Shall we have constables knock on all of these doors and ask them whether they have any information about Jenkins or Lord Wakefield?" asked Nicholson.

Lenox considered the idea. "I suppose you'd better."

"I'll just arrange it, then. Back in a moment. Have a cup of tea."

Dallington and Lenox made their way down toward the table of refreshments, talking quietly. "I'm free," said Dallington. "Perhaps I'll go along."

Lenox thought for a moment. "Might we send Pointilleux?"

Dallington frowned. "Do you think it's the right time to train him, on such a sensitive matter?"

"He's inexperienced, but he's bright, and I'd like to reward him for his loyalty to us. He's made it plain that he would like to get out of the office and do some work. On top of that, whether it's you or he who goes, the Yard will insist upon taking the lead."

"True enough."

"That would also give the two of us time to step over to McConnell's laboratory."

Nicholson returned after a few moments with Sergeant Armbruster, the rather portly, worried-looking officer who had so dearly wanted hot soup for himself and his men as he was managing the scene of Jenkins's murder. He had also conducted the canvass. Nicholson reintroduced them and said that the sergeant and his men had already visited most of the houses on the list.

"Which ones haven't you visited?" asked Dallington.

"I'm not entirely certain, sir," said Armbruster. "It will be in the report we made. I'm happy to go out again, though as I said to Inspector Nicholson, we found little enough the first time, and I generally work here, in the back offices, not out in the field. Perhaps it would be better to send a fresh pair of eyes."

"Sometimes it only takes a second round of questions," said Nicholson sharply.

The sergeant nodded quickly. "Oh, yes, sir. Did you want me to go now?"

"I do. You can take two constables from the pool."

"And a lad of ours, if you wouldn't mind," said Lenox.

Armbruster took out a brightly polished gold watch, whose chain was stretched taut over his belly. "Of course, sir," he said. He looked rather dispirited, and Lenox wondered what his plans for the evening had been.

Lenox and Dallington left the Yard not long after—Nicholson was going to read over Armbruster's initial report again, and gave them a copy so they could do the same—and stopped into Chancery Lane, where they informed Pointilleux that he would be accompanying several members of the police force on a canvass. He reacted with a momentous wordless nod, took the information Dallington handed over, and set off at a rapid clip to meet Armbruster and his men.

After he left, Polly appeared in the doorway of her office. She was wearing an unadorned blue dress and had her hair under a bonnet. There was ink on her fingers. "How is the case proceeding?" she asked.

"It seems to me that we have a great deal of information and not quite enough," said Dallington. "How has it been here?"

"Very busy," said Polly. Suddenly she looked tired. "LeMaire has left. And there was a new matter for me, a young governess whose mistress has accused her of an inappropriate friendship with the gentleman of the house, quite inaccurately. She was close to hysterical, the poor dear. Penniless, it goes without saying, but I felt we must assist her."

Dallington was moved. "By all means. Can I help?"

Polly looked at him quizzically. "Can you spare the time?"

When the three had met the year before—Polly had been an independent detective then, fresh to the business and full of new ideas—a friendship had sprung up between all three of them, but especially, perhaps, between Polly and Dallington. It made sense. They were of the same age, the same class. Both had been rather battered in their turn by the gossiping classes of London's salons. Above all, they had the same wry, not altogether serious way of looking at the world. It was enough to madden some people—those who took the world very seriously indeed. Lenox wondered what Alfred Buchanan had been like, Polly's short-lived husband. He must remember to ask Jane.

For a while, as Lenox recalled, it had seemed inevitable that Dallington and Polly would fall in love. Indeed, there was a moment when it seemed to him that they had already fallen in love. Like most ironists, Dallington was at heart a romantic, easily moved, and there had been glimpses in his face of something like passion, which Lenox had observed when Polly was talking, or even merely when she was in the room. As for Polly, early widowhood had trained her to wear a mask, but Lenox had imagined that he detected a softness in her, too.

Yet here they were, several months later, and the two were only colleagues—considerate of each other, particularly he toward her, but if anything slightly more distant than they had been in the first months of their friendship. Was their business the cause of this very faint separation? The struggles of the agency? Had something passed between them?

At any rate, Lenox could see in his protégé's eyes that at least on one side there were still feelings of love lurking beneath whatever conceptions of professionalism and respect had stilled them. He wondered if Polly felt the same way. He hoped she did. There were few men he had met finer than John Dallington, and few men who more deserved a wife's love. Nevertheless, it was not difficult to conceive of him as one of those eternal bachelors, aging into affectionate courtliness, going home to an empty sitting room every evening. There was something proud—untouchable—in his bearing. Lenox wondered if too many doors had been barred to him, in his wild days, for him to be quite comfortable with the traditional gestures of wooing. He was like Polly, in this regard: Each had a mask of proud self-sufficiency, and underneath it a need to be loved.

"He certainly has the time," said Lenox quickly. "There's nothing else we can do today on behalf of Jenkins and Wakefield, whereas it seems as if there's a great deal to do here. Dallington, I'll go to see McConnell. We can meet again here in the morning."

"If you're sure?" said the young lord.

"Absolutely."

"Then perhaps I will stay and help Polly."

So it was that Lenox rode alone to McConnell's in the waning spring light, jotting a few overdue thank-you notes as the carriage moved through the West End.

At the door the doctor greeted him with a grim smile.

"What?" asked Lenox, reading McConnell's face. "The port?"

"Yes. Poisoned. Come in and I can show you." McConnell led Lenox up to his laboratory again, where he demonstrated the chemical test he'd used, as well as the controlled test he'd done on an identical port that he'd sent his butler down to Berry Brothers to buy that morning. "Can't be too careful."

"There's no doubt, then?"

"None at all. The Yard's chemists are bound to find what I did. In fact, the quantities were unusually high. The marquess must have had a copper-bottomed constitution to survive as long as he did. Have you found the fellow who poisoned him yet?"

"Not yet," said Lenox.

"I can't imagine Berry Brothers will be altogether pleased to know that their product has become . . . well, a weapon of murder."

"The manufacturers of the Webley will sleep well enough tonight, I'm sure," said Lenox. He paused and stared at the beakers and glass bowls on McConnell's wooden tables. "The question I have is whether Wakefield had time to murder Jenkins before he was murdered himself—or whether Jenkins knew that Wakefield was in some kind of trouble. He may even have been trying to help him. Though I doubt he could have imagined someone was poisoning the man."

There was a knock on the door downstairs, and a moment later Shreve, the McConnells' butler, appeared in the doorway of the library. "A visitor, sir. He is most insistent upon his need to see Mr. Lenox."

Behind Shreve was a bobby. "Is one of you Mr. Lenox?" he asked.

"I am, yes."

"Inspector Nicholson sent me here to look for you. You're to come with me at once. There's been another attack at Portland Place."

CHAPTER TWENTY-FIVE

Lenox looked at the doctor. "I know we've asked too much already, but if you could—"

"Of course," said McConnell.

The three men went outside to Lenox's carriage, which was waiting in the weak warmth of the spring sun. The bobby knew nothing of the circumstances of the attack, not even whether there had been another murder or not. He had just been told to come and fetch Lenox. The drive didn't take long, and as they pulled into Portland Place Lenox looked anxiously through the window and after a moment said out loud that he thought there wasn't another corpse; there was a single constable at the door of Wakefield's house, not the whole circus that would gather in the event of a death.

He was right. Inside the house Nicholson was talking in a low tone to a young man. Both looked up at the arrival of Lenox and McConnell, and Nicholson said, "Ah, here's Mr. Lenox now. He's been working closely with us to investigate your father's death. Lenox, this is the . . . well, the Marquess of Wakefield."

The young man stuck out his hand. "Joseph Travers-George," he said. "Thank you for your assistance. I know that Scotland Yard are doing all they possibly can to get to the bottom of all this. Rotten business."

The new marquess spoke emotionlessly, as if he were thanking Lenox for his assistance with a banking transaction, not a criminal investigation. This squared with the upbringing he had no doubt received, an emphasis on stoicism, and then his father had been no prize. Whether or not it was seemly, not all deaths were mourned equally.

Still, it seemed odd. Lenox felt a breath of interest in the back of his mind. Some enormous proportion of a detective's education could be reduced to a single Latin phrase of two words: *cui bono*. Who benefits, as it was most often translated into English, though Lenox associated it more strongly with money than that translation would imply—who gains, perhaps. Who is enriched? It was easy to say this to a young constable at the Yard, of course, but it took the grind of years to really impart that knowledge to a man, case after case in which some sordid crime led back to a few thousand pounds, a few hundred, even just a few. *Cui bono*. It was the phrase that entered Lenox's mind as he shook the hand of the former Earl of Calder. This young chap had inherited one of the largest fortunes in England two days before, and one that he couldn't have expected to descend to him for many years, given the rude health of his father.

There was every chance that he was a mere bystander to the circumstances. But the alternative was not impossible, either.

The lad was only twenty, but you could see his middle age coming pretty plainly; he was already overweight and slightly too red, with a globe of a stomach and limp light hair. He looked as if he would grow short of breath easily. Nevertheless he was very well dressed, in a suit tailored by some excellent master of the craft, for it made his shape as close to youthful as it was ever likely to be, unless he decided to stop eating for six months, or took a sudden fancy to exercise and cold baths.

Lenox introduced McConnell and then said, "There's been an attack?"

Nicholson nodded, lips pursed. "Yes. On the butler, Smith, poor fellow. He'll survive, but it was a nasty piece of work. He's resting upstairs, but you'd better let him tell you himself. He's fit enough to talk."

Smith was in a guest bedroom on the third story of the house. There was a constable posted outside his half-open door. The room was neutral, irreproachable—like much of the rest of the house, without any evidence of Wakefield's personal taste. "Will you live in London?" Lenox asked the new young marquess as they walked toward the room where Smith was recovering.

"No, no. I'll finish at Cambridge and move to Hatting. This isn't a family house. My grandfather bought it not thirty years ago. I mean to let it as soon as I can."

The light was low by Smith's bed, but Lenox could see that he was bare-chested underneath his blankets, and that there was a long bandage across his torso. He looked pale. The cook, a pretty woman, was sitting by his bed, and didn't rise when the men entered, a breach of normal convention that showed, perhaps, the seriousness of her concern for her colleague.

"How do you do, Smith?" asked Lenox. "I'm terribly sorry to hear that you were attacked. You've seen a doctor?"

"Yes, sir. He was not overly concerned."

"Nicholson said you wouldn't mind telling us what happened?"

"No, sir." Smith struggled to sit up a little straighter against his pillows, and the cook quickly helped him. There was a strong smell of beef broth in the room; he had been eating, anyhow. "How much would you like me to tell?"

"All of it, if you don't mind doing so a second time."

"Not at all, sir. This afternoon I was preparing the second-largest bedroom for the inhabitation of Lord Calder—excuse me, Lord Wakefield." The young inheritor nodded his forgiveness of the slip, himself probably still unused to the new name. "There was a noise in the hallway, and I knew that the other staff were all in the basement. Or thought they were. I went out to see what it was, just in time to see somebody walking into the master bedroom—that which was Lord Wakefield's, you understand."

"Where we found the port?"

"Yes, sir, precisely."

"Please, carry on."

"I went down the hall. The door to the master bedroom was ajar, and I called out to ask who was there. There was no response, so I pushed the door open and saw two men coming toward me."

"Two men," said Lenox slowly. "What did they look like?"

"Both of them had their faces concealed," interjected Nicholson.

The butler nodded. He looked pale, thinking of his attackers. "They had dark scarves around their mouths," he said, "and caps on."

"What else were they wearing?" asked Lenox.

"Nothing distinctive, sir. Dark trousers, dark shirts."

"Eye color?"

"I cannot recall, sir. I was very taken aback when I saw them, as you can imagine."

"Might one of them have been Francis—or Hartley?"

"Inspector Nicholson asked the same question, sir. The answer is that I cannot be sure. I don't think so, but it all happened very quickly."

"What happened, exactly?" said a voice behind Lenox. It was young Travers-George.

"I asked them who they were and what they wanted. They didn't answer. I had been cleaning the furniture in the blue bedroom, so I was holding a tin of polish and a cloth. I dropped them as they approached and started to back out through the door, but they caught me and took me up. One of them held me with a knife at my throat while the other looked through the room, very quickly."

"What was he looking for?"

"I don't know, sir. He looked through all of Lord Wakefield's effects. He didn't take anything. I don't think he took anything, that is."

"Did he mention the port, or seem to look for it?"

"He didn't mention it, though he did look carefully through the liquor stand, sir."

"And so how did you come to be wounded? And how did they leave?"

"I heard footsteps in the hallway, sir, and I suppose I panicked. I cried out for help. I jerked out of the grip of the man who was holding me. I must have taken him by surprise, because he stumbled backward and slashed out at me. The knife caught me across the chest."

"Thank God it wasn't the throat!" said the young cook. Her name was Miss Randall, Lenox recalled, a quiet soul with a heavy Lancashire accent and dark ringlets of hair. "It was me in the hallway! I might have got him killed!"

"There, now," said Smith to her, patting her hand. "I'm glad you weren't hurt yourself."

"Did you see the two men?" Lenox asked the cook.

"They came barreling out past me quick as you like," she said, her eyes wide at the memory. "Terrible huge men."

"Did you get any better look at what they were wearing, or what they looked like?" he asked.

She shook her head. "The same, sir. They left great horrible smudges all over the floor."

"Footprints?" said Lenox quickly. "Where?"

Nicholson shook his head regretfully. "They've already been cleaned."

"We had the young lord coming, sir, we didn't want it a mess," said Smith apologetically, and then added, "Your Lordship."

"I appreciate the thought," said the young man.

Nicholson said to the butler, in a grim voice, "You'd better tell Lenox what they said on the way out, too."

"What was that?" asked Lenox.

Smith looked hesitant but then said, "They mentioned a detective."

"Nicholson?"

"I'm not sure, sir," said Smith. "The one who had been looking through the room—not the one who'd been holding me, you see, sir—stopped for just a moment and said, 'Tell that detective to keep his nose out of it. Tell him a man with a wife and daughter should know better.'"

Lenox felt his heart freeze. He looked at Nicholson, who shook his head and said, regretfully, "I don't have a wife or a daughter. I fear they meant you."

CHAPTER TWENTY-SIX

A panic descended on Lenox. It was the newspapers, he thought—his name appearing in the newspapers that morning as a consultant on the investigation. But why wouldn't they warn the Yard away? Why not Nicholson?

"Are you certain that's all they said?" he asked. "A wife and a daughter? They didn't mention any other person?"

They hadn't, according to Smith.

"And that was all they said to you?"

"Yes, sir. That was their final word. They left me alive, thanks be, and then must have bolted past Miss Randall on their way out."

Lenox excused himself and ran from the room, scribbling a note that he handed to his driver, which asked Jane to take Sophia and go to her friend the Duchess of Marchmain's—Dallington's mother, who also happened to have one of the largest and best-guarded houses in London, with a vast staff.

When he returned he found that McConnell was checking Smith's wounds; finding them to be still damp, he dressed them in fresh bandages, but didn't seem concerned about the butler's prognosis. "Ugly, but not serious," he said. "No major blood loss. You'll certainly be sore for a few days, I'm sorry to say, and there may be

some slight scarring. But your recovery should be uncomplicated."
He came over to Lenox and said, in a softer voice, "What can I do
to help? With Jane, I mean?"

"Thank you, Thomas. You could go and tell her to get to Duch's
house, or yours, anywhere really. I doubt there's immediate danger,
and I did send a note—but you might beat it there, and I would feel
more comfortable knowing she and Sophia were safe."

"Of course," said McConnell. "Instantly. The wounds look painful, but they really aren't dangerous—not enough to keep me useful
here."

"Thank you for coming."

"Of course. Good luck."

As McConnell bade good-bye to everyone in the room, Lenox
pulled a chair over to the bed and soon with a greater sense of ur-
gency was leading Obadiah Smith once more through the questions he had about the assailants, their dress, their accents, their
hands, their footwear, their height. Painstakingly he amassed slightly
more information than he had before. They'd both had lower-class
accents. That would seem to discount Wakefield's friend Francis as
one of them, though he could have shammed an accent quite easily: Indeed it might have been savvy to do so.

When this conversation was concluded they left Smith to rest,
the loyal Miss Randall sitting with large worried eyes trained upon
his pale face.

Downstairs in the lovely, impersonal hallway of his father, the
new marquess thanked Nicholson and Lenox. "When do you expect to have this business wrapped up?" he asked.

"It's impossible to say, My Lord," answered Nicholson, his tone
careful. "It could be hours or it could be years. We try not to hold
out false hope. But in this case I'm optimistic that we might come
to a solution within the week."

"Excellent. The sooner it's out of the papers . . . well, I'm sure you understand." Travers-George hesitated. "It was port wine that killed him?"

"Yes, sir, we believe so."

"Are you familiar with a friend of your father's named Francis?" asked Lenox.

The lad frowned. "I'm not familiar with any of my father's friends, blessedly," he said. "Our relations were not close. We didn't see eye to eye on several important matters pertaining to the family's estate. Thankfully those matters are in my hands now."

Thankfully! "What matters?"

Travers-George shook his head. "They cannot be of material interest to your investigation. Family affairs."

"What about the name Hartley? Does that ring a bell?"

"None whatsoever. I'm afraid I really will be of very little use in sketching out the details of my father's personal life, unfortunately."

"A final question, then. Did you know that he kept a hold on the *Gunner*, which shuttles between London and Calcutta with mail and goods?"

"The ship where he was—was found?" For a moment there flickered into the son's face a slightly more human aspect, as if it were just occurring to him that his father was gone not merely in name but in flesh. "What was he shipping?"

"We're still trying to discover that information," said Nicholson.

"I didn't know that, no. I can refer you to Robert Barker, of Prowse Street. He manages our family's investments—including my father's. Although I cannot guarantee that my father did not keep some of his income apart."

"Thank you very much for your time," said Nicholson.

"I'm at your service," said the new Lord Wakefield. He looked very conscious as he said this that the reverse was the case. Lenox could very nearly see his self-confidence expanding to fill his new, illustrious place in society—only faintly blemished by his father's conduct, a blemish that his own sober deportment could efface very quickly. "You may find me here at any time."

Out on the pavement Nicholson and Lenox paused. "What do you make of it all?" asked the man from the Yard. He was pulling a pipe and a packet of shag from his pocket, and soon he had lit up and was drawing the smoke into his lungs, then exhaling it with a great sigh of relief. "Strange business."

"Do you really think the case will be solved within the week?" asked Lenox.

Nicholson smiled ruefully. "It's best not to antagonize a fellow who could have your chief apologizing for you inside of ten minutes, if he wanted to. A lord and all."

Lenox understood. "Of course. I only ask because in truth I'm as puzzled as ever."

"Today's attack seems straightforward to me. Francis, or his proxies, wanted to fetch the port before we found it—and possibly any letters they could find on Wakefield's desk. Perhaps even the parcel with the gun in it, I suppose."

"Why did they wait until two days after the murder?"

Nicholson shrugged. "Access to the house. There have been officers and visitors in and out since the day of the murder."

"So they chose to enter in broad daylight?"

"It was bold, certainly. Misguidedly bold, it would appear, since they didn't get the port and we have some clues as to their appearance. What I'm curious to know is who Wakefield was mixed up with."

"Did you ask the neighbors whether they had seen anything of the two attackers?" asked Lenox.

"Yes, and they must be the blindest godforsaken neighbors in the whole of London, because again we came up nil, damn them." Nicholson sucked on his pipe angrily. "Though in fairness it's not as if the two men burst out of the house with drawn knives. They only needed to lower their scarves from their faces to their necks and they would seem like any other pair of fellows on foot in the city."

It was a chilly night, the moon slender and shrouded, and soon they parted. Lenox told Nicholson that he meant to look into Asiatic Limited—something about that hold on the *Gunner* still made him uneasy—and Nicholson said that he would call on Robert Barker, of Prowse Street. The fact was, though, both men felt rather stymied. A gunshot in Portland Place, a body stuffed in a trunk, poisoned wine, and now this attack upon a servant: It ought to have been simple, with such a surfeit of incident, to decipher the links between Wakefield's death and Jenkins's death. Instead it was one of the most difficult cases Lenox had encountered in his career. Whether that was luck or cunning remained to be seen.

He arrived back at Hampden Lane with his heart beating more quickly than usual, wondering whether he should send Jane and Sophia and the servants down to the country for a little while, shut the house altogether, and take a room at the Savoy himself.

He was ruminating on this idea as the carriage turned into his street, and to his surprise he saw that his house looked busy inside and out. For a moment—one of the worst of his life—he thought they might be the police, that it might be a crime scene, but then he saw that they were workmen.

He mounted the steps of his own house as a stranger might, passed on either side by men who were busy with—well, with what? Some were carrying parcels, other tools. Several were propping up a tall ladder.

"Jane?" he called as he entered the house.

He found her in the dining room, consulting with a gray-haired gentleman in a suit. "Charles," she said, "there you are. This is Mr. Clemons—shake his hand if you like, yes—he'll be making our house secure."

"Mr. Clemons," Lenox repeated.

"Yes, Mr. Lenox." Clemons passed him a card. "We're a security firm."

"Security?"

"They installed Duch's safe," said Jane, "and they work with the Queen. Haven't you worked with the Queen, Mr. Clemons? Have I got that correct?"

Clemons inclined his head. "We have been so honored, madam."

"I take it my wife has hired your services?" asked Lenox.

"I have," said Jane. Lenox could tell from her businesslike demeanor—there were few women in England as fiercely determined, when she set her mind to a thing—that she had no interest in his opinion of the project. "They'll be here several hours, and at least until this case of yours is finished they'll leave a rotating service of men at our doors and in our back garden. Mr. Clemons has assured me that they're all armed to the teeth."

"With safeties on their firearms," said Clemons quickly. "They are professionals, Mr. Lenox—primarily ex-servicemen."

"They're putting bars on the windows, too," said Jane. "Here, come and say goodnight to Sophia—unless you need anything else, Mr. Clemons?"

"No, madam, thank you."

As they climbed the stairs, Lenox said, "You've acted very quickly."

"About three months too slowly, in fact. I ought to have done this the moment you started that agency."

"Are you quite angry at me?" he asked.

She had reached the top of the stairs, and she turned, her face dark. "I am, yes. But I love you, more the fool am I, and nobody will come into our house to hurt any of the three of us—you may be absolutely sure of that."

CHAPTER TWENTY-SEVEN

Lenox arrived at the office the next morning with the first light. He wanted time to sit quietly and gather all of his thoughts about this perplexing case, and his uncluttered office, with a pad of paper and a full inkwell, seemed the place to do it.

When he arrived, however, it was to find the office inhabited: by Pointilleux, asleep with his head on his desk in the office's large main room, where the four clerks' desks faced each other. He was surrounded by towering stacks of worn cloth-bound books. Quietly Lenox peered at the binding of one and saw that it was a record of London property transactions.

"Good morning," Lenox said gently, standing a few feet back so as not to startle the lad.

Pointilleux rose bolt upright in his chair, blinking rapidly, and then, seeing where he was, shook his head and pushed the wavy hair from his forehead. "I apologize. I am extremely fatigue—I have fallen asleep." He shook his head again. "I think I must acquire a cup of tea."

Lenox, who could sympathize very well with the feeling that it was vital to acquire a cup of tea, went over to the small portable stove they kept in the corner of the room and lit the flame. (Another innovation of Polly's, that.) He spooned three tablespoons of black tea, the Bengalese kind they kept in the pine teabox on Dallington's insistence, into a large earthenware teapot. It had an ugly pattern of lilies on it, a relic of Lady Jane's own kitchen, actually. Suddenly the office didn't seem such a bleak place to Lenox—the tea, the teapot, Pointilleux. For no good reason at all, he felt a sense of optimism. They would make it.

At that moment there was a footstep on the stairwell, accompanied by a telltale metallic clatter, which sounded like the milkman. Lenox met him at the door just as the water started to boil and took their standing order with a smile and a word of thanks, two bottles of half-skimmed.

When he and Pointilleux both had their cups of tea, Lenox asked, "Were you up late, or did you fall asleep early?"

"I lose track of the hours. But I think I have discover something for you."

"On the canvass with Armbruster? Or here?"

"The canvass is not very effectual, I must tell you. There was a difficulty that Colonel Armbruster—"

"Sergeant Armbruster," said Lenox. "You've promoted him several steps and into a different service."

"Yes, Sergeant Armbruster," said Pointilleux, "the error is mine. Sergeant Armbruster was sad to be doing such work beyond his normal working hours. He was not conscientious of the job very high. Several of the house we do not knock on the door, because they are dark, and because he has knocked on these doors before and talked to their . . . their . . ."

"Residents?" offered the older detective.

"Yes. Their residents."

Lenox could remember Armbruster's unhappiness at missing his supper, on the night of Jenkins's murder. He didn't seem a very determined fellow; it was easy to imagine him cutting corners to get home a bit earlier. What odds then that he had glided his way past some important clue, or witness?

"Go on," he said.

"After we are finish the canvass, therefore, I go back and observe the houses for my own satisfaction. I observe several things. For instance, I observe that at 75 Portland Place, next door to the house of Lord Wakefield, there are a tremendous amount of men coming and leaving, five or six an hour."

"What time of the day was it?" asked Lenox.

"Six o'clock."

"There might well have been a party. What else did you see?"

"At 80 New Cavendish Street, where we have not knock with Colonel Armbruster, there is a very great . . . you would say, row. Argument."

"Did you hear its subject?"

Pointilleux shook his head. "No. Except, as I get closer, I see a small sign in the window—*To Let, Inquire Jacob Marshall, 59 Abbot Street*. It was then I realize that I have seen this sign elsewhere, three times. At"—Pointilleux looked at a scrap of paper on his desk—"80 New Cavendish Street, at 90 and 95 Harley Street, and at 30 Weymouth Street. Jacob Marshall."

Suddenly Lenox realized, from a very faint sparkle of triumph in Pointilleux's eye, that the lad had stumbled onto something he considered significant. "And now you're looking at London property records," he said.

Just then there was another footstep on the stairwell. Lenox glanced at the clock on the wall—it was scarcely past seven—and was surprised when the lock of their office door turned. It was Dallington and Polly. They were red-cheeked and laughing, though they came up short when they saw Lenox and Pointilleux in conference. Dallington was carrying a large parcel.

"Hello!" said Dallington, only momentarily nonplussed. He looked very happy. "We thought we were getting a very early crack, but nothing compared to you two. We came in to work on the cases, though I think we've beaten back the worst of the workload I left poor Polly—Miss Buchanan—with. Is that a pot of tea that I spy? And look, I've brought croissants!"

Dallington opened the box he was carrying. Polly, who was removing her gloves, said dryly, "He only bought sixteen, so we had better cut them each in half to be sure we have enough."

But she looked happy too. Lenox went to the teapot and poured out two cups for them. "Something to eat, just what the doctor ordered for Pointilleux. He's been here all night."

"I do not deem these croissants," said Pointilleux, who had stood and was inspecting the box.

"They jolly well too are croissants!" said Dallington indignantly. "This one has jam!"

Pointilleux gave a look as if to indicate that this fact was a point in his favor, rather than the young lord's, and appeared to be on the verge of saying so when Lenox interjected. "Let's get back to the case," he said. "Dallington—Polly—do you want to hear the details, or continue with your own work?"

They both wanted to hear, which meant telling them not only of Pointilleux's description thus far of his activities, but also of the attack on Smith the previous day. Dallington was startled to hear the news and asked a great number of questions. At last, Pointilleux was allowed to continue.

"Jacob Marshall, then," said Lenox.

"Yes," said the Frenchman seriously. "Jacob Marshall. I visit his office in Abbot Street, but find nobody present. So I decide to investigate of my own. I borrow these volumes from the library of the French Society, and return here."

"What did you find?"

The triumphant gleam came back into Pointilleux's eye. "What I find is that every single house on the list of Mr. Jenkins—of Portland Place, of Weymouth Street, of New Cavendish Street, of Harley Street—is the property of one man: William Travers-George, the Fifteenth Marquess of Wakefield."

Lenox raised his eyebrows. "You're sure?"

Pointilleux had a sheet of paper. "I have checked double and tri-ple. I am sure."

"By jove, you've done splendidly," said Dallington.

Lenox was staring into his cup of tea, thinking. "Wakefield owned all of those houses," he said, more to himself than to any of the three other people in the room.

Dallington was still offering congratulations to Pointilleux. "Shake my hand. If you don't want to call them croissants, we shan't, upon my word."

Lenox still had Jenkins's original list in his pocket. He took it out and looked at it for a moment. "Look at this," he said.

"What?" asked Dallington.

"Look at the list again."

He held it out for the others to see, and all four of them gazed down at Jenkins's handwriting on the singed paper.

Wakefield
PP 73-77; New Cav 80-86; Harley 90-99; Wey 26-40

Lenox pointed out what he meant with a finger. "Look at the num-ber 77," he said. "Jenkins underlined it. I missed that the first dozen times I looked at the paper, I think."

"Why has he underline it?" asked Pointilleux.

"I'm not sure—but Dallington, do you remember what's at 77?"

"What?"

"The nunnery."

Dallington raised his eyebrows. "A witness there, perhaps. Some-one he was working with."

Lenox nodded. "We must go back and see what they know, and I don't care if they've each taken a thousand vows of silence."

"If you give me half an hour to finish helping Polly, I can go with you."

"You're more than welcome," said Lenox, "but it's not necessary. I can fill you in later. In the meanwhile, Mr. Pointilleux, you have certainly earned the right to accompany me, if you like."

The boy's eyes flew open with excitement. "Of course!" he said, and he stood to get his coat, turning this way and that to look for it.

"I wonder what Jenkins was onto," Lenox said to Dallington. "It's a dark business."

"Yes," said the young lord.

Lenox shook his head dourly. "What's more, after all this I have a terrible feeling I know where his papers have gone."

CHAPTER TWENTY-EIGHT

At just after eight o'clock, Lenox and Pointilleux left Chancery Lane. It was a bright morning; passing down the street was a long double line of schoolboys in matching navy jackets, each carrying a slate board with a piece of chalk tied to it. The last two little fellows in line had crimson armbands with the word "Dunce!" written on them—a common enough punishment, though Lenox thought the exclamation point unnecessarily mean-spirited. Still, it was preferable to the bin, a device many London schools still used despite the efforts of the reformers to ban them. These were the cramped dome-shaped wicker baskets in which idle students might be enclosed and then raised to the ceiling by a system of levers and pulleys. They would be gone soon enough, he imagined. Lenox would have shot anyone who tried to put Sophia in one.

Their first stop was the offices of Asiatic Limited, where an elderly clerk named Bracewell assisted them, after they showed a letter from Nicholson with the official seal of Scotland Yard imprinted upon it in black wax. Bracewell could find the records for the *Gunner*—at the name he looked up at them sharply, perhaps contemplating the money his concern was losing every day that she was in dock—but it would take some time to find out who was permitted to retrieve Lord Wakefield's goods in Calcutta.

"Two to one, sir, it is the Pondicherry Limited, which distributes nearly every piece of cloth and bottle of liquor we ship. Nevertheless I am happy to check. If you return tomorrow morning someone will have the ledger in question."

"Thank you," said Lenox.

"My pleasure."

This job done, they hailed a cab, and Lenox directed it to Portland Place. Pointilleux looked extremely focused. After they had ridden some blocks, he said to Lenox, "Still you do not prefer to tell us where Mr. Jenkins's papers have gone?"

Lenox shook his head. "I want to be sure first. We must go see Nicholson. Or I must, I suppose."

"I am happy to come, too."

"I'm sure you are."

When they arrived at 77 Portland Place, Lenox stepped out of the cab and stood still for a moment, looking at it with fresh interest. It must once have been a normal London residence, a low-slung brick house, rectangular in shape. The nuns of St. Anselm's had made it extremely secure—a fence that reached as high as the roof, bars over every window, heavy padlocks on the black gate in front. He wondered how long they had been there.

As they crossed the street toward 77, dodging an omnibus, Lenox saw a woman standing out front: Sister Grethe again. Behind her in a small lodge near the door was another woman, who must have been the same porter Armbruster had encountered on his canvass.

Lenox approached the gate with Pointilleux behind him, and automatically Sister Grethe pulled a card from the folds of her habit—the same one Lenox had seen before.

"No, thank you, no," said Lenox, waving it away. He pointed behind her. "We need to speak to the porter."

Sister Grethe turned and looked at the porter, then gestured in her direction questioningly. Yes, Lenox indicated. The sister went and knocked on the porter's door, and soon the woman came down. She was young and heavy, with thin, downturned lips that gave her a no-nonsense look.

"Good afternoon," said Lenox. "My name is Charles Lenox. I'm assisting Scotland Yard in the investigation of the murder of Lord Wakefield, who lived two doors away. We believe several of the residents of the convent might have valuable information—might have witnessed something."

"The sisters are at prayers just now."

"So you told my colleague on the evening of the murder. They don't stop often, I suppose?" said Lenox with a smile.

"They're right pious, yes," said the young woman suspiciously.

"May I ask your name?" said Lenox.

"Sarah Ward."

"Miss Ward, it's urgent that we speak with the sisters. Or at a minimum with some representative who can tell us when we might have a conversation with each of them individually."

"They ain't to be bothered," said the porter.

Sister Grethe was watching this exchange dumbly. Lenox felt a growing irritation. "In this case I'm afraid I must insist."

The young woman looked uncertain, and went on hemming at the notion—but at last she said she would try to find someone.

They waited a very, very long time. "Why can this sister not be help to us?" whispered Pointilleux eventually.

"She only speaks German. And she's taken a vow of silence."

To Lenox's surprise, Pointilleux turned to her and said something in German, in a lively tone. Sister Grethe merely stared at him. He tried again, and she handed him the same card Lenox had already seen, then turned back to the street.

Pointilleux read the card. "She behave as if I speak to her in strange language, but my German is excellent," he whispered unhappily.

"Do you know the term 'vow of silence'?" asked Lenox.

"I am French. I know about my church more in my little toe than every Englishman put together in their head."

Finally Sarah Ward emerged. Behind her, in a dingy habit, was a middle-aged woman. She looked as if she had been sleeping, not praying. "May I help you?" she asked.

Lenox introduced himself and asked her name—she was Sister Amity, she said—and then asked whether they might interview the sisters of the convent, beginning with Sister Grethe, to whom his assistant would be happy to speak in German.

Sister Amity looked alarmed. "Absolutely not!" she said.

"But if you only—"

"Should you choose to address your impertinences to us again, we will be forced to contact the police! Now—good day!"

Lenox frowned. "I'm afraid then that we, too, will be forced to return with the police—for we really must speak to all of you. You may have been witnesses to a crime without knowing it, and your house was the property of a murdered man."

"We have a long lease signed upon it," said the sister.

"Did Lord Wakefield often come by?"

"Absolutely not. Nor should you, if you have any sense of decency. Good day."

With that, Sister Amity turned and went back into the house. Sarah Ward gave them a gloating look and returned to her lodge. Sister Grethe continued to look at them without any change in her expression, which irritated Lenox so profoundly by this stage that he had to stop himself from slamming shut the gate as they left.

They would return with Nicholson. It was all they could do.

The carriage rolled through the bright morning toward the Yard. Lenox was in a brown study, absorbed in a deep contemplation of the details of the case, until finally Pointilleux said, "Can you not tell me where the papers are, of Inspector Jenkins?"

Lenox looked at him. "Not just yet. I may be wrong."

Nicholson was at Scotland Yard when they arrived, reading through the results of the canvass upon which Pointilleux had accompanied Armbruster and several other men the evening before. He looked fatigued. "We've had the new Lord Wakefield's solicitor in already this morning, to inquire about our progress," he said.

"That's no good," said Lenox.

"Why is it not?" asked Pointilleux.

Lenox looked at him sternly. "If you have questions while we are speaking to Inspector Nicholson, please save them until you and I are alone."

Pointilleux raised his eyebrows in surprise, then nodded. "My apologies," he said.

"Nicholson, I wonder if you could send for Armbruster. I wanted to ask him directly about the canvass."

"I don't know if he's here at the Yard. Let me ask."

"Tell them to look in the canteen, I suppose."

Nicholson smiled, then stepped out to send one of his constables off to search for the sergeant. While they waited they discussed the *Gunner* and the Asiatic Limited Corporation.

At length Armbruster appeared. "Sirs," he said. Then he gave a not particularly favorable look to the Frenchman. Too zealous the night before, perhaps. "Mr. Pointilleux."

All three men had remained seated when Armbruster came in, and Nicholson's office, smaller than Jenkins's though with the same lovely view of the Thames, barely had room to hold a fourth chair. Instead Lenox moved to a nearby filing cabinet, leaning against it and offering the sergeant his chair.

"You had a question about the canvass?" asked Armbruster, sitting back and looking up at Lenox expectantly.

"A few questions," said Lenox. "Though my more pressing concern is what you've done with the papers Inspector Jenkins left behind."

CHAPTER TWENTY-NINE

Papers?" said Armbruster. "What papers?"

Nicholson looked at Lenox with consternation. "You cannot think that Sergeant Armbruster killed Inspector Jenkins?"

"I doubt he did that—or at least, I do not know. He may have. What I do know is that I would like to see Jenkins's papers."

"Papers!" said Armbruster again. "I don't know who you think you're speaking to, but I've been at the Yard for thirteen years. My father and two of my brothers have worked here alongside me."

There was a crimson flush in Armbruster's ears, however, a note of hysteria in his voice—this fellow was involved. Lenox pointed at his stomach. "I would bet five quid that you bought your pocket watch this week," he said. "Am I correct?"

"That just goes to show," said Armbruster, appealing to Nicholson. "I've had this for ages."

"You really must explain your suspicions," said Nicholson to Lenox.

"About the watch? Or about Mr. Armbruster? The matter of the watch is simple enough. He wasn't wearing it Thursday evening, when Jenkins died. I remember specifically seeing a brown stain on his shirt at the time—soup, I think—and there was no watch chain across it."

"That scarcely seems indicative of any great crime," said Nicholson.

"I have also noticed across the years—anyone who wears a pocket watch will—that there is substantially more wear at the clasp than anywhere else on the watch. All of those openings and closings, thumb and fingernail rubbing down the metal. Mr. Armbruster's has no such blemish."

"That's easy," said Armbruster, looking more confident now. "On both counts. I don't wear it often. Had it for ages."

"Now you've worn it the last two days. And it looks, to my eye, to be made of solid gold."

"A gold wash," said Armbruster quickly.

It was here that he betrayed himself.

Nicholson asked, mildly, if he might see the watch. This evidently seemed reasonable enough to Armbruster, but as soon as Nicholson handled the object, it was apparent to the other three men that he did so with a vastly more intimate knowledge than they could have. He had the watch open and its workings under the squinch of his eye in an instant, and after he had turned the watch over and tapped it with his knuckle, then checked the maker's mark, he passed it back to Armbruster.

"You see?" said the sergeant hopefully.

Nicholson shook his head. "My own father worked in a jewelry shop. I grew up behind the counter with him. Your watch is gold. And new, as Mr. Lenox said; it was made in the year 1876, according to its maker's mark. What's more, I doubt there's a sergeant on the force who has a more expensive watch."

Armbruster shrugged, feigning nonchalance. "I had a bargain, I suppose. And by ages I meant . . . months."

"Do you remember where you bought it?"

"Not the exact name of the shop. I hope it wasn't stolen."

Nicholson looked up at Lenox. "Still, I cannot accuse a man on the basis of a new watch. Armbruster—sit down." This latter injunction was given sharply, because the sergeant had started to rise from his seat. "Why do you suspect him?"

Lenox, hands in the pockets of his jacket, leaned back against the filing cabinet. "As you know, it is difficult to gain access to the inner corridors of this building," he said. "When we couldn't find Jenkins's papers, I wondered whether perhaps he had taken them home or had them upon his person when he was murdered. But Madeleine Jenkins confirmed that he never brought work papers home with him, and the note to me suggested, I believe, that he wasn't carrying them about London with him. They were in his office, then, locked securely away."

"Except that they weren't," said Nicholson.

"Precisely. And there was that space upon his desk—the empty space you and I both saw, where they might have been. Since I saw that, I have believed there must have been someone working within the Yard who took them. Someone with access to the office and a key to its door."

"It wasn't me," said Armbruster indignantly.

"At first I thought it was most likely one of Jenkins's close associates—perhaps Hastings, perhaps Bryson—but I no longer think so. May I ask where you live, Sergeant Armbruster?" said Lenox.

"In Hammersmith. Why on earth do you want to know that?"

"You told us yesterday, didn't you, that you aren't accustomed to working in the field? That you are generally employed in the back offices?" Armbruster was silent at this. Lenox went on, "Take those facts together, then: You live nowhere near the part of London where Jenkins was killed, you generally work in this building, which is not a hundred steps from the Tube station where you would find your train home, and yet you were first upon the scene of the crime, as Inspector Nicholson here told us when we arrived. That was why you had charge of it, was it not?"

"It was," said Nicholson. "He sent the fellow who found the body to fetch a constable and watched over it himself."

Lenox nodded. "It must have been then that you looked through Jenkins's pockets. You were very thorough—you even untied one of his shoes. But I suppose you were interrupted before you could get it off."

Nicholson's gaze had hardened now. "What were you doing near Regent's Park that evening?" he asked.

"And what were you doing when I arrived," said Lenox, "with a thick sheaf of papers, clamped tightly under your arm?"

"I didn't have any papers," said Armbruster. There was menace in his heavy face now.

"In fact you did," said Lenox. "And if I had to guess why, I'd say it's because you watched Jenkins's office closely, saw when he left, slipped in, took the papers, and then followed him to North London to be first on the scene when he was murdered. You had to hold the papers—there was nowhere you could safely leave them. The only questions that remain are where the papers are now, and whether or not it was you who killed him."

There was a tense silence in the room. "This is all mad speculation," said Armbruster at last. "You have no proof that I've done anything."

Pointilleux, who had been sitting quietly, widened his eyes slightly and then said, "I see now! This is why you have done such a bad job with the canvass, last evening!"

"I didn't do any such thing," said Armbruster.

"You did!"

"You had better give it up, Armbruster," said Lenox. "If you were merely working for someone, you can avoid being hanged, anyway."

For a fleeting moment the threat seemed to work. The sergeant's face wavered. But he held firm. "This is all nonsense," he said. "Inspector Nicholson, if you require nothing else?"

"I require a great deal else," said Nicholson. "Sit there. Your desk and your home are going to be searched thoroughly before you leave this office."

"As you please," said Armbruster, and he sat back, unperturbed.

Lenox's heart fell. They could search both his desk and his home all they liked, but they wouldn't find anything—the fleeting reaction in the sergeant's face told as much. "Was it Wakefield who was paying you?" he asked.

"Nobody was paying me."

"Or Hartley? Francis?"

"You're talking rot," said Armbruster. "I was in the neighborhood on a social call, and I happened to see a fellow in distress. I ought to be getting a ribbon from you lot, not an earful about how I killed him. It's a disgrace."

"Yes, it's a disgrace," said Lenox.

Nicholson had gone to fetch two constables from the pool. When he returned, he said, "They're going over his desk."

"They won't find anything," said Lenox.

Nicholson shook his head. "No, I don't think so either. And yet this chap lied to us now several times—about the watch, about the papers, for now that I put my mind to it I remember as well that you were carrying some kind of papers, Armbruster, and why on earth would that have been? You'd no need to take work home."

"They were probably personal papers," the sergeant said. "I can't even remember them myself."

It was maddening: to have someone who knew the truth about two murders sitting here before them, and to be unable to make him give it up.

CHAPTER THIRTY

That afternoon was Jenkins's funeral. Lenox and Dallington rode together to it, and Lenox used the time to tell his protégé about the interview they had conducted with Armbruster.

"Where is he now?" asked Dallington.

"Still in Nicholson's office, waiting for them to search his desk and his house. He's not happy about having to sit there for hours, but they can't arrest him. For all I know he's marched out of the office already. He seemed more confident as time went on, I'm sorry to say. There was a moment when I thought he might break down, but if he doesn't we're flummoxed."

Dallington turned his head, his face philosophical. "Still, it was well done to spot him, the scoundrel."

Lenox hesitated, then said, "No, it was badly done. I realize that now. I would have been much better off observing him, building a case against him." He shook his head. "I was too excited to have put it together, after Pointilleux described how incompetent the canvass was."

He half-expected Dallington to object to this self-criticism, but the younger lad said, "Perhaps, I suppose."

In all the months of the agency's existence it was the closest he had come to offering any criticism of Lenox. He felt it keenly. "Armbruster will betray himself in the end, I hope. Something in his office or in his house that he didn't count on us finding."

"I hope so too," said Dallington.

The funeral was at a church called St. Mary's. They arrived a bit early and found Nicholson standing on the church's steps, changed from his daily clothes into a subdued gray flannel suit, with a black bowler hat on his head. He greeted them.

"Any news?" asked Lenox.

"None. He won't talk, and there's nothing unusual in his desk. I've left instructions he's not to move. But as you said, I doubt we'll find much. All society's going to hell anyway," said Nicholson moodily. "Marquesses murdering and getting murdered. Police sergeants stealing papers."

Dallington smiled gently. "And they say the Queen and Princess Beatrice have been seen smoking cigarettes at Balmoral."

Nicholson shook his head. "It's extremely distressing to think of it coming from inside the Yard." He looked at Lenox. "Do you think Armbruster killed Jenkins himself?"

Lenox shook his head. "I think he did a job for money. The new watch tells us that. He took the papers and he made sure—or tried to make sure—that there was nothing incriminating on Jenkins's person. At the scene and since, he's dragged his feet and tried to slow down the investigation."

Nicholson nodded. "The soup, the slow and incomplete canvasses."

"But I would hazard that was his full role. I could be wrong, of course."

"Who paid him, then?"

Lenox shrugged. "Andrew H. Francis, I suppose."

"Yes. Him." Yesterday and that morning the Yard's clerical staff had done extensive research in the directories of London and still hadn't found Andrew Francis—or at any rate not one who corresponded to the description they had of him, young, aristocratic, wealthy, well dressed. Lenox had begun to wonder whether it was a pseudonym. "The fellow shot an inspector of the Yard, poisoned a nobleman and arranged for him to be shipped to Calcutta like a slab of mutton, and we can't find hide nor hair of him. Either he's a genius, or we're a pack of fools."

"We'll find him," said Lenox. He wished he were as confident as he sounded.

"How?" asked Nicholson.

"By carrying on. After the funeral I mean to start with what Pointilleux found—that list of houses that Wakefield owned. If Jenkins thought it was significant, I'm certain it was."

They spoke for another few minutes, and then the bells of the church chimed, and all of the people engaged in similar conversations on the steps turned toward the enormous oak doors of the church and began to walk inside.

The service was long. There were several hymns, followed by a warm eulogy from the Lord Mayor of London, a redoubtable figure in black velvet breeches with a silver-headed cane. The turnout was excellent in this respect—there were three Members of Parliament present, the entire upper echelon of the Yard's administrative staff, and more off-duty bobbies and inspectors and sergeants than could be counted. Behind the final pews of the church were a few loose lines of standing men, and their stolidly endured discomfort over the eighty minutes was its own kind of testimonial to Jenkins, the church too full because he was so mourned.

Of course, though, it was difficult to take much pleasure in the attendance when set off forward and to the left, in the specially wide pews where the local lord must have taken his place on Sundays, was Jenkins's family: Madeleine; two small boys; a baby girl in a white lace dress and matching bonnet, blessedly unaware, for now, of what she had lost.

After the service was over, the people in the church made their way outside and stood on the steps again. The traditional funeral procession began. First a long series of empty carriages passed down the avenue outside, each, including Lenox's own, sent by its owner as a mark of respect; after the carriages a line of five deaf-mutes dressed in black and red carried long wands, men who hired themselves out for funerals such as this one every day of the week; then the casket itself came, borne by a dozen pallbearers. Lenox looked among their faces and saw several men who worked at Scotland Yard.

Last was another carriage. Accompanied by a few ancient relatives, Madeleine Jenkins and her children stepped into it. They would follow the convoy to a cemetery nearby for the interment.

As she went, the bells of the church began to ring, thirty-nine times in this case, one for each year of Jenkins's life, and then nine solemn strikes of the largest one, the tenor, to send the departed man on his way to his God.

The crowd on the steps watched silently until the final carriage was out of sight, and then breathed a collective exhalation, which could hardly be helped from bearing a slight air of relief. That was over, at any rate. By ones and twos most of the men and women began to get into a line of waiting cabs. There would be ham and bread and ale at Jenkins's house now—a few hours to celebrate the man, with quiet stories and jokes, after these somber hours of grief at his death.

Lenox and Dallington decided it would be quicker to walk. The house—Treeshadow, Lenox recalled—wasn't far, and it was a lovely spring day. They'd lost Nicholson, who was of course among dozens of his own daily colleagues on an occasion such as this one.

Dallington lit a cigarette. "You won't find a more Christian fellow than me, but I can't stand a funeral."

"Really? I find it comforting."

"I don't mind the hymns. I just don't think anyone should be allowed to talk. It always seems like so much hocus-pocus."

"Hax pax max deus adimax," said Lenox, and smiled.

"What on earth are you trying to say?"

"That's where the word 'hocus-pocus' comes from. It's a nonsense phrase that traveling magicians used to say to impress people as they did their tricks. Sounded enough like Latin, I suppose. I know it because my brother used to say it to me when I was four or five and we were arguing. It always scared the devil out of me. As he knew."

"Edmund did that? I can't imagine it."

"Small boys are dirty fighters. Tell me, though, how are Polly's cases coming along? You were able to help her?"

"There's still a great deal more to do this evening," said Dallington, though he didn't look as if the prospect of the late night's work gave him as much displeasure as it might have in other circumstances. "But I tell you, she's a marvel. LeMaire's a fool to leave. If Polly has anything to do with it we'll be minting money by New Year's. Every one of these cases came to her by a reference from a previous customer, and I think every one of the people she's helping now will refer her to a dozen more."

"What are the cases, specifically?" asked Lenox.

As they strolled on in the soft sunlight they discussed these—many of them small domestic matters, worth a pound or two to the firm, but in aggregate, they agreed, creating something more valuable: a reputation. There was the woman in Kensington whose post kept disappearing after it was delivered, the lost dog in Holborn, the Oxford Street tearoom whose owners suspected their cashier was stealing from them—but dearly hoped she wasn't, because she was their beloved daughter. Small or large, Polly handled all of these matters with intense dedication, Dallington said.

They neared Treeshadow after a little while, identifiable from a distance by the great bustle outside of it. When they arrived at the house Dallington discarded his cigarette.

Lenox stopped him with a hand. "John, before we go in—I only mean to stay for twenty minutes, and then I should be off. You must stay longer for both of us, if you don't mind, and then you ought to return to Chancery Lane to help Polly."

"Where are you going?"

"Those nuns are going to tell us what they know once and for all. Preferably this very day."

CHAPTER THIRTY-ONE

I f an alert Londoner had been asked to pinpoint the precise geographical center of his city's aristocratic society, in that month of that year of that century of English life, after a little hesitation he might have pointed to a slender street in the West End, only six houses long and none of them impressively large. It was called Cleveland Row.

Drop a fellow in this ostensibly unremarkable little corridor, and he was guaranteed to be within a minute's walk of a title, of a fortune, of a beauty—and sometimes of all three united within a single body. At its east end the street opened onto the corner of St. James's Street and Pall Mall, which were lined with the cavernous and sumptuous gentlemen's clubs of London; at its west end it let onto the pathways of Green Park, which offered a direct approach, not three minutes' walk, to Buckingham Palace. The Row backed onto Clarence House, where the Prince of Wales lived, and the Queen's own chapel next to that; it looked forward to the Earl of Spencer's chalk-colored mansion, where the great pageant of London society held its weekly gatherings.

Cleveland Row was Lenox's destination, as he drove away from Jenkins's house half an hour later in a cab. (His own carriage was still in the funeral procession, now heading to the cemetery.) There were few places he felt more at home. It was a ten-minute walk from Hampden Lane, where he and Jane lived, it was half a block from several clubs to which he belonged, including his favorite, the Athenaeum, and he'd visited Spencer House only the week before.

He had the cab stop at a sprightly brick residence with bright green shutters. He paid, stepped down, and rang at the bell. The house's windows were glimmering with light, and after only a moment a butler answered.

"Charles Lenox, to see Father Hepworth," said the visitor. "Here is my card. Is he receiving?"

"Please come in, sir," said the butler. He gestured toward a small brittle chair upholstered in red velvet. "If you would care to sit while I ascertain whether Father Hepworth is occupied."

Lenox waited in the small entrance hall, occasionally peering down the red-carpeted hallway the butler had followed upstairs. Even this little room was dense with beautiful objects: a convex mirror in a burnished brass frame, a stone urn carved with cherubim (and stuffed unceremoniously with umbrellas), small paintings of religious scenes in gilt frames.

After a few moments there was a footstep on the staircase, and when Lenox half-rose, he saw that it was not the butler again but Hepworth himself. "Lenox!" he said. "What an unexpected pleasure! Come up, won't you? I was just about to have tea."

"I'm pleased I caught you," said Lenox.

"On the contrary, the pleasure is mine. Come along, this way."

The upstairs room into which Hepworth led Lenox was decorated in much the same style as the entrance hall, though the objects here were grander in scale, including a row of magnificently ostentatious reliquaries along one wall, all of them bejeweled, some of them carved, some of them painted. One of Holbein's portraits of Sir Thomas More (a great hero to Catholics, of course—he had died rather than grant Henry the Eighth permission to divorce) hung near the fireplace.

Catholics: It was an odd but no doubt exhilarating moment to be one of these in England.

Of course, to some degree it guaranteed that you would be loathed—such was the tradition of the country. It had been Catholics who plotted to kill Queen Elizabeth, and before that Catholics who had so brutally slaughtered the brave Protestants who died while Elizabeth's sister, Queen Mary, Bloody Mary, had reigned. (Nearly three centuries after it was written, Foxe's gruesome *Book of Martyrs*, which depicted those deaths in horrible, explicit detail, was still one of the bookshops' five bestsellers year after year.) The bias against them had long been unswerving, though recently it had softened somewhat. Since 1829 they had at least been permitted to vote and own land.

More than that, in the last twenty years things had begun to change in ways that were, depending upon one's perspective, either exciting or alarming. First, in the 1830s and 1840s, a great number of Protestants of the "high church" variety—that is, those who didn't mind a little bit of incense in their services, or insist upon plain vestments for their priest—had suddenly darted in a mass to the Catholic Church, led by the great controversial Tractarians of Oxford University, Newman and Pusey. Reviled in London and beloved in Rome, these intellectuals had stubbornly insisted upon their decisions, even as their conversion cut them off from the society of scholars and aristocrats to which they had once belonged.

Slowly others had followed them, one by one, forsaking society, fortune, and often even family to do so. The great poet Gerard Manley Hopkins had converted; Irishmen in search of work emigrated in more and more significant numbers to England, bringing their religion; in 1850, the pope, Pius IX, had finally reintroduced into the country proper dioceses and parishes, where there had been only uncertain and makeshift churches before. There were men in Parliament who believed the toleration of all this would lead to England's ruin. It was a badly kept secret that Queen Victoria herself was panicked about the invasion.

At the center of this web of Catholic life in England sat Father Dixon Hepworth.

Of course, London had its own holy overseer—the Archbishop of Westminster—but it was Hepworth, not the archbishop, who mattered. The reason was a very British one, class. Hepworth came from an old and noble Suffolk family, and when he had converted at Oxford he hadn't lost their love, which meant that, unlike most Catholics, he still had a place in society, even if some of the more religious houses of London stopped sending their invitations to him.

On top of that he had charm, wit, and wealth—and despite being ordained, he knew better than to push his religion forward in the wrong situation. He was a philosophical fellow, a bit beyond fifty, bald and rather athletic, with the practical face of a man of business. He was extremely devoted to his collection of art and artifacts, but there seemed to be nothing especially artistic about him in person. He had a mistress of long standing named Eleanor Hallinan; she was a dancer in the West End, very beautiful, with no more of an eye toward Christ than a goldfish might have had. He never preached, rarely visited with the poor, and spent most of his days here, in Cleveland Row—but his power was unassailable. He presided over the city's Catholic institutions, whether from the board or with a softer kind of influence, and the Vatican never filled a significant vacancy in the country without consulting him first. The archbishop could make no such claim.

Lenox had known him for decades now, and liked the fellow; and if there was one man who could apply some slight pressure on a group of stubborn nuns, it was Hepworth.

The priest was sitting on an armchair and leaned forward from its edge, face full of interest, hands clasped before him. "What can I do for you?" he asked.

"Have you heard of the murder of Inspector Thomas Jenkins?"

It took just a few minutes for Lenox to describe to Hepworth the sequence of interactions he and Scotland Yard had had with the sisters of St. Anselm's, and the absolute refusal of Sister Amity to speak to them, on the one hand, and the absolute inability of Sister Grethe to do so, on the other.

As Lenox spoke, Hepworth's face had slowly taken on a look of consternation. After the story was finished, he leaned back in his chair. "St. Anselm's, you say?"

"Yes."

"You're sure that's what they said? At 77 Portland Place?"

"Yes," said Lenox.

Just then the door opened, and a footman came in behind a rolling table, which was topped with a silver half-globe. He retracted this when the table was between Hepworth and Lenox, revealing a teapot, a plate of sandwiches, and several piles of toast. Lenox realized how hungry he was when he saw it.

Hepworth stood up, buttoning his blue velvet jacket. "If you wouldn't mind pouring your own tea, I think I can help," he said. "Wait here for two minutes—less, probably."

As he waited, Lenox fell gratefully upon a stack of cinnamon toast wedges, piping hot and running with butter. When fully half a dozen of these were gone, he poured himself a cup of the light, fragrant tea, stirred in his milk and sugar, took a long sip, and sat back with a sigh of profound contentment.

To think: In Rome there wasn't a cup of the stuff to be found.

Hepworth reappeared just as Lenox was pouring himself a little more. He was carrying a large leather book and accepted Lenox's offer to give him a cup of tea only with some distraction. He sat down and opened the book, flipping through it.

"Is anything wrong?" asked Lenox.

Hepworth took a sip of tea and was silent for a moment. "Yes," he said at last.

Lenox felt a surge of interest. "What?"

"Only what I suspected, when I heard your story—and what this book has confirmed. The Catholic Church has no record at all of a convent called St. Anselm's in London, on Portland Place or anywhere else."

CHAPTER THIRTY-TWO

Within the precincts of Regent's Park there were several churches, Hepworth explained, including St. Thomas's on Longford Street, which was the closest building to 77 Portland Place that the Catholic Church owned. There was no order of nuns nearby, however.

Lenox was silent for a moment and then said, "The Church owns the land upon which St. Thomas's sits, you mentioned. Would the Church ever rent a building?"

Hepworth shook his head. "No, we buy them. They have a fair number of accountants there at the Vatican, you know—just as sharp as our fellows near the Inns, only they wear long robes."

"Where is the closest convent to Regent's Park?"

"Half a mile from Portland Place, just off Bayswater Road. It's called Her Sisters of the Holy Heart, a Benedictine order. I know it well myself. They've been working in close concert with the Temperance Christians on behalf of the horses who drive the London cabs. It doesn't sound like much, but you wouldn't believe the bloody lives they lead, the poor beasts. They rarely live longer than a year or two. And it's excellent for the reputation of our Church for the sisters to be working with Protestants."

Lenox's mind was racing. "Might St. Anselm's be some sort of renegade offshoot of the church?" he asked.

"I cannot conceive that such a group would have escaped my attention," said Hepworth seriously. "What's more, it's no small matter to establish an exchange with convents in other lands. Germany, you said?"

"Yes, Germany." Lenox thought of Sister Grethe. "But it's possible?"

Hepworth shrugged. "Anything is possible, I suppose. Do they advertise their presence there? Is there a sign on the gate? A cross?"

"Nothing at all of that sort. On the contrary, it looks designed to keep people out."

Hepworth shook his head slightly. "It sounds like very few convents I know."

The light outside was waning now. Somewhere south of them, Lenox thought, the wake for Jenkins was still going on. What had he known about the various houses in Regent's Park that Wakefield owned? And who had killed him?

Lenox stood up. "Thank you so much," he said. "I hope I can count upon your discretion?"

"I'm troubled to learn of this place," said Hepworth. "I ought to speak to someone in my Church."

"Absolutely. But if you could wait a day or two—three at the outside. I can send you word."

Hepworth nodded. "Yes. All right," he said. "On the condition that you keep me apprised of anything you learn. Do we have a deal?"

"We have a deal."

They shook hands, and Lenox left Cleveland Row with a hundred ideas in his head. He didn't know whether it would be wiser to wait and speak to Dallington and Nicholson, or to go directly to Portland Place himself.

In the end, he hailed a cab and directed it toward Wakefield's neighborhood. He couldn't resist. Still, he'd learned his lesson from his premature interrogation of Armbruster, and from Armbruster's subsequent silence—he only intended to observe.

Over the years Lenox had learned how to blend himself into any street in London. There was a special brand of loitering that the natives of the city, across every neighborhood, seemed to have in common. As he reached Portland Place—having been dropped a few streets shy of it, so that he could walk—he turned down the brim of his hat, turned up his collar, lit a small cigar so that he would look as if he had an excuse for idling in one place, and took up residence in a doorway across the street from numbers 73 to 77 Portland Place: Wakefield's grand double-wide mansion, St. Anselm's with its high black security fence, and the nondescript alabaster row house between them.

As the sky darkened and the gas lamps came on, Lenox watched. There were subtle changes to any inhabited place, if you looked at it closely enough. Lights came on at the convent, window by window, though it was impossible to see through them because they were made of ground glass. Meanwhile, at Wakefield's lights had already been on, but more appeared, and just shy of six o'clock smoke rose from the chimney. Lenox wondered if the new master of the house—young Travers-George—felt comfortable staying there, after the attack on the butler. It would appear so. Bold, that, particularly after the murder of his father. Lenox himself would have taken refuge in the safety of a large hotel, at least for a few nights.

Increasingly, however, his attention was drawn to a house he hadn't considered before—the one that lay between Wakefield's and St. Anselm's.

That morning Pointilleux had said, with some confusion, that he had observed a tremendous number of visitors at 75 Portland Place, several men an hour.

The pattern was the same this evening. Every few minutes, it seemed—Lenox took out his pocket watch after a little while so that he could start timing it more precisely—a person would arrive at the anonymous house, look up and down the street quickly, and then enter. Mostly these were men, though some were women. All were well dressed.

It took Lenox some time to realize what bothered him about it, and then it came to him.

Nobody knocked on the door.

With mounting excitement he watched, still timing the intervals, as over the course of forty minutes three more men came up to the door. Little enough was happening at Wakefield's or St. Anselm's (as his brain still stubbornly thought of it), but there was this riot of activity between them. Could it be meaningful?

Then he realized a second strange fact: Since he had arrived on Portland Place, more than a dozen people had entered through the front door—but not one had left by it.

He took a moment to study the house in greater detail. It was the same height as Wakefield's house, three stories, though half as wide. It was a town house like so many in this part of Regent's Park, with handsome white columns in front, a well-kept air, and tall, curtained windows. These curtains were thin enough that Lenox could see someone moving behind one of the upstairs windows repeatedly, a short figure.

Was it a party they were having? If it was, why did none of the guests knock? And was the family of the house likely to have parties on two successive nights?

Slowly, slowly, Lenox felt his brain begin to comprehend the contours of the mystery. It was always painful, this part—knowing the answer without yet knowing it. For a long while he watched, motionless, his third cigar lit but forgotten in one hand, his other hand tensed around the pocket watch.

Then, finally, he understood.

His eyes darted toward the convent. Was it possible? Yes, he decided—in fact, it was probable.

No wonder Jenkins had underlined that number: 77. Now, though, it was 75 Portland Place that held Lenox's eye. He took in more details—the brass doorknobs, the handsome row of small green bushes lining each window. It was one of those houses at which you could still imagine them doing the old Jane Austen dances, the ones Lenox just barely remembered watching through the banister of the stairwell during his childhood: advance and return, hold hands, bow and curtsy, corkscrew, thread the needle, back to the start. A house that valued the old ways.

Behind the grandeur of Portland Place was an alleyway, Lenox knew. With a purposeful stride he made his way for it. To stand directly behind one of the houses that Wakefield owned would have been too conspicuous, so he lingered at the end of the alley for a few minutes instead, trying hard not to peer too intently down it at the back of St. Anselm's.

Ten minutes passed, then another ten. Then it came: confirmation. It was all Lenox could do not to celebrate then and there.

He left the mouth of the alleyway and made his way back toward the brightness of Portland Place, taking up his old spot in the doorway. He was tempted to go to Scotland Yard as quickly as he could and find Nicholson, but he forced himself to wait and watch a little while longer. A man and a woman entered the house a few minutes apart. Then there was a long period of inactivity, during which he grew restless. Why shouldn't he walk up to the house himself, and open the door as boldly as all of these other people had?

But caution ruled the day. Best to measure twice.

By the time he hailed a passing cab, it was nearly eight o'clock. He directed it to Chancery Lane, where he hoped he would find Dallington and Polly still at work on Polly's cases, and perhaps even Pointilleux. It was probably too late by now for Nicholson to be in his office, and Lenox needed to tell somebody what he thought he'd discovered.

He took the stairs two at a time. He was energized. None of the setbacks of the case mattered any longer. When he reached the door he pushed through and was pleased to see that Polly and Dallington were in the clerks' room, Dallington sitting upon one of their desks, Polly standing a few feet from him with her arms crossed.

"I think I've discovered something," said Lenox. The other two exchanged glances, and only then did he realize that there was an air of tension in the room. "What?" he asked. "What is it?"

Dallington's voice was bitter when he spoke. "The firm is just you and me now, it would appear. Polly is leaving us, too."

CHAPTER THIRTY-THREE

Lenox looked at Polly with a kind of despair. He realized he was crestfallen at this news, far more so than he had been at Le-Maire's abdication. Even in just the few months they had been working together, he had come to trust her implicitly. He couldn't imagine what Dallington must be feeling. "Is that correct?"

She shook her head once and turned away, and Lenox could see that despite her aloof expression there was some high emotion stirring in her breast. She looked back at him, skin pale but cheeks red with feeling. "I've had a proposal," she said.

"Of marriage?" asked Lenox, confused.

"No, no," she said. "A business proposal."

"From whom?"

"I would prefer not to say."

Dallington laughed severely and stood up from the desk he'd been leaning on. "Yes, why tell us? We're the competition now, after all."

"Please don't be unfair, John," said Polly. "You must see that we're struggling."

"Businesses always struggle at the beginning. That doesn't mean you walk out on your friends."

"I wouldn't, in the normal course of things," said Polly. Her voice was tightly controlled, as if she were trying not to cry. "I should hope you would know that."

Lenox held up a hand. "Can somebody tell me what's happened?"

Polly explained. That afternoon, a gentleman's assistant had left his card for her there at the office, inviting her to come take tea with him at the Langham. ("Where else, of course," Dallington interjected. "Vulgarity upon vulgarity." The Langham was a new and enormous hotel, which had cost some three hundred thousand pounds to build—an astonishing sum.) She had gone, thinking it might be a case, and, given the name upon the card, which was known to all of them, almost certainly a remunerative one.

When she had arrived, however, the gentleman in question had presented her with a different idea altogether: that they go into business together. It was simple, he said. He believed in her talent, in her innovations, in the specialists she had hired, and above all in the idea of a detective agency. There was money to be made.

But the agency she had founded with Lenox, Dallington, and LeMaire had gone about the business all wrong. Bad press. Too little backing. Four overseers rather than one. He knew business, he said, and a firm like theirs needed a single guiding hand—a single guiding vision.

To his surprise, Lenox realized that he was inclined to agree at least with this latter point. Too much of their time had been spent coming to agreement upon small matters. Four voices upon each subject was too many.

Polly went on. This businessman, Lord—and here she nearly said his name, but stopped herself—he had a plan. He already had an office selected, and showed her several designs. It would be called Miss Strickland's, as her own business once had been.

Above all, it would be substantial. Ten detectives working under her—all trained precisely to her specifications. Specialists of every variety. Security. Clerks. He could guarantee an enormous splash, and an immediate and significant client: himself. His multitude of businesses saw dozens of incidents, large and small, that were beyond the purview or the interest of Scotland Yard but interrupted his efficiency.

That was the beauty of his idea, he explained: It was a wonderful idea for a business in its own right, but even if it operated at a slight loss, for some time, it would make him money. An in-house detective agency.

And Polly, in addition to a handsome salary, would own half of the business.

It took her five minutes to describe all of this, a little longer than it might have otherwise because Dallington, uncharacteristically, interrupted her continually with a succession of small, wounded sarcasms.

When she had finished, Lenox was silent for a moment. Then he said, "If I were your brother, I would tell you to do it."

He looked at Polly and saw that all the anxiety and tension in her face washed away at his words, replaced by relief. "Thank you," she said. "That's it exactly. I would be a fool not to consider it. It has nothing to do with my . . . with my faith in either of you, or in our agency."

"Ten detectives," muttered Dallington. "What a load of nonsense."

"Can you not tell us the identity of this benefactor of yours?" asked Lenox.

She shook her head. "I cannot. It was a condition of the offer he made me."

"And it was you he wanted, not either of us," said Lenox.

Even as he asked the question he wished he hadn't, because the answer was very obvious—and what's more, probably astute. Polly was sharp, young, and she had run a business of this sort before. With very great grace, she said, "He wants just one person—and had heard my name through a friend, I think. I believe it might just as easily have been either of you he approached, but a friend told him my name, and then he had his assistant research my history, and—"

"I understand, of course," said Lenox.

"Then you're farther along than I am," said Dallington. "I could never turn my back on either of you."

Lenox looked around the office, with its tidy rows of books upon the shelves, its hopeful lamps at each clerk's desk, its well-ordered air of prosperity. Not six months before, he had been in Parliament! Strange to think of that, anyhow.

He found that he didn't want to look at Dallington. His friend was nearly vibrating with disappointment, and Lenox understood, without quite articulating it to himself, that it wasn't simple professional disappointment.

"How long do you have to decide?" he asked.

"I said that I needed two nights of sleep," said Polly.

"Then you should have them," said Lenox. "Why don't we conduct our business as we usually might tomorrow, and meet the morning afterward? That will give all of us time to think."

"Yes," she said. "Thank you. Time to think."

"And time to steal our list of possible clients, too," said Dallington.

Polly's face, which had been apologetic since Lenox arrived, flashed with anger for the first time. "You're a scoundrel to say that to me," she said.

Without looking at either of them again, she walked toward her office and went inside, closing the door behind her. Dallington, who had gone pale, stared at the door for a moment.

There was a long silence.

"It will be all right," Lenox said. "Whatever happens."

Dallington didn't look at him but went on gazing at Polly's door. Finally he said distractedly, "Yes, yes. Of course." But he looked older than he ever had before, his youthful face suddenly hollow and worn, the carnation always at his breast a mockery of the naked emotion in his eyes. A lock of his black hair had fallen onto his forehead.

Lenox realized that it was Jane, not he, who would be the best companion for Dallington at the moment. "Will you come have supper in Hampden Lane?" he asked. "We can let Polly's temper settle. Whatever comes of this professionally, we are all too close now for our friendships to end. She'll see that in the morning, as will you."

"D'you think so?" asked Dallington, still not looking away from the door.

"Get your things. We can find a cab outside, and I'll tell you about Jenkins."

Some spell broke at that name, and after a beat Dallington shook his head and turned to Lenox, forcing a smile. "Yes. Let's have supper."

In the cab on the ride toward Hampden Lane (despite all of the distractions of the evening, Lenox found himself studying the horse that pulled it, after Hepworth's aside about the taxi horses of London) Dallington recovered some of his righteous indignation, though it was redirected now. He spent most of the way inveighing against the anonymous lord who had approached Polly.

"Sheer theft," he said. "It's our idea, a detective agency."

Lenox shrugged. "That's the marketplace, I'm sorry to say."

"I wish I knew who he was, the upjumped bastard," said Dallington.

The conversation continued in that vein for some time. Only when they were in front of Lenox's house—where two men in dark cloaks stood at attention, Clemons's men—did Dallington say, "What was it that you discovered, after all? I'm sorry I didn't ask before."

"St. Anselm's isn't a convent," said Lenox.

Dallington frowned at him, puzzled, and for the first time fully engaged by Lenox's news. "Then what is it?" he asked.

"I think—I may be wrong—that it's a brothel."

CHAPTER THIRTY-FOUR

Lady Jane was in the back sitting room alone when Lenox and Dallington entered, writing letters. She was very busy just at the moment, Lenox knew; she was planning a garden party the next weekend for a cousin of hers, a willowy young woman named Emily Gardner.

But no woman in London had finer manners.

"Hello, you two," she said, rising and smiling. "John, I'm so happy that Charles has brought you home with him. You must stay to eat, of course."

"We're both hungry," said Lenox quickly.

Dallington returned Jane's smile. "If it's easier we can send out for a chop."

"Nonsense. What would your mother say to that, knowing I had you under my roof? I'm going to speak to Kirk and make sure he has the wine open."

Sophia was already asleep. It was Mrs. Adamson's evening out. Lenox realized with a pang how little he had seen of his daughter in the past few days, and wondered whether he had time in the morning to accompany her on her walk through the park. It looked to him like it might rain, though. In any case he would visit the nursery.

While Jane was arranging supper, Lenox and Dallington went to Lenox's study at the front of the house. He poured them both drinks. Dallington drank off half of his whisky and water in one gulp.

Polly was still on his mind, Lenox guessed, but all Dallington said when he had swallowed was, "A brothel?"

Deliberately, Lenox laid out the facts. At 77 Portland Place there was a house masquerading as a Catholic convent, for unknown reasons; its privacy and security were both fiercely protected—just think of that high fence—and the young women in it only emerged, from all Lenox had seen, under strict supervision.

"Rather like the novitiates at a convent, handily," said Dallington, who looked skeptical.

Lenox bore onward without acknowledging this: At the house next door, 75 Portland Place, a steady procession of gentlemen arrived each evening, mixed in with a few women. All of them opened the door without knocking, and none of them ever appeared to leave.

"You never saw anyone exit that house?"

"No. And I was there above an hour."

The two houses were connected—and connected as well to the house of the man who owned them, who had lived at 73 Portland Place, a person both of them knew was capable of any violence or iniquity.

Then Lenox described what he had seen as he lurked at the mouth of the alleyway behind Portland Place: two men, in quick succession, leaving from a small unmarked door at the rear of 77 Portland Place. Both were men he had seen enter the house next door.

Dallington raised his eyebrows. "Interesting. So you think that the clients arrive at 75 Portland Place, walk through an interior passageway to the convent, and find there . . . what, some Parisian red house?"

"Yes," said Lenox. "And Jenkins, the poor soul—"

"Somehow found out."

Dallington's face was grave now. Lenox nodded. "Yes, and paid for his life with it."

Dallington took another sip of his drink and strolled away from Lenox, toward the windows overlooking Hampden Lane. It was a clear night outside, the breeze light and constant. A landau rolled by, clicking across the stones of the street. "There's something I don't understand," said Dallington.

"What?"

"Why all the secrecy? Any officer at Scotland Yard could name half a dozen addresses near Regent's Park where men go for that sort of thing. Or think of Helmer's place down by the docks, which as we saw was pretty brazen about its business. Why the whole business of inventing St. Anselm's? Why not just locate the whole enterprise at 75 Portland Place?"

Lenox nodded. "I've been thinking about that a great deal, and I have a dark thought."

"What?"

"I wonder whether the young women are there by choice."

Dallington stopped and looked back at him. "You think they're kept there against their will?"

"It would be just like Wakefield, I think. He loved money and had no great regard for women."

As he said this, Lenox realized that the phrase "by choice" implied that some of the prostitutes of London—some of those women of the East End streets, or the more superficially genteel West End parlors—did the work as he did his, out of a sense of vocation. There were one or two, perhaps, but it was absurd to imagine that anything but a lack of choice had driven most of them into their work. He thought of Gladstone, who even as Prime Minister had visited with prostitutes, hoping to draw them into new lives—or Dickens, who had built a refuge for "fallen women" in Shepherd's Bush. Both men had been mocked for what seemed, to some, like an unnatural interest in these young ladies. Lenox wondered. Gladstone, at least, he felt sure was acting out of principle. Very likely Dickens, too. According to the *Times* there were eighty thousand women in London alone practicing the trade.

Still, there was a difference between a woman who could buy her dinner at the end of the day and a slave.

"And this Francis fellow—Hartley, blast him—you think he was Wakefield's partner."

"Yes," said Lenox. "I don't know whether he killed Jenkins on his own, or if he and Wakefield planned it together, but all the while Francis was plotting to murder Wakefield, too, and conceal his tracks."

"Mm."

"What I do know is that I suspect we'll find him, at last."

"Where?" asked Dallington.

"At 75 Portland Place."

Just then Jane called them from the hallway. They ate supper at one end of the large table in the dining room, by low light, and as they talked, some of the unease in Dallington's face started to disappear. They would have to end things with Polly on a happy note, if indeed things were going to end—it was important. As he had this thought, Lenox realized as well that he considered Dallington more or less a member of his own family, a brother, a nephew, a cousin, a son, some mixture of all those things. As it would have with a member of his family, it made him nervous that his young friend cared so much. It was funny how change came in life— usually not in great calamitous bursts but in the gentle onward motion of the years, half-visible, mostly unconsidered from day to day. Marriage, children: They were like a series of ships out upon the sea as you stood upon the dock, moving so slowly toward you that they never seemed as if they would arrive. Except that then they were there all at once, huge and close, pausing for a moment and then sailing on toward the next person.

For dessert there was a sponge cake in cream sauce, and after that tea for all three of them. Then Jane returned to her letters, and Dallington and Lenox went again to Lenox's study, where they sat by the fire with glasses of brandy. They brooded over the case together, discussing St. Anselm's.

"It will be an enormous scandal if I'm right," said Lenox. "A nobleman, a convent that isn't a convent, that particular part of London. Not to discuss all of the men who will be there during a raid—should there be a raid."

Dallington nodded, then, after a moment of thought, said, "You mentioned that it was mostly men who entered the house—but a few women, too."

"Yes, the rate was about seven or eight to one, I'd say. It's been puzzling me, too."

"Surely they couldn't make use of any such—any such house?"

There was a moment of uncomfortable silence, as they stared into the fire, and then Lenox said, "There must be some explanation for it. They were dressed just as well as the men."

Suddenly Dallington's face grew angry. "Do you know what," he said, "if it's true, we ought to go over there tonight and stop the whole damned thing. One more minute of it is too much."

"Yes. Except we need Nicholson—we need the Yard."

"Let's go fetch him, then. Let's go fetch them."

Lenox was silent for a moment, and then looked at his watch and nodded. "Yes," he said. It was nearly ten o'clock. He realized that his sense of deliberation this time had been misplaced. "You're quite right. You're absolutely right."

CHAPTER THIRTY-FIVE

Nicholson had had a long day—a very long day, between burying one colleague and placing another under suspicion of theft and murder without the least scrap of evidence—and it redounded to his credit that when he saw Lenox and Dallington at his door, late that evening, he invited them in without demurral.

He lived in a set of rooms off the Strand, a bachelor's apartments. It was a place with little enough ornamentation, except that along one wall there were a dozen framed watercolors of ducks and geese. Most of them were identifiably set in the ponds and marshes of Hampstead Heath, just to the north of the city.

"My hobby," said Nicholson shortly, when he observed Lenox looking at them, "watercolor."

"You painted these?"

"Yes, in the mornings before work. On Saturdays I go and sketch, and on weekdays I work from my sketchings."

"They're extremely handsome."

"Thank you."

"They're very like life," said Dallington. "As if they might fly out of the frame, I swear."

Nicholson, smiling at this, sat them down and offered them something to drink—they declined—and then asked why they had come. As they explained their theory about the houses Wakefield had owned, he listened carefully. When they were finished, he asked a few questions; then, after a moment's pause, he retired briefly to his bedroom, where he exchanged the soft gray flannel suit he had been wearing for his stiff navy-colored uniform.

"Let's go immediately," he said.

The three men went by Lenox's carriage to a small police way station near Regent's Park, where Nicholson enlisted the help of three constables who were just coming on duty. A fourth he sent to Scotland Yard to fetch the police wagon, just in case.

All of this passed so quickly that it was scarcely an hour from the time Dallington suggested going to the time that they stopped at the corner of Portland Place. The broad thoroughfare was shimmering with the kind of lamplight that only the city's most affluent streets brought forth at night—a lady would have been confident of walking unmolested down the pavement, as she might have at midday, at least for these few hundred feet. The grand pale crenellations of Wakefield's house rose proudly above the corner. A few lights were on upstairs.

"We ought to give Wakefield's son some warning," said Nicholson. "They're his houses now, after all."

Lenox and Dallington objected, but Nicholson was firm—which both men understood to be fair, considering that it was he who could lose his job if the new marquess grew indignant and took a complaint to the right people.

In the event, a footman informed them (the butler, Smith, was still upstairs recovering from the wounds of his attack), the new marquess was out.

"Has he kept you on?" asked Nicholson.

"For now, anyway, sir," said the footman.

"Hard luck if you were to lose your place because your master was murdered."

"Harder luck still for him that was killed, sir."

Nicholson smiled. "It's true enough. Do you know when he'll be back, Lord Wakefield—the younger one?"

"No, sir. He said he wouldn't be late."

"We may stop in again, then."

"Very good, sir."

As they went next door, to the anonymous house, Lenox felt a kind of charge, an excitement. They might find anything inside. Nicholson paused, then said, "Shall we knock or walk in?"

"Walk in, I think," said Dallington.

"I had rather knock," said Nicholson.

At that moment a carriage stopped in front of the house, and a gentleman stepped down, past sixty, with a fox stole around his neck. He took in their small congregation, and perhaps the uniforms Nicholson and the constables were wearing, and got straight back into the carriage, tapping the door with his cane so that it moved immediately. Lenox noticed that there were black velvet curtains hanging over the doors—this was how men of rank, with a family crest painted upon their carriage, traveled discreetly.

He looked at Nicholson, who was grinning; the hasty departure hadn't been lost on him. "Straight in, then," he said, and, walking ahead of them, opened the door.

They came into a small entryway. Rather as at Hepworth's, ironically, the first impression was of extreme opulence. The walls were hung with an ornately patterned red-and-gold flock, and on a marble-topped table in front of them was a silver salver with several dusty bottles of wine and brandy on it, apparently left there to each person's discretion. Handled glasses stood next to it. Dallington took one and poured himself a glass of wine.

In a distant room of the house there was music. A viola, Lenox thought.

If the first impression he had was one of wealth, the second was of the room's strange configuration. It was entirely enclosed, a sealed chamber, offering no way any farther into the building. There was something uncanny about it—something Gothic, as the dim light of the two candles on the marble-topped table flickered.

They stood there for a moment, the six men crowded into this small space, and then Lenox had an idea and stepped toward the wall, saying, quietly, "Feel for a seam."

He ran his own hand along the wallpaper to the right of the table carefully, until at last he found an unevenness. He prodded on it, then pushed when a door gave way. At the same moment one of the constables found a matching door on the left.

The six men looked at each other. "Which way?" asked Nicholson.

"Left, first, I think," said Lenox. "Toward St. Anselm's."

"Half of us might go right," said Dallington. "I'll go, and you two come along."

"Send someone back here to meet when you find anything," said Nicholson.

"Just so."

Lenox, Nicholson, and one of the constables made their way through the door to the left. It led into a narrow hallway, paneled in mahogany, with a few lights in widely spaced sconces along it. The sound of the music grew stronger, and at one moment there was a sharp bark of laughter in a distant part of the house, upstairs perhaps.

They came around the curve of the hall and saw a brighter light, and a door—and sitting by it, next to a small table with a silver bell on it, a woman.

It was Sister Amity.

Lenox fell back behind the other two men, ducking his face into his collar. Apparently it worked, because she addressed Nicholson as she stood up. She was no longer wearing a habit, but a dark gown. No wonder it had taken her so long to come outside to meet Lenox and Dallington—she must have had to change clothes.

"What is the password?" she asked Nicholson.

"Scotland Yard," said Nicholson, and when she moved in front of the door, a panicked look dawning on her face, he pushed his way roughly past her.

First the constable and then Lenox followed, Sister Amity recognizing him at last and giving him a look of helpless loathing. Nicholson turned back and asked the constable to keep hold of her, lest she run off to warn someone of their presence.

They came into a wide room. The scene that confronted them there was extraordinary.

It would be some time before the Yard would piece together the full architecture of the house. Off to the right, where Dallington and the two constables had gone, there was a single room, a different woman standing outside of it and asking for the password as Sister Amity had. They had pushed past, too (Lenox would learn in just a few moments, when he and Dallington reconvened), and found a strange and magnificent gambling parlor. At its center had been an enormous table with a felt top, where four men and four women had been seated in an ingeniously designed series of private booths, so that each could see the table and its cards, but none of them could see each other. Servants stood attentively nearby, bearing champagne, wine, brandy. There had been hundreds of pounds in play upon each hand, far more than even the most exclusive gambling parlors in London permitted

But that was nothing to what greeted Lenox and Nicholson. It was a long, slender ballroom that had been converted into a kind of Roman bath hall, with separate hot and cold baths, both decorated in marble, with fauns, cupids, spouting dolphins. An overweight man with a black eye mask was swimming lazily in one of them, two women at his side—two undressed women. Up and down the sides of the pools there were private stalls made of oak. Some of them were flung open, their owners unconcerned about observation; others were closed. Near the large fountain at the end of the room was a table laden with caviar, chocolate profiteroles, cold roast fowl, and every kind of hothouse fruit, oranges, quinces, pomegranates.

What struck Lenox, painfully, was how extremely young the women looked—for there were women everywhere, in various states of attire. The servants, too, were women, dressed in diaphanous white robes, and from the discarded robes at the side of the baths Lenox perceived that there was probably no distinction between the servants and the prostitutes.

They stood there for a moment. Nobody observed them; it was a large room, its lighting atmospherically low. Nicholson ran his fingers across the intaglio on a table just to the right of the door: sc. Looking around, Lenox saw that there was a similar seal on the wall, on the doors of the stalls.

"It must be a kind of private club," he said.

Nicholson nodded, staring. Then he said, "But have they done anything illegal? Are we even sure these are prostitutes?"

As if to answer those questions, behind them Sister Amity had just managed to slip the grasp of the constable and reach for the silver bell that had been sitting near her in the hallway from the front door—and she rang it, sharply.

The whole place broke into chaos. Men fled from the stalls, half-clothed, and ran without a backward glance toward the rear of the building.

A moment too late, Nicholson leaped forward, then turned to Lenox and said, despairingly, "We'll lose them all through the back door!"

"No, we won't," said Lenox.

CHAPTER THIRTY-SIX

The headlines in the newspapers the next morning were lurid. The mildest of them blared HEDONISM FOUND IN THE HEART OF MAYFAIR, which Lady Jane, reading it with a forgotten piece of toast in hand, said was like printing an announcement that water had been found in the ocean. The *Times* called for the immediate resignation of the two Members of Parliament arrested, and the less dignified publications reported, breathlessly, that several aristocratic marriages were in shambles. One especially yellow rag declared BERTIE IN SLAVONIAN CLUB BLOW-UP, but Lenox was happy to inform Jane that the Prince of Wales had in fact been nowhere on the premises. Even the sporting pages had a crack: THE HIGHEST-STAKES GAME IN EUROPE, one said of the gambling parlor, which was otherwise mostly an afterthought. There were rumors that the king of a large northern European country had been present during the raid.

It wasn't Nicholson's fault that these details had spilled out. The arrests in Regent's Park had been too noticeable, and the press had arrived almost immediately, following them to the gates of the Yard, ready to offer any guard or officer high fees for information about the bold-faced names who were in trouble. There would be weeks of newspapers sold by this.

"The Slavonian Club," said Lady Jane, shaking her head contemptuously. "Give people enough money and they'll make the doomsday sound decorous."

Lenox smiled and took a sip of tea. "If you pay as much as these fellows must have, a certain air of respectability is part of the service, I suppose. And they could delude themselves into thinking they were part of something mysterious, rather than merely sordid."

Lenox had been up late into the night, helping Nicholson on the scene. The club had soon been swarming with constables, for the first girl they met had burst into tears and said, in a foreign accent, "Ah, thank God, you have come."

There had been an ugly welt along her bare shoulder, Lenox noticed.

The two parts of the club were completely segregated, the gambling parlor only a lucrative side business compared to the sprawling brothel that took up most of the two houses.

Otherwise the space of the two houses had been dedicated to the use of the men who were members of this Slavonian Club, as a few would admit it was called—though there was no paper trail on the site; none of them had a card of membership, or even a bill.

In the basement at 75 Portland Place was a taproom, with newspapers, couches, and fireplaces, nothing very scandalous. Upstairs, however, there had been a series of bedrooms, each decorated in a different way, one with an Egyptian theme, another like a Turkish harem, another with the ambience of a Paris dance hall. These were apparently for the gentlemen who desired either more privacy or space than the fountain-side stalls provided.

Then there were two bedrooms on the highest level of the house—and these, though they were empty when Nicholson led them in, were the ones that darkened Lenox's memory of the night. They looked like dungeons, and hung on the walls were instruments designed to inflict pain.

Next door at what London had thought was St. Anselm's, meanwhile, was a much less sumptuously decorated space; in it were two long, dormitory-style rooms, lined with hard, low cots. It was very cold. Downstairs was a dining hall, though as it emerged the women who slept in the cots were rarely permitted to eat more than a bowlful of thin soup a day except when they were next door, "at the Club," their hunger an incentive for them to win the favor of the men who could invite them to eat from the buffet, so that there was fierce competition among them to please the club's members. Some of the more timid-looking girls Lenox had seen had thin, haunted faces.

Not one of them, it turned out, had been there voluntarily. Not one of them spoke more than a few words of English, either. All of them were very beautiful.

The only other space they had found within what Lenox thought of, still, as St. Anselm's, was a narrow corridor leading between the two houses, similar to the one that led inward from the street. This one let out into the back alley.

It was here, at the last moment, that Lenox had reminded that fourth constable to bring the police wagon, rather than to the front of the building—and here that the fellow had managed to block off the exit just in time for Nicholson and Lenox and then all the others to catch up and begin making arrests.

Nicholson was still at the Yard, Lenox expected. He and Dallington had left only after three o'clock the morning before. The structure of the place had become clear enough after exhaustive interviews: There were five women of middle age in charge of the prostitutes, including Sister Amity, whom they all seemed to fear terribly. There was also a staff of four people. (This excluded the staff at the gambling parlor, whom Nicholson permitted to leave, along with their patrons, their crimes being, or at least seeming, in the moment, rather more venial.) There were seventeen of the younger women, too—the *enslaved girls*, as the papers called them—who were now being sheltered in a house owned by the city of London.

To Lenox's frustration, two people hadn't been in the house at all. He was simply curious about the first, Sister Grethe.

The second was Andrew Hartley Francis.

The four young men on staff had all been able to prove immediately and beyond a shadow of a doubt that they weren't called Hartley, or Francis. They were all quite plainly of the wrong class, too, mostly East Enders who had been drawn by an advertisement each had answered, promising high wages in exchange for absolute discretion.

("We didn't think anything about it was illegal," said one of them indignantly at some point after midnight.

"Then what on earth did you think you were doing?"

"It was for the toffs, wasn't it?" he had answered bitterly. "They have all sorts of clubs.")

In the end twenty-five people had been arrested, among them several with very illustrious names indeed. Most of these men remained silent, confident in their solicitors; it was the Earl of Kenwood who gave them the most information, desperate to be released before anyone learned that he had been arrested. (A hope in which he was to be disappointed.) Club membership was only available by personal recommendation, he told them; the fees were spectacularly high, something nearly to boast about, Lenox heard in his voice; the girls changed often enough to keep it interesting; of course they were well paid, of course, why else would the fees be so high . . .

He himself—a thin, pointy-faced man in his sixties who owned most of Hampshire—had been referred for membership by Wakefield.

"Before he died, you know, poor chap."

"You were friends?"

"Not close—but there are so few fellows in the House of Lords who have any idea of fun, and he used to stand me a drink now and then."

Lenox understood. Wakefield and Kenwood operated at very different levels of malice, Kenwood a more insipid and less violent person, but nevertheless these sorts of men always did find each other. They had as long ago as Oxford; look at the Bullingdon Club, whose new members destroyed a different restaurant or pub or college common room each year, solely from the pleasure they took in drunken destruction.

Kenwood's volubility stood in stark contrast to that of the four women who had presided over St. Anselm's. None of them spoke a word. Nicholson had realized at some point that it would be a difficult case to prosecute, as had his superiors at the Yard. The owner of the two houses, Wakefield, was recently dead, and his son could hardly be held legally accountable for what he was on the brink of inheriting.

The key, Lenox knew, was the tales of the young women. None of them had been able to offer these yet, however, for none of them spoke more than very bad English. It wasn't even clear what country they came from. A fleet of government translators was coming to the Yard that morning, and they would try to speak to the young women in a variety of languages.

"You'll be away all day?" Lady Jane asked, over the breakfast table.

"Yes."

"You must be tired."

"On the contrary, I have a great deal of energy," said Lenox, standing. There was a lovely morning light coming through the windows, the room softened by its gentle natural hue. "Though I wonder how it all relates to the deaths of Wakefield and Jenkins."

Jane looked up at him. "Poor Mrs. Jenkins," she said. "Do you think it would be inappropriate of me to call on her? We've never met."

"On the contrary, I think it would be very kind."

"The day after the funeral must be difficult," said Jane. "At least a funeral is something to . . . well, not to look forward to, I suppose, but something to plan, something to expect. The days ahead must seem so empty once even that part of it's over."

"I expect so."

She was staring out the window, and when he came around the table to kiss her good-bye, she said, "Do be careful, would you?"

He kissed her, then took a last swallow of tea. "Always, my dear. Do you feel safe here? With Clemons's precautions in place? You could still take Sophia to the country, you know."

"We're safe. But solve the case quickly, Charles. For my own part, I don't know that I could face the day after your funeral."

CHAPTER THIRTY-SEVEN

That morning, a team of constables had gone out to every house the Marquess of Wakefield owned in London, checking each of them top to bottom. None of the others proved more than a simple domicile. One did have an unusually high number of cats in residence—twenty-nine—but that was, apparently, legal, and the owner who answered for them, a man named Withers, promised that he kept them all confined to the house and in excellent health.

Still, the Commissioner of the Yard was in an utter state, according to Nicholson. There had been word from very high, indeed from the Palace itself, that the matter was to be resolved and quieted as quickly as possible. The presence of the Slavonian Club in the heart of London was an embarrassment not just to its members but to England; already emissaries from the Vatican were on the way according to Hepworth, with whom Lenox had exchanged notes that morning.

As a result the translators were at the sheltering house very promptly. They were a varied group. Some were darker skinned, others more clearly of British descent; some wore the tweeds and spectacles of the academy, others looked slightly less reputable, and one, a fellow named Chipping just down from Caius College, affected an Oriental robe.

Lenox, Nicholson, and one of Nicholson's superiors were present to watch. One by one, the translators stepped forward and said, in some language, a phrase Nicholson had written: "If you understand the language I am speaking, please come to me, and I will translate your story for these police officers. Regardless of what you tell us, the Metropolitan Police of London guarantee your safety."

So the young women—clothed now in plain wool dresses, and having eaten a breakfast delivered with vehement generosity by Her Sisters of the Holy Heart that morning—began to divide up and tell their stories. Lenox sat and listened to them, translated from Turkish, French, Arabic, and German, among other languages. Three of the women didn't respond to any of the languages; they grouped together and spoke among themselves. All of them looked, to his eye, as if they might be from India.

The whole process took many hours, but the tales of life inside the Slavonian Club were depressingly similar: privation, cold all through that winter, enforced prostitution, the alternating viciousness and kindness of the gentlemen who visited the club, each of those beset by its own brand of difficulties. Several of the women were extremely reluctant to speak, as if this might be a trap. That was understandable. There were some weak friendships among them, but women who spoke the same language had always been divided at Portland Place. Punishment had been rife, and all of them recounted the violence of Sister Amity, who beat them with a switch if their paint was careless, if they attempted to speak to each other, if any of the gentlemen were dissatisfied. When these beatings left marks, the women stayed in the dormitories until they were gone. Going more or less hungry, Lenox gathered.

But all of this came out slowly, whereas the most interesting thing of all, to him, came out almost immediately. That was the story of how they had ended up in London.

Aboard a ship.

None of them knew the ship's name, but Lenox felt, instantly and with tremendous certainty, that it must be the *Gunner*.

One young Turkish woman, with beautiful delicate cheekbones and troubled dark eyes, told her story, which was similar to the rest of them. Like the other women, she had been a courtesan in her homeland, too, though, also as with them, that had been in very different circumstances—in luxury, as in most of their cases. It wasn't difficult to imagine, given their beauty.

"A client came in," said the Turkish woman through one of the translators. "He was very handsome. He had lovely manners. He persuaded me to come and see him the next evening, that he wanted to give me something. He paid my mistress twice what she had asked, and left a card with his name upon it. He made me promise to come. He said he loved me—love at first sight. I was intrigued by him.

"When I arrived at the teahouse where we were to meet, he was absent. I grew uneasy after a few minutes and left, thinking it was better, that I knew nothing of this man or his promises. It was then that they took me—several very rough people, it was instantaneous, there wasn't time even to cry out. They pushed me into a carriage, and before anybody on the streets could notice, or help, we were gone. I had nothing with me—not my gowns, not my family's letters, nothing of my old life except the clothes on my back. From there I was taken to a ship. The room aboard was dark, and windowless. There were four other girls in it. It was a small space, we barely fit if all of us stood at the same time. There was a bucket in the corner, but nowhere to empty it. Twice a day they took the bucket, and we were given food. We spent a great deal of time sleeping."

Lenox asked, through the translator, "And how did you sleep?"

"I do not know the word," said the young woman, looking directly at him. "In a kind of netting that hanged from the ceiling."

Lenox nodded and said, "Give her my thanks. Tell her to go on."

As she went on, though, he was preoccupied by the pile of hammocks they had found next to the trunk that held Wakefield's body, feeling certain that these were the same hammocks that these women had been transported in Wakefield's hold. Or at the very least, a similar one.

It was easy to imagine the ruse. The *Gunner* picked up and dropped off mail from several ports between England and India, and while they were in dock they could have taken the women. Any of the officers might have played the grandee in love with the courtesan, or indeed Wakefield himself could have done it. And a man of Wakefield's type would have known the most expensive houses of that type in every city, or could have learned their names easily enough.

He thought of what Dyer had told them, with perhaps more honesty than he had intended: *All of us are here for the money. Anything that gets in the way of it is a nuisance.*

"We were all terribly ill during the voyage," the woman went on. "When we arrived I knew we were in England, because of the voices. We were pushed into crates. These must have been loaded onto carriages, because I could feel that horses took us across the city. I feared then that we would be killed. But we were only taken to the house, the house where we lived.

"The women rotate very quickly," she said. "Always new ones. I myself have marked the days in my head—it has been just forty. I think that they cannot risk that we begin to learn English. I am anxious when I contemplate where the other women have gone, the ones who preceded me. I am thankful now that it is over."

Lenox nodded at her. She was very composed—some of the other girls were in tears—but somehow it made her tale worse.

As the translators continued to gather the women's stories, Nicholson murmured to Lenox, "I wish they would come back and tell us about the *Gunner*."

Lenox looked at his pocket watch. Almost from the first words the young women had spoken, he had advised Nicholson and his superior to send a team of constables down to the docks to arrest Dyer and the men of his ship. "I hope they haven't resisted arrest. They're a bloody-minded crew, from the sound of it."

"Do you think these women can somehow verify that it was the *Gunner* they were stolen onto? They must have seen a face, scratched their names into the walls—something. I feel sure Dyer is involved with all this."

"Yes," said Lenox.

Even so, he and Nicholson both knew they were still missing the whole picture. The difficulty was that Dyer and his men had a cast-iron alibi for the night of Jenkins's murder: They had been at sea, their ship coming in about an hour after his body was found. A hundred different objective observers had confirmed as much.

And then the next morning, somehow, Wakefield's body had come to rest in a trunk in the ship's hold.

"There's been a question rattling around in my brain for a few days now," Lenox said to Nicholson. "How did Jenkins come to have Wakefield's claim ticket for the *Gunner*?"

"I don't know, but he must have felt it was important—he left it in his note for you," said the inspector. "He could have kept it with his notes."

"Or else he had just gotten it when he was murdered."

"What do you mean?"

"I wonder if he had just seen Wakefield when he was murdered. I wonder if Wakefield was—though it's difficult to imagine—helping him."

"Can you explain?"

"It has seemed singular to me all along that Jenkins and Wakefield were closeted together at Portland Place in the past few weeks. As Wakefield's butler described it, too, their conversations were at least friendly, if sardonic. All that business about 'the very profound honor of a visit from Scotland Yard,' if you recall."

"Mm."

"That doesn't sound like an interrogation, an accusation. Is it possible they were working in alliance? What if he gave him that claim ticket so that Jenkins could stop the *Gunner* when she came into dock?"

Nicholson was staring intently over his fingertips, thinking. "So then Wakefield was giving up Francis—Hartley—and Dyer, to save his own skin. Yes, it seems possible. All the more so because of the primary thing that he and Jenkins have in common."

"What's that?" said Lenox.

"That they were both murdered."

Just then a constable appeared at the door. He came over to Nicholson. "It's the *Gunner,* sir," he said, out of breath.

"Well? What about her?"

"She's gone, sir. Shipped out of London early this morning for Calcutta."

CHAPTER THIRTY-EIGHT

It was one of the most maddening cases Lenox had ever negotiated. On the one hand, he had uncovered so much of the truth, he felt—Armbruster's involvement, the dark reality of St. Anselm's, the role of the *Gunner*. On the other hand, they had nothing. Armbruster was comfortably entrenched behind his denials. They had scoured London—even now two of Nicholson's constables were still searching—and found nobody called Andrew Hartley Francis.

And now the *Gunner* was gone.

They were at the very beginning again, without anything more than a few educated guesses about who might have killed either Inspector Jenkins or the 15th Marquess of Wakefield.

Dallington had spent the morning at Scotland Yard; he and Lenox reconvened at the offices at Chancery Lane just after noon. It felt empty without Polly or her silently hulking assistant, Anixter, nearby, though Pointilleux was full of effusive greetings for them, and thousands of questions, which they did their best to answer. In fact, Polly was still in some evidence—on Lenox's desk was an envelope with his name on it in her handwriting. Inside was a note that said:

Whether or not we are partners tomorrow, we are still partners today, so I will give you a piece of advice. Every paper in the country ought to know that you and John were with Inspector Nicholson last night. PB.

She was—as usual—quite right. As quickly as they could, hoping to slip into the evening papers, Lenox and Dallington drew up a list of fairly reliable journalists and charged Pointilleux with circulating among their offices at Fleet Street to spread the word.

"Make sure you tell them that the Yard is paying us for our consultation on the case," Dallington said, "and that we're available for interviews about our heroic actions—off the record."

"Are we?" asked Lenox, uncertain.

Dallington nodded grimly. "Yes. I'll be damned if LeMaire gets to win, after all of this. No offense, Marseille."

"Only this false name is offense of me."

Both Lenox and Dallington were tired, but they sat in the conference room drinking tea together all afternoon, piecing together every last detail they knew about the case. At some stage Pointilleux returned. He was cross. Among other things, it was an overcast day, and evidently it had drizzled on him as he attempted to get the omnibus back to the office. "I am soak," he reported angrily. "The sky of this country is too wet."

On top of that, he said, the journalists had dismissed his accounts without listening as closely as he would have liked. Lenox wasn't disheartened by that—he could have told the young man that London journalists had little use for politeness—and in fact he was positively encouraged to hear that three of the nine men had said they intended to stop by the offices that afternoon or that evening to hear more, though it meant staying late.

At four o'clock Nicholson arrived. He looked absolutely dead on his feet, but he had brought them a report from the Asiatic Limited Corporation. Apparently one of the members of the company's board had pressured the Yard into releasing the *Gunner* the day before, complaining of the delay and the loss of profits as the ship bobbed idly on the Thames.

"Nobody bothered to inform me the blasted ship was going, though," said Nicholson resentfully. "Anyway, I've brought you their full company files on the *Gunner*, at least. I have a copy for myself, too. I mean to look over it later. I need to go back to the Yard just now and see what's come of all these interviews."

"And at some point you need to sleep."

"In 1877, fingers crossed," said Nicholson, and a shadow of a smile appeared on his face. "It's been made clear to me that my advancement depends upon the resolution of all this. People are angry, you know. Very angry."

"They ought to be pleased that we found the club."

"Well, they're not."

When Nicholson had gone, taking with thanks a few biscuits from the plate they pushed on him, Lenox took up the file he had left from Asiatic Limited. Dallington came and looked over his shoulder. There were many long pages in tight handwriting detailing the ship's voyages, accounts, diagrams and drawings of her, lists of past mates.

Lenox sighed. "Shall we divide it up and go through it?"

"I bet we find Francis's name."

"And another false address for him, no doubt."

For half an hour they sat in silence, reading; then, with a cry of delight, Dallington said he'd found something.

It was an overhead illustration of the ship's hold, dated 1874, on a large piece of paper, the size of a decent map, folded over twice to fit into the file. As Lenox came around the table to look, Dallington planted his finger next to a name. It was the space on the plan for aft hold 119, with *Lord Wakefield* written in tidy cursive letters.

"Look," said Dallington, "he had hold 118, too. Did we look in that one?"

"I think we did," said Lenox.

Together they went around the holds in a circle, reading them aloud together, most of the names unfamiliar, *Donoghue Spirits, Jones, India Hemp Corporation, King, Davies, Taylor, Berry's Herb and Pharmaceutical, Smith, Warrington, Fielding, Brown,* but then a few familiar, *Dyer, Wakefield,* one marked *First Lt.* and even one that said *Helmer.* The chap from the docks. That gave Lenox pause. It might be worth speaking to him again.

And then, when they had nearly circled back around to Wakefield's holds again, they came across a name that stopped them both. And not Francis's.

Earl Calder.

They looked at each other. "Just one hold," said Lenox.

"Very close to Wakefield's."

"Yet for all the world he acted as if he couldn't distance himself from his father quickly enough. It was as if the name were poison to him. It can't be a coincidence."

"No," said Lenox quietly, thinking.

"Shall we go see him?"

Suddenly it struck Lenox anew how strange it was that Calder had stayed in Portland Place for the past few evenings. He said as much to Dallington and then added, "After all, his father was murdered, an inspector of the Yard killed on the pavement out front, the butler attacked upstairs. The place is bedlam."

Dallington had stood up and was pacing the room, thinking. "Yes. Either he's a fool, a very cool fellow—or he knows he's not in danger. Let's go to Portland Place, I say."

"What should we ask him when we get there?"

"What in the devil he's doing leasing a hold on a ship that brought captive women into his country's capital, while he was supposed to be sitting tripos at Cambridge and worrying about whether the Field of the Cloth of Gold was in 1200 or 1300."

"It was in 1520."

"Nobody likes a swot, Lenox."

Lenox smiled. They were both standing now, energized by the possibility that they'd come upon something new. Then something occurred to him to dampen his enthusiasm. "I suppose we owe it to Nicholson to wait," he said. "It sounds as if he's already on thin ice."

"They can't hold him responsible for us."

"They can, unfortunately. As you pointed out, he's paying us."

Dallington frowned. "True."

Lenox looked down at the files on the table. "Perhaps we should get through as much of this material as we can, and go see Calder—or Lord Wakefield, I suppose he is now—tomorrow. With Nicholson. At least we can look for Calder's name again."

They sent Nicholson a note at the Yard telling him what they had found, and mentioned that they were going to investigate the Asiatic's files very carefully, if it would spare him doing the same. They dedicated the next hours, then, to doing just that, Pointilleux joining them after he had finished a bit of filing on Polly's behalf.

At half past six they sent out for a pot of oysters and three pints of ale, and when the barmaid came to fetch back the tankards and the pot, Dallington ordered three more from her. They didn't find Calder's name again, though Wakefield's did appear several times. Just before eight o'clock one of the newspapermen came around, a fox-faced reporter for the *Evening Sentinel*, and listened to their story. Between that interruption and the density of the documents Nicholson had dropped off, it was ten o'clock in the evening before the three men finally left—dispirited, but promising each other that they would see about Calder the next day.

CHAPTER THIRTY-NINE

Seven years before, in 1869, the august medical school in Edinburgh had admitted women for the first time. There had been anonymous threats of violence against these women, and no lesser figures than the Queen and William Gladstone had plotted together to see if they could keep the Queen's own sex from joining the medical profession, but the next fall these prospective students came to the college nevertheless to enroll. A gathering of hundreds of people met them at the gates, heckling and booing, waving signs in protest. This crowd threw rubbish at the women, old eggs, rotten fruit. At moments it had seemed likely to cross the line that divided a protest from a riot.

Afterward there were fines handed down by the courts. A pound each, a heavy penalty, for disturbing the peace—from the women, not from the protesters.

Since Sophia had been born, Lenox sometimes thought of those women, of the injustice of that fine. He harbored little doubt that women were weaker than men, being more prone to the vicissitudes of emotion—though sometimes, watching Lady Jane out of the corner of his eye, even this assumption seemed slightly doubtful—but despite this conviction, having a daughter had made him reconsider the idea of them working. There were women's colleges at the universities now, after all. Why shouldn't she attend one of those? He knew for a fact that his daughter was more intelligent than a boy nearby on Hampden Lane of the same age, Alfred O'Connell, who seemed to pass most of his time sucking on his fist. Sometimes Lenox even wondered: Should he be able to vote in an election, for instance, and his own daughter not?

It was because of Sophia, he thought, or obliquely perhaps even because of those young women in Edinburgh, that he had a sneaking sense of sympathy for Polly's probable departure from their firm. From the first time they met he had admired her intelligence and her ambition. It was hardly surprising someone else should have noticed those qualities. Still, it was very surprising, outlandish even, to consider a woman being offered the control of such a large enterprise, and at such a young age. Polly was twenty-six now—the age Sophia would be in a quarter century, that far-fetched-sounding year, 1900. He wondered what the world would look like to her then. Perhaps her physician would be a woman.

It was in this philosophical mood that Lenox waited for Polly and Dallington to arrive at the office in Chancery Lane the next morning. It was an ugly day outside, the sky gray-black in color, with wind and rain whipping between the narrowly spaced buildings, umbrellas turning inside out, the men and women without them retreating further and further into their cloaks as they walked. Apart from a few flickering candles outside of each shop or restaurant, it was hard to see much even from just a single story above the street.

LeMaire had taken with him his loyal Irishwoman, Mrs. O'Neill, and with her had gone the morning pot of coffee (and her anxieties about Dallington's bachelor diet). So Lenox made coffee himself, and tea as well. As he was pouring himself a cup of the latter, Polly arrived alone, and they had a friendly if slightly stilted moment of conversation about the weather, full of goodwill toward each other, each apologetic for separate reasons. If she were going, best that she went on good terms.

Besides, he thought there might just be one more arrow in his quiver.

Only a bit later Dallington came in. His greeting was stiffer. "Mrs. Buchanan," he said.

She colored and then said, with exaggerated deference in her voice, "Lord John."

Lenox smiled faintly. "Come along, let's sit and have a conversation," he said. "Polly, thank you for your note. A reporter came by in the evening."

"Oh? For whom?"

"The *Evening Sentinel*."

This wasn't a very august newspaper, but Polly said, stoutly, "Excellent."

They sat down together then at the polished conference table, and Polly once again expressed her regret that she had to make the choice to leave. She believed in their joint venture. It was only that the opportunity before her was too significant to throw away. And with LeMaire gone—well, it was true that things would be more difficult, there was no other way of looking at it.

Lenox nodded at this, Dallington glowered. As if in response to his mood, the steady rain outside began to grow wilder, lashing at the windows, soaking the buildings into darker colors.

Thoughtfully, Lenox rotated his cup of tea in its saucer for a moment. Then he looked up and spoke. "We hold you in the greatest possible esteem, you know, Polly. I don't think either of us doubts that if you leave, you'll be successful. There's even a chance that you'll push us out of business. At any rate we won't continue in these offices. We don't need so much space, and always worked from our homes before."

With an anguished look, Polly said, "I never intended—"

"No, of course not, and what's more, for you this is a business, whereas, to speak candidly on a subject I don't think any of us would like to linger upon, John and I can afford to act as amateurs. For that reason I won't beg you to stay. But I do have one request."

"What's that?" asked Dallington suddenly.

"I would like to know the identity of your new partner."

Polly shook her head. "His privacy was an absolute condition of his offer."

"You have my word as a gentleman that I will keep the information in the very strictest of confidence. Nobody who isn't present in this room now will ever hear the name you tell us from my lips." And suddenly the room, awash in natural light, took on a solemn air. "Dallington? Would you commit to the same?"

"I would never tell," he said.

Polly looked at them each in turn, and then exhaled. "Very well," she said. "It's Lord Monomark."

Lenox leaned back. There was the beginning of a smile on his face, though his brow was furrowed, as if he were taking in the news. In truth it was precisely as he had thought. "Monomark," he said. "I wondered if that might be the name you'd say."

Polly looked at him, confused. "You did?"

It had come to him last night at home, as he glanced over the newspapers. Polly had described the man who offered her control of this agency as one whose name they would all know, and someone with enough interests that an in-house detection agency would make financial sense. Then there was something suggestive about the meeting-ground of the Langham—a grand hotel, moneyed, the kind of place one might expect a newly arrived fellow like Mono-mark to take a prospective associate.

"And finally, of course," said Lenox, "the articles."

"The articles?" said Polly.

"How much do you know about Monomark?" he asked.

"A fair amount," she said. "He was born the son of a grocer, ap-prenticed as a printer, bought several paper mills before he was twenty, made them very profitable, and now owns a dozen newspapers too. The Queen made him a lord last year."

Lenox stood up and went to the window, looking out. He saw how it had all played out now—indeed, should have seen it from the start. The two most damaging articles about the new firm had both appeared in the *Telegraph*, one of Monomark's papers, and there had been half a dozen other negative ones in his smaller papers.

Lenox had attributed the negativity to a political grudge, but now he thought it was probably more complicated. Monomark was above all a man of business, and he would never have made Polly the offer he did—dozens of detectives and staff, expensive offices— for reasons of personal satisfaction, without believing it to be a profitable idea.

Perhaps even very profitable. As he stared outside at the rain, Lenox began to wonder whether Monomark had heard of their new firm, envied the idea, and then set out systematically to destroy it, so that he might replace it.

"Two articles," said Lenox. "One just after the opening of the firm, the other just after Jenkins's death. For that matter, there may have been others. I don't read the *Telegraph* every day, at least not closely. And in both of them the inspector with whose successes I am most closely linked in the public mind was chosen to discredit me—Jenkins, with quotes on the record."

Polly realized what he was implying, and indignation began to dawn on her face. "You think that such a conspiracy against you is more likely than Monomark having a genuine interest in my abilities?" she asked.

Dallington put in his oar. "Of course it's jolly well more likely!" he said. "Monomark and Lenox were at each other in Parliament constantly."

Lenox shook his head. "Monomark has no love for me, but no, I think in addition to any idea of retribution toward me he must have seen your abilities from the start. Perhaps he resented that I would profit off of them, rather than himself. He's a difficult man, but far from a stupid one. I think he has been determined since January to scuttle our firm and start his own, and I think he's very nearly succeeded."

Polly looked uncertain. "That's business, I suppose."

"But could you trust someone capable of that?" asked Dallington.

"We don't even know that it's true," said Polly.

"You don't find it odd that he was so insistent upon his privacy?" asked Dallington. "He must have known that Lenox would figure out his motivations, once he knew who had made you the offer!"

"But—"

"And once the business was started—a favorable article in the *Telegraph*, I would guess, and a standing half-page advertisement on the third page of the paper. Have I got that right?"

Polly colored, and was about to reply when Lenox held up a hand to silence them. "I have a plan," he said.

CHAPTER FORTY

Word had gone out to the naval bases at every dock between London and Calcutta, by the new overland telegraph that had been built from England to India a few years before, that the *Gunner* was to be stopped and thoroughly searched if she put into port; Wakefield was dead; the Slavonian Club was closed, and though the staff in charge of it were still silent in their cells, as the days passed the crown's prosecutors grew more confident that the stories of the young women who had been kept there against their will would tell decisively against their captors.

That left just the murders. Just. It would have been lovely to pin them to Captain Dyer, whose very ship had concealed one of the corpses, but he couldn't have killed Jenkins—the *Gunner* had still been a night's travel outside of London.

Could it have been Calder?

Again and again, since the night before, Lenox had tried to piece together a scenario in his mind by which the young marquess might have become involved in the scheme of transportation and imprisonment that Wakefield and Dyer had apparently been operating for years now.

Nicholson, Dallington, and Lenox went to Portland Place at

midday to interview the young gentleman. Obadiah Smith, Wakefield's butler, was again at his post when they arrived, answering the
door for them, pale after his attack but moving well. He brought
them into the living room and asked if they wanted anything to
drink or eat.

"A glass of brandy wouldn't go amiss," said Nicholson.

"Right away, sir. I'll inform His Lordship that you're waiting for
him."

It took Calder several minutes to come, much longer than the
brandy. When he entered the room it was with Mr. Theodore Murray, the family cousin who had been handling their business earlier
that week when Lenox visited.

"How do you do?" said the young marquess. He looked rumpled,
harassed. "Can I help you with anything? I assure you I've told the investigators from the Yard absolutely every detail I know about this . . .
this scandalous club, the one that was operating just next door. I
was as shocked as anyone, you can imagine the horror of it. The
shame of being in the papers, my God. They searched up and down
this very house looking for a passageway leading next door and
didn't find one, though at this stage it's hard for me to put anything
past my father. The family is in an outrage. Thank goodness for
Teddy here—preparing a statement to the press on our behalf. Feels
it's important—what was it, Teddy?"

"We feel it's important to emphasize the long line of Wakefields
who have served the country and the crown," said Murray.

"A line that's bloody well going to start again," said Calder—or
Travers-George, as he must be called now, since he had moved on to
more august titles than the honorific belonging to the marquess's heir.

As this thought flashed across Lenox's mind, he realized something. Suddenly there was a sinking feeling in his stomach. "May I
ask who your heir is now?" he said.

"My aunt's son, Frederick, though he must be thirty years older
than I am. Lives in Devon."

"And now he'll be called the Earl of Calder, I suppose?" said Lenox.

"I doubt he'll use the name. Though he's entitled to, until I have a son, at any rate."

What Lenox had realized was that Wakefield—the dead marquess—would himself have been called the Earl of Calder until about seven years before, when his own father died. That meant that the hold in the *Gunner* marked on the schematic with the name Calder could easily have been his, if their illegal plot had been going on long enough. In fact, it would have coincided with the period when Wakefield left England for nearly a year after Charity Boyd's death—a voyage that for all Lenox knew might have been when the original conspiracy between Wakefield and Dyer was first plotted.

As that repugnant business had expanded, the marquess could have added more holds in the ship. For legal reasons those would have been the ones marked under his new name: Wakefield. Lenox would check with the Asiatic to see how long the particular storage hold under Calder's name had been held. Longer than seven years, he would guess. Which meant that their discovery was probably useless.

In the moment of silence that followed, Nicholson was about to begin asking the new Lord Wakefield about the *Gunner*, Lenox could tell, and with a subtle motion he gestured for him to stop and instead himself addressed His Lordship, whose pink, small-minded, essentially mediocre face seemed to him all at once exceedingly unlikely to hide the imagination or devilry of a criminal, a murderer.

"We primarily wanted to see how you were holding up under the strain of all this," Lenox said. "Inspector Nicholson pointed out that it must be very difficult."

The young man flushed with gratification. "Well, that's awfully nice of you," he said. "Yes, it's been jolly hard. We're bearing up."

"Has anyone unusual come to the house? Perhaps Mr. Francis, the fellow we asked about before?"

"Only reporters, unfortunately. Our eyes are open. And of course there have been all sorts in and out of the two houses next door. Teddy is already arranging to sell them, thank goodness. I'm going to sell this one, for that matter, if I can. I would far rather shake down around Mayfair. It's where all of the other fellows from college are getting digs after examinations have finished."

As the three detectives started back toward Scotland Yard together a quarter of an hour later, Lenox explained in the carriage why he suddenly suspected Calder's innocence.

"I didn't want you to ask any probing questions and have him put in a complaint about you," he said to Nicholson.

"Quite right, thank you." Despite the thanks, Nicholson looked glum, and a moment later he added, "Though it does seem hard luck when we thought we were onto something."

They reached the Yard and went to Nicholson's office for a little while then, where they sat mulling over the details of the case together—all of them in that mood of frustration. Jenkins must have uncovered Dyer and Wakefield's scheme, they assumed. Did that mean Wakefield had murdered him? Or had Jenkins and Wakefield been working together, and both been killed for it by the same person?

At about two o'clock, two of Nicholson's constables came in, Leonard and Walker. They had been doggedly pursuing Andrew Hartley Francis this week even after Nicholson's attentions had moved elsewhere, asking anyone they could find of Wakefield's acquaintance if they knew the man. Up until yesterday, none of them had even recognized the name, however, much less the person himself—not Wakefield's acquaintances in business, not his cousins in the nobility, not the members of his clubs.

With any luck they were arriving with better news now. Nicholson greeted them. "Any sign of him?"

Leonard, who was the tallest constable on the force, as thin as a blade of grass, shook his head morosely. "None at all, sir."

"Nobody even familiar with the name?" Nicholson said to Leonard.

"Afraid not, sir. I'm not sure who else we can ask, though I suppose we'll carry on trying."

Walker said, "We might send word to the police in a few of the larger cities, sir. Manchester, Birmingham. Asking if they know the name. For my part I don't think he's in London."

"He may be on the *Gunner*, for all we know," said Dallington broodingly. "Sitting in the crow's nest with a flask of whisky, laughing at us."

"I'll wire to Manchester and Birmingham," said Nicholson.

After a few more words of conversation, Walker and Leonard left.

What they had said lingered in Lenox's mind, however. Just as he and Dallington were about to leave half an hour later—Nicholson was headed toward the interview rooms, to see again if he could get a word out of Sister Amity or any of her cohort—he said, "What's become of Armbruster?"

"He's back on the job today," said Nicholson. "He's one of the reasons I'm in everyone's bad graces now. He wasn't lying—his father was at the Yard, and both of his brothers. I've yet to pass him in the hallways, the scoundrel. I'm sure he was involved."

"Of course. All three of us saw his reaction when we confronted him. Dead giveaway," said Dallington.

And then all of a sudden Lenox was excited, exhilarated. It was a feeling he knew well: that he was close. The pieces were sifting together in his mind, clicking into place. He was close.

It was that phrase, *his father was at the Yard, and both of his brothers.*

"You have a strange look on your face," said Dallington.

"Do I? I'm thinking."

"I hope you're thinking about a slice of steak pie, because I'm famished. If only the canteen here weren't so monstrous."

Nicholson, standing up and putting on his coat, smiled and said, "They don't do a bad suet pudding, mind you."

"Quiet, quiet," said Lenox, not angrily but in a low, urgent voice. "Please give me a moment."

Nicholson raised his eyebrows and sat down again, hands in the pockets of his coat. "Take as long as you like," he said.

From the start the most elusive figure in all of this had been Francis—and yet at the same moment he had been everywhere, meeting at all hours with the marquess in the weeks before his death, ordering the port that had slain the nobleman, sending the parcel with the gun that had killed Jenkins.

His address, a dead end, a false lead.

His name, unrecognized by every conceivable member of London society who might have known it.

Even its strange confusion—was it Francis, was it Hartley?—had sent them searching for the same man twice over.

Then Lenox knew. He looked up at Dallington and Nicholson. "I've got it," he said.

"What?" asked Dallington.

"Andrew Hartley Francis doesn't exist," Lenox said hurriedly, grabbing his own coat down from its hook and throwing it over his shoulders. "What's more, I know exactly where we can find him."

CHAPTER FORTY-ONE

It was back to Portland Place they went, one of the final trips that he would have to make to that accursed street for some time, Lenox hoped as they drove. They knocked on the door of the Wakefield mansion. The butler opened the door and frowned, surprised to see them back so quickly.

"Are you here to see His Lordship again, sirs?" he asked.

Lenox shook his head. "Thank you, no, we are in a hurry. But would you be so kind as to pass a message to him from us?"

"Of course, sir. What is the message?"

"Tell him that we've just had a wire—we were away from the Yard—that Armbruster has said he'll confess to Nicholson. He wants a deal, doesn't want to go to jail. We're going back now to hear what he has to say. I know His Lordship was concerned with a quick end to all of this embarrassing business. Please tell him we've stopped by just as a courtesy."

The butler nodded and then carefully repeated the message back to Lenox. "Was that all, sir? Anything else to pass on?"

"No, that will do nicely. Thank you," said Lenox.

As they walked back to the carriage, Dallington said, "What now?"

"Now we wait at the corner," said Lenox, "and hopefully not too long a time. There was a clue in Asiatic's diagram of the *Gunner's* holds after all, you know. Give it ten minutes. Less, even."

"Will you tell us what you're expecting?" asked Nicholson.

"I'll tell you that I'd be very curious to meet a man named Jarvis Norman," said Lenox. "For the rest, wait just a few—no, even less than that! There we are! Follow that cab, driver!"

From the servants' quarters of the house on Portland Place, the butler and another person had emerged. The butler was wearing a bowler hat and a spring jacket over his regular uniform. Immediately he had flagged a cab and stepped into it with his companion, the cab Lenox now asked the driver to follow.

The person with the butler, Lenox thought, was the young woman who had been so concerned after the attack on him—Miss Randall, the cook.

"We're following them?" asked Dallington. "What about Calder? The message?"

"The message never got to Calder," said Lenox. "Nor did it have to. It did its work, as you'll see."

The cab they were following turned onto Shaftesbury Avenue and clipped along briskly toward the east, overtaking omnibuses and landaus, under orders, Lenox suspected, to move as quickly as possible. It turned onto Margaret Street. They were headed in the direction of the Seven Dials—one of the less savory parts of the metropolis.

"Please explain, Lenox," said Nicholson. "At the end of this cab ride are we going to find Francis, finally?"

Lenox, who had been staring intently after the cab in front of them, turned toward his two colleagues. "I doubt it," he said. "What occurred to me at the Yard was a strange fact—that despite his omnipresence in the case, every single piece of information we have ever received about Andrew Hartley Francis comes from a single source."

Nicholson objected. "That's not true. All five of Wakefield's servants described the same fellow—dapper, young, a gentleman, dark hair, in and out of Portland Place all the time."

"That's the source," said Lenox. "Wakefield's staff. It should have come to me before now—they must have known about the businesses next door, all of them. Too risky to have it any other way. And at the head of the beast was that man—in the cab in front of us."

"The butler?" said Nicholson.

"Obadiah Smith," said Dallington.

Lenox nodded. "It's him. I think it's him behind it all. Smith."

"Why?" asked Dallington.

The cab ahead of them took a right turn, and Lenox's carriage followed the same turn after a safe delay. Lenox, after peering out of the window to make sure they hadn't lost their quarry, said, "One of the first things he told us about himself was, not incidentally I think, one of the first things Armbruster mentioned about himself, too."

Nicholson brightened, his bony face animated. "That they both had fathers who worked at the Yard! Of course!"

"Armbruster still does, apparently. That explains how they might have known each other—how Smith might have brought Armbruster into league with him, if he needed a corruptible police officer. Then there's Jenkins's shoe."

"What about it?"

"It's been bothering me all along that someone untied his laces. How on earth could they have known he had a letter in his shoe? But consider: What if Jenkins, just before he was shot, had received that claim ticket for the *Gunner* from Wakefield. They *were* working together—Wakefield was helping Scotland Yard, as out of character as that might seem. Jenkins must have offered him a choice to go to prison or to betray his circle, and he chose the latter."

"Honor among thieves."

"Quite. When the *Gunner* arrived that night, Jenkins would have been able to meet it at the docks, find the hold that matched the claim ticket—and the girls that must inevitably have been inside the hold. Jenkins was very close to saving those women from their fate. Only he was killed.

"But back to the shoe. What would he have done with the claim ticket as he was leaving Portland Place, that evening he was murdered? He was a cautious man, Jenkins. His notes were locked safely away in his office, but now he had this extremely valuable piece of paper, given to him by his key informant. Perhaps he knew that he was in danger—perhaps Wakefield did, too. He would have written me a hasty note, included the claim ticket, and tied it in his shoe there at Wakefield's house—in Wakefield's very sitting room."

Nicholson finished the thought. "Where one of the servants would have been lurking, watching."

Lenox nodded. "Exactly. Smith would have told Armbruster, in the bustle of the crime scene, to check the shoe, if he could, get the claim ticket out of it, and the note. Armbruster nearly managed to get it away. If he had, we never would have heard the name of the *Gunner*, much less searched her holds before she shipped for Calcutta. We would still think Wakefield had murdered Jenkins and fled for the Continent. A tidy crime. Indeed, one of the most brillant I can recall, in its way."

Dallington frowned. "Yes, but Wakefield had already been missing for more than a day on the night Jenkins was killed," said Dallington. "Nobody had seen him."

Lenox laughed bitterly. "According to whom? To Obadiah Smith. It all circles back around to him. Think of it, the brazenness of it! The gun that killed Jenkins—sitting on the table in the front hall. The port that poisoned Wakefield—Smith would have been the fellow who ordered all the wine and spirits for the house, and more significantly the fellow who poured it every night."

"And the attack on Smith himself?" said Nicholson.

"To divert attention—and to scare me off, with that 'warning.'

The wounds were ugly but superficial, McConnell told us as much from the start."

The three men sat in silence for a moment. Dallington looked slightly stunned. "He seemed such an easygoing fellow."

"He was always very affable with us," said Lenox. "And extremely eager to help, if you recall—to point us toward Francis."

Nicholson shook his head. "But why? How? Wakefield and Dyer had their scheme running smoothly, the women at the Slavonian Club smuggled into London aboard the *Gunner*, St. Anselm's. How does Smith come into it?"

Lenox shrugged. "I'm not precisely sure. But you recall the names on the schematic of the ship's hold, John?"

"Some of them, anyhow."

"There was one we skipped past—between Berry's Herb and Pharmaceutical and, I don't know, Jones, or Hughes."

"Smith," said Dallington in awe. "He had a hold of his own on the ship."

"I would bet that the Smith on the schematic is named Obadiah in the Asiatic's files. Legally, he was bound to use his own name. As was Wakefield. And it must have given Dyer some assurance that their names were there, that he had some proof he hadn't acted alone, if he were caught."

The cab ahead of them turned down a dingy side lane. The street was too small to follow down without attracting notice, and Lenox quickly called up to the driver to continue on for another twenty yards, then jumped from the door as it slowed. He ran back just in time to see Smith and the cook—his wife? his lover?—unlocking a red door halfway down the street.

"Let's arrest him," said Nicholson.

"He may be armed," said Lenox. "If I had to guess, he and the cook are going to take what they can put their hands on and flee—the Continent, probably. As long as Wakefield and Jenkins were silent in their graves, Smith was safe, but he's Armbruster's big card to play, to keep himself out of jail."

"Honor among thieves," murmured Nicholson once more.

They went to the red door. The street was empty, unnaturally quiet for the center of the city. Lenox felt his heart racing. He wasn't as young as he had once been, and he let Nicholson turn the handle of the door.

The entranceway of the building was covered in dirt and dust, dark as midnight except for a kerosene lamp casting a sallow triangle halfway up the wall. From the second floor came muffled voices.

"Softly on the stairs," murmured Nicholson.

As they mounted the steps, however, it was clear that Smith wasn't expecting to be followed, or at any rate didn't feel obliged to keep his voice down. He was nearly shouting, and a hoarse woman's voice was responding. Miss Randall, Lenox supposed. Their words were indistinct.

On the landing of the second story Nicholson took out his bludgeon. They stood by the door for a moment and listened.

"I tell you, we have to go this minute!" Smith was saying. His voice was different here, in the eastern rather than western half of London, and Lenox had the flashing thought that in another lifetime he might have been an accomplished actor, so convincing had his act as a pleasant butler been for so long, a figure of minor importance, unworthy of attention. "Armie will have them here within the hour."

"He won't peach on us."

"He will!" Smith's voice was becoming hysterical. "I heard it from the Yard with my own ears. Good God, are you hoping to be hanged? Every woman in that house will be lining up to point a finger at you."

There was a pause. "Very well. Let me pack my bag, then."

"Finally, some sense."

Nicholson had waited long enough. He nodded at Dallington and Lenox and after a moment of hesitation burst through the door, calling out, "Scotland Yard!"

The two amateur detectives followed closely on his heels. Smith, standing in the middle of the room, was the first figure they saw, his face white with anger and surprise, and behind him Miss Randall.

Between them was a high stack of banknotes, bundled into piles—and next to it a satchel.

And then Lenox almost burst into laughter: because sitting in an armchair next to the fire was a third person, the one Smith had been addressing, and who had been returning his words in perfect English. It was Sister Grethe.

CHAPTER FORTY-TWO

The look of incomprehension that had been habitually fixed on her face was gone. She raised a gun at them.

Lenox disliked guns, though not as much he disliked knives. He had been shot at a dozen times in the course of his career as a private detective, and witnessed several other weapons fired, and in his experience the shooters tended to overestimate their own skillfulness, unless the range was very close. Whereas even the most modestly coordinated simpleton could make a knife hurt, at close enough quarters.

Here, unfortunately, the range was very close.

"Gun!" cried Lenox, and dodged left as sharply as he could.

Dallington, no fool, did the same, and within an instant both of them were muddled into a crowd with Smith and Miss Randall, at whom, they hoped, Sister Grethe wouldn't be inclined to shoot.

But Nicholson, with real bravery, took the opposite tack, charging her. Just as Lenox heard the bang of the gun go off, Nicholson bowled over both the old woman and the chair she was sitting in.

There was a fraction of a second in which Lenox was sure Nicholson was dead—then, behind him, the bullet ricocheted off the ceiling over his head, chipping clear a large chunk of plaster. He felt his chest constrict and his breath stop, then start again. The plaster fell, and at the same moment the gun dropped to the ground and skittered across the floor.

Smith darted forward, but Dallington, who was just behind him, used the butler's own momentum against him, shoving him in the direction he was moving so that he stumbled, out of control, past the gun and into the wall.

Just as Miss Randall began to realize that she might try for the gun on the floor, Lenox leaped forward and grabbed it.

For a moment they all stayed exactly as they were—breathing hard, tense, recovering from the rapid sequence of events. Sister Grethe and Nicholson were still in a crumpled mass on the floor, Smith not far from them on his backside. Dallington stood ahead a few feet. Lenox and Wakefield's cook stared at each other warily— but he had the gun.

Once, in the case of the September Society, one of the shots intended for Lenox had hit him—a superficial wound, but there was a scar as its evidence, and sometimes when they were arguing Dallington would remind Lenox that it had been he who tackled the shooter. There had also been a case in '64 when Lenox had come within a hair's breadth of being shot by a gamekeeper on a farm in Nottinghamshire: The squire who owned the hunting preserve had noticed only after several rather dim-witted decades that nearly all of his family's silver had vanished, and twelve hours after taking up the case Lenox had discovered that it was sitting, a veritable treasure, under the frigid one-room hovel in which the gamekeeper lived. The gamekeeper had been less delighted than his master by that piece of detection and opened fire upon them. Unsuccessfully, thank goodness.

Still, this was been the closest a bullet had come to striking him since those two occasions. That piece of plaster had been very low above him.

"Is everyone unharmed?" he asked.

Nicholson nodded, and Dallington said, "Think so, yes."

They looked around at the conspirators. "You're all under arrest," Nicholson said. He stood and went to the window, lifted it, and blew his police whistle. Then he turned to Sister Grethe. "You especially."

"Can you be especially under arrest?" asked Dallington.

Grethe spat in his direction, disgustedly. "Lovely," said Nicholson.

"I'm beginning to suspect she's not a real nun," said Dallington to Lenox and Nicholson.

"Possibly not."

"To begin with, her English is better than she lets on," said Dallington.

She swore an oath at him, violently—and in English.

That evening, when Lenox arrived home, he passed by the two sentries in front of his house with a nod and turned the new second key in the new second lock, thankful that these precautions were no longer necessary. They had their criminals. He and Nicholson and Dallington had agreed: The exact details of their crimes could wait until the morning. Let them simmer overnight. Armbruster, too; he was back in custody.

Lady Jane greeted him at the door, with a kiss on the cheek. She held a blanket she was sewing for her cousin Addie's new infant. "I decided just now that I'd like to have a dinner party in two weeks," she said.

"I was nearly shot today."

Her face paled. "What?"

"It doesn't mean we can't have a party."

"What happened, Charles?"

"Maybe a smallish party, given the circumstances."

"No, don't talk like that, please—what do you mean, nearly shot? Are we in danger? Ought we to leave Hampden Lane?"

"No—no, no, no, I'm sorry, my dear. It all ended well enough."

She had an arm around him and was looking up at him. Now she leaned her face into his neck. "I don't like this new job."

They walked down the hall and went to sit in her drawing room, and carefully he relayed the story of the afternoon to her. He spoke in a tone of voice that downplayed the real sense of danger he had felt—the thudding of his heart, the mixture of euphoria and dismay he'd felt in the hours afterward—while giving her all of the facts.

But she knew him well. "You must be terribly shaken."

"It's different than Parliament, certainly."

She stood up and poured him a brandy then—his second of the day, since Nicholson had sent out for a bottle of it when they returned to the Yard, admitting himself that his hand was still trembling.

"But you were the one who charged her yourself," Dallington had said. "You saved all three of us."

"Not at all," said Nicholson.

"He's quite right," Lenox interjected.

Nicholson nodded philosophically. "Well—a toast to all three of us being alive, then."

"Hear, hear."

Lenox described this conversation to Lady Jane, too, and she said that she intended to send Nicholson a hamper from Fortnum's, and asked Lenox whether he would prefer sweets or savories.

"I have no earthly idea."

"You've been with him every day for a week."

"I know that he likes ducks. Living ones, however."

"You're hopeless."

At last they exhausted the subject of the day's events, and Lenox said, "Is there anything left for me to eat?"

"Of course. What would you like?"

He looked up and thought for a moment. Suddenly he felt a powerful sense of relief—he was alive, when he might have been dead. No matter the circumstances, that made it a notable day. He was very glad to have Jane, very glad. He squeezed her hand. "I think I would like scrambled eggs, toast, and a cup of very strong and very sweet tea," he said.

"You'll have it in eight minutes," she said, jumping to her feet. "We should have given it to you straightaway."

Eight minutes later—or perhaps a few more, but he could be charitable—the food and drink were on a tray before him, steaming and filling the room with the rich smell of warm butter and freshly brewed tea leaves.

He tucked in voraciously. "What kind of party did you have in mind?" he asked between bites.

"Only a supper, next weekend. But it's the last thing we need to think about just at the moment."

"No, it would be very fine, I think. My brother can come. I've seen too little of him recently. Too little of all of you!"

After he had eaten they sat on the sofa for a passage of time. Lenox picked up a newspaper and began to read, which he found restful, and Lady Jane returned to sewing the blanket. She paused midstitch after some time and looked at Lenox curiously. "Who was she, then?" she asked. "Sister Grethe?"

Lenox smiled. "She wouldn't say at first, but we found out soon enough."

"How?"

"When we returned to the Yard, I asked several of the older bobbies if they remembered Obadiah Smith, a constable for the Yard. Two did, but no more than the name. But another fellow, Clapham, said Obadiah Smith was the least savory, most crooked officer he'd met in all his days at the Yard. It was then that I realized who Sister Grethe might be, if that man's son cared enough to stop for her before leaving London."

"Who?"

"His mother."

CHAPTER FORTY-THREE

With Smith in custody, people began to talk quickly.

He spoke himself as well. "It was Armbruster who managed it all," he claimed.

"Armbruster?"

His smooth, ingratiating voice had returned in custody. "The only thing I did in this whole nasty sequence of events was to give His Lordship the port from Mr. Francis. Quite unintentionally."

"So we are still to believe there was a Mr. Francis."

Smith looked at them guilelessly. "Of course there was," he said.

Miss Randall followed the same line. She was the second person they questioned the next morning—with many to come after her. Her presence the afternoon before had reminded Lenox of the other three servants in Wakefield's employ. They had described Francis identically the week before, his visits, his dress. They had all been working from the same script. Now they were all under arrest.

As for Armbruster, he knew when the game was up.

"They tell us you orchestrated it all," Nicholson said, as Dallington and Lenox leaned against the wall behind the table where the two colleagues faced each other. It was a rather nicer cell, and there were the remnants of a decent breakfast nearby, an orange peel, a crust of toast, the civilities accorded someone who oughtn't to have been there. "They say that you brought in the girls with Wakefield, shot Jenkins, poisoned the marquess."

"Have you gone completely mad?" asked Armbruster.

"No more of that," warned Nicholson. "You have"—he looked at his own pocket watch, a brass one, well polished and well loved by the looks of it—"twenty minutes to tell us everything you know, or I can't promise anything short of the rope. You've made quite a lot of your friends in this building look foolish. Nobody other than the three of us has any cause to show you leniency."

For a moment Armbruster's face went rigid with anger. Then, though, it yielded. He was a weak-willed person, Lenox thought— gluttonous for food, as was obvious from his figure, and apparently gluttonous for money.

That had been the root of it all. He and Smith had known each other since childhood, both the sons of peelers. Eighteen months before, Armbruster said, Smith had taken him into his confidence: They were starting a high-end brothel in the West End and needed some protection from the Yard's interference. Armbruster had accepted what seemed in the moment like easy money, nothing life-altering, a pound or two a week, and in exchange had kept an eye on the area and smoothed over several minor incidents.

Then, on the day before Jenkins's death, Smith had wired him with an urgent request to meet.

"What did he ask you?" said Nicholson.

"He said that there was going to be a murder the next day. I told him I couldn't be involved."

"I'm sure you did."

"I did! With Christ as my witness, I did. But he said that it was my own neck on the line—that the person who'd betrayed them had given my name away, too. And he offered me fifty pounds." Armbruster shook his head mournfully. "That stupid watch. I don't know what's wrong with me."

Lenox felt a flicker of pity for the man at those words.

Then he remembered something. "You took Jenkins's papers from the Yard before you followed him, though," he said. "That means you knew who Smith meant to kill."

"Is that true?" asked Nicholson.

"I—"

"The truth, mind you."

Armbruster hesitated, then said, "Yes. I knew it was Jenkins. He would have had us all up to the gallows, you know."

Dallington snorted. "Better to go to the gallows than see a good man murdered."

"What became of his papers?" asked Lenox.

"I burned them."

"What did they say?"

"It was a thick file. He knew everything about the Slavonian Club—everything. My name was all over them, Wakefield's, too. Jenkins had obviously been working on it for months."

"Was Smith's name on them? Or Dyer's?"

Armbruster thought. "I don't know. I only looked at the papers very quickly. But I don't think so, no. It was all detail about those houses—the three houses that have been in all the newspapers."

It seemed clear enough to Lenox. Jenkins had discovered Wakefield's crimes, and used the threat of prosecution against the marquess to try to chase down all of the criminals involved in the operation. Wakefield had turned on his friends to save his skin. Both of them had died for it.

"And it was you who untied the shoe?" Lenox asked Armbruster. "Before everyone arrived?"

The sergeant hesitated again and then nodded. "Yes. When I arrived to find the body, I knocked on Wakefield's door on the pretext of searching for witnesses. Smith told me to look in the shoe. He was flustered—had just shot Jenkins and run, not wanting to linger, obviously, in such a public place. I could look in the shoe without drawing notice, because I was leading the investigation, of course." He shook his head. "But then Nicholson arrived. Another thirty seconds and none of us would be sitting here. I would have had that claim ticket in my own pocket."

They took fifteen minutes more to sketch in the details of the day Jenkins had died; for his part, Armbruster seemed sincerely not to know anything about Wakefield's death.

There was a narrow hallway outside of the cell—surprisingly bright, with a clock and a portrait of Sir Robert Peel on the wall— and here Nicholson, Lenox, and Dallington stood, discussing what they had learned.

It all fit together, but there were still questions. Nicholson, shaking his head, said, "If he were planning to betray Smith, why would Wakefield meet with Jenkins right in front of him?"

Lenox shook his head. "I've been thinking about that, too. Smith was cleverer than Wakefield. I've been following Wakefield's trail for years—he was violent, heedless, cavalier. Smith is cold-blooded."

"And?"

"If I had to guess, I would say that he probably took the precaution of seeing Jenkins when Smith was out. What he didn't consider was that Smith had been responsible for hiring all of the rest of the staff, too—Miss Randall, the three others. They were his. Wakefield wouldn't have bothered about details like that. He would have assumed that he only had to watch out for Smith, that the others were simply normal servants. In fact all four of them were spying on him."

"For that matter," said Dallington, "we have no idea what Wakefield told Smith. Perhaps he told him he was only going to give up Dyer—that they were in on it together, against Dyer and the men of the *Gunner*. But as Charles says, Smith was cleverer than Wakefield by half."

"Or us, nearly," said Nicholson. He hesitated. "I also wonder how Smith and Wakefield connected."

There was a pause as they considered the question. Then Lenox said, "Armbruster is sitting there. Let's ask him."

So they returned to the room and posed the question to the sergeant. A disconcerted look came onto his face—one of concealment, calculation. He knew something. "I'm not sure," he said.

"No more games, I told you," said Nicholson.

There was a long pause. "Does the name Charity Boyd mean anything to you?"

Lenox nodded. "The woman Wakefield killed. Yes. Why?"

Armbruster paused again, as if considering his options. "There's no reason to drag that case up, you know. Wakefield's dead. He's the one who killed her."

"This is your final warning," said Nicholson. "We—"

Lenox thought he understood. "The officers who helped investigate the murder," he said. "Was one of them Obadiah Smith's father?"

Armbruster nodded very slightly. "Yes."

"And another one of them was your father."

Now the sergeant looked pained. "Yes. But it was only Smith who helped Wakefield, I'm sure of that—sure of it. My father's nearly seventy now, anyhow. You've no cause at all to bring him into this."

Lenox turned away in disgust. He remembered the witness who had seen Charity Boyd's death, only to recant his testimony. How easily a brief encounter of intimidation from someone in a uniform might have changed his mind. And how easy to imagine that once a fruitful relationship had been established between Wakefield and Obadiah Smith Sr., the rest of the family—the constable's son, his wife—might have found their way into Wakefield's employ.

Except that Smith had probably become something very like a partner, it seemed to Lenox. Dallington evidently had the same thought. In the hallway, he said, "I suppose Smith made himself indispensable."

Nicholson nodded. "For all we know, the entire enterprise was Smith's idea."

"Yes," said Lenox. "Wakefield had the houses, Dyer the ship, but they needed Smith to run the operation. I know Wakefield—there's no way he could have been bothered with all that work. He was essentially an idle man, unless some piece of violence was called for. Smith and his mother—they were the ones in charge of the whole thing, until it came crashing down. They must have been minting money before that. Think of that pile of notes we found Smith ready to pack. Thousands of pounds."

Nicholson shook his head. "I wonder how Jenkins discovered the truth. It was a damned fine piece of detection, however he did it."

The other two nodded, and they stood there in silence for a moment, considering their departed friend.

CHAPTER FORTY-FOUR

As the women's stories of captivity seeped out into the press, the charitable hearts of the British public were stirred. A collection was taken up through the newspapers, a fund established by which all of them might have their return fares to their homelands provided, along with a six-month stipend to put them on their feet. There was talk, moreover, of a suit against Wakefield's estate, some reparation. Most of the women left as soon as they could. They gave forwarding addresses, though Lenox doubted that these would stay good for very long. Two or three women elected to stay in London—and one, in fact, a young German lady, would eventually become the well-known mistress of one of the gentlemen who had been arrested on the night of the raid at the Slavonian Club, Clarkson Gray, a bachelor of long standing descended from a line of immensely wealthy manufacturers in West Bromwich.

Several weeks after the fact, Lenox saw Gray at the Travellers Club. Gray gave him a pained look. "Bloody bad show, that was," he said, without any other greeting. "I'd no idea they weren't paid. None at all. And with the fees of the place! She's a damn fine girl, too. I'm trying to make up for it to her, you know. And she knows she can go back any time she likes. I've told her so earnestly. She prefers it here."

That encounter was still in the future as Lenox and his two partners slowly drew the net around Smith in the days after his arrest, carefully interrogating the various people who had been involved. Sister Grethe was, indeed, the grieving widow of Obadiah Smith Sr., or in any event the apartment in which she had shot at them was rented to a woman with the same name as his wife, Gwen Smith. She wouldn't confirm anything, but several of the captive women had been only too delighted to identify both Smith and his mother in person, telling long, complex tales of their roles in the day-to-day operations of the Slavonian Club. One of the girls had laid eyes on Sister Grethe—a person who in their early encounters had always seemed bovine to Lenox, placid—and fainted dead away with fear.

She was the least of their worries, though. She had fired a gun upon them, and she would end her life in prison. The question was how to be absolutely sure that her son would do the same.

His subordinates in Wakefield's house turned on him one by one, admitting that they had fabricated Andrew Hartley Francis's character together, and also that they had been directly in Smith's employ, their salaries doubled and trebled by him—rather than by Wakefield. (When Lenox remembered how spare the house had been, how little work it must have taken to keep up, he saw the appeal of the job.) Yes, one of the footman told them, he had seen Jenkins put the note in his shoe, and reported it to Smith. He'd had no idea Jenkins was going to be murdered—only Smith had threatened them with their own deaths if they said anything, and promised them grand lumps of money if they could stick it out until the new marquess was installed in the house.

Nicholson, one afternoon, wondered out loud why Smith had stayed around, acting as butler. "I suppose it would have been too suspicious if he disappeared just at the moment Wakefield did."

Dallington nodded. "What's been on my mind is why, if the Slavonian Club is only eighteen months old, they've had holds on the *Gunner* for so long."

Lenox shrugged. "There are plenty of illegal things to do with a hold on a ship, I suppose. They simply grew more ambitious. Perhaps they were always bringing in women, and decided to eliminate the intermediate step—to run the brothels themselves, rather than take all the risk of finding women for the brothels."

"There's opium, too," said Nicholson, "and any other number of drugs. We've had a fearful time stopping the trade."

They were in Nicholson's office, eating a bite of lunch together. A definite companionship had sprung up between the three men, now that the case was concluded, and they talked easily, enjoying each other's company.

"Did we ever learn why they named it the Slavonian Club?" asked Dallington.

"It was in the papers, you know," said Nicholson. "It's a place on the Continent. 'Even more hedonistic than its neighbor Bohemia,' or some rubbish of that nature, was what I read."

Lenox added grimly—and it was this he would ultimately think of when Clarkson Gray rationalized his behavior at the Travellers'— "And there's a word buried right in the name, too. Slave. Whether that's an accident or a cruel joke, who can say."

They might easily have sent Obadiah Smith to trial with the evidence they had. There were witnesses who could place him at the Slavonian Club, a constant presence, and the other servants were all quick to blame him. Nevertheless, it seemed a little thin. The houses belonged to his employer, Lord Wakefield, and he could plausibly plead that he had no idea of the crimes that had taken place there. He and Miss Randall allotted all the blame to Armbruster— and to the servants beneath Smith, who they claimed were conspiring against him.

There was also no trail of paper tying him to the business other than the hold in the *Gunner,* and though that was registered to O. Smith, according to the Asiatic there was no address or other identifying tag to confirm that it was the same man; apparently the captain of the *Gunner* managed the holds. As for all the money they had found in Smith's possession—that was another piece of highly suspicious circumstantial evidence, but there was nothing illegal about it, on its face.

It was in the state of frustration induced by these tenuous pieces of evidence that Lenox passed the next week, searching for a way to break down Smith's story once and for all. What they knew about his connection to the club would perhaps be enough to send the man to prison for a few years, but on the more serious charge of the murders of Jenkins and Wakefield, he had covered his tracks too cleverly. As it stood, they would have to hope that Armbruster was a persuasive witness. He was the only person who could definitively declare that Smith was a murderer. The problem was that it wouldn't be difficult to make a jury doubt the word of a man so plainly corruptible.

One of Smith's fellow plotters wouldn't prove quite as elusive as the silver-tongued butler, however. On a morning the next week, as Lenox was puzzling over all of the case's details in the offices at Chancery Lane, a telegram came from Nicholson. It said:

DYER SHOT STOP GUNNER HELD AT LISBON STOP

"Dallington!" he called out.

The young lord popped his head around the doorframe. With Jenkins's murder solved, he had resumed his normal schedule of work and was investigating a housebreak at Brixton. "Yes?"

"Look at this."

Dallington took the paper, read it, and whistled. "Shall we go see Nicholson?"

Nicholson had a limited amount of information, but some, and more came in during the next few days. The *Gunner* had sailed into the port under camouflage, painted with a new yellow-and-white check above the sea line (which meant that it had been done in the week since she left London) and calling herself the *Ariana*. The British admiral stationed in Lisbon had received the word from Scotland Yard to look out for the ship, however, and one of his assistants had spotted her right away, despite her attempts at concealment.

The admiral had decided to let her run into port, rather than challenging her out at sea. As she tied on, a lieutenant had called out, "All men of this ship are under arrest, by order of Her Majesty the Queen."

There had been a stirring on deck then, followed by two noises in quick succession: a gunshot, first, and second, a splash, the sound of a pistol hurled far overboard.

They found Dyer in his cabin. He had been shot in the back. None of the two-hundred-odd men aboard the *Gunner* would say a word, other than to confirm that the captain had ordered the ship repainted and renamed since they left the Thames.

"Can't say why," the ship's lieutenant, Lawton, had said. "Captain's orders."

Indeed, it became clear that the magical use of this phrase, *Captain's orders,* was the reason Dyer had been killed by his own men. The British representatives at Lisbon heard it hundreds of times as they investigated the ship. It was a clever maneuver: By maritime law, the illegality of the ship's new, unregistered name, and the illegality of anything in the holds, were the responsibility of the captain alone.

And indeed, one of the things that the navy found was a group of several women, living in hammocks—in the hold licensed to Lord Wakefield, the hold where Lenox and Dallington had found his body.

This detail puzzled them, until they learned that the women had all lived for several months at St. Anselm's—at the Slavonian Club. That, evidently, was how Smith, Wakefield, and Dyer had ensured that none of the women mastered English. Every time the *Gunner* came and went, it exchanged new women for the old.

Where had Dyer been taking the women now, though? They didn't know themselves, of course. Lisbon wasn't part of the course the *Gunner* usually sailed on its route to Calcutta. Why, then, had Dyer risked putting into port there, when the disguise he had arranged for his ship showed that he was already worried about being caught?

The answer must be money, and Lenox surmised, on the day he and Dallington went to see Nicholson, that Dyer must have gone to Lisbon to sell off the women in his holds. From there he could have sailed the *Gunner* to Calcutta—confident that no ship could outrun her on that route—and then left her with the Asiatic. He and his crew might well have dispersed there, leaving the company to replace them, perhaps eventually returning to London overland.

With all this in mind, Nicholson asked the British navy in Portugal to investigate the city's brothels, to ascertain whether there was any that might have taken women from the *Gunner* in the past. ("Though asking the British navy to look at a city's brothels seems like a redundant request," Dallington had pointed out.) With the assistance of the Portuguese police, who were eager to aid the country that brought so much foreign trade into their cities, they raided half a dozen houses and questioned the women working there.

Finally, at one of these, belonging to an aristocrat named Luis Almonte de la Rosa, they found success: Several of the women had been at the Slavonian Club, and were paid no more now than they had been there. Emboldened by the assurances of the navy that they could have their freedom, they recounted their own stories of the *Gunner*, which had brought them first to London and then here.

The emergence of this second criminal consortium, far away in a different country, returned the story to the headlines for several days. After that it gradually faded, in abeyance until the trial of the last living member of the criminal trio who had planned it all began.

CHAPTER FORTY-FIVE

The weeks after Smith's arrest were rainless and bright, the soft, light days of spring hardening toward the heat of summer, women walking with fans in hand, men in suits of lighter cloth. Along Chancery Lane, the dogs belonging to each shop lingered in the shadows of their doorways, their instincts for adventure and alarm dormant while the sun was up.

At the detective agency one story above street level, business had resumed.

"What about you, Dallington?" asked Lenox.

They were sitting at the conference table. "Two new cases over the weekend. One a woman of middle age whose husband has been missing for four years—she wants proof that he's dead, so that she can remarry. The other is from a fellow who saw our names in the papers. He was defrauded of three hundred pounds by an itinerant salesman. Offers to split whatever we can recover. It will probably lead nowhere, of course, but I thought I might put Pointilleux on the trail, if we don't need him here."

Lenox nodded. "And Polly?"

For Polly was still there; she had declined Monomark's offer. Now, as a fly buzzed against the warm windows, and she sat in the meeting that Lenox had begun by reporting that he had no new cases, she looked as if she might regret it. Briskly she tapped her pen twice against the sheet of paper in front of her, then offered up her usual list of small and middling clients, many of them women— good, steady business.

Eleven percent. Since the day LeMaire had announced he was leaving, the words that had rattled around Lenox's mind were those two, *eleven percent.* That was the trivial proportion of the revenue the firm took in for which he was responsible. Could he blame the Frenchman for leaving? Or Polly if she had chosen to go?

The difficulty was that the previous autumn he had viewed this return to detection as a pleasure, a fulfillment of his private wishes— not as a business.

Today that changed.

"Thank you," he said to Polly when she had finished. Then he paused. "As you both know, my official, paid involvement in the Jenkins murder concluded on Friday. I'll still be helping Nicholson, but only in an unofficial capacity. That makes this a good moment to address the future of the firm, I think. I told you I had a plan, and I do."

Both Polly and Dallington looked at him more alertly, eyes enlivened by their curiosity. With each other, in the last week, they had been stiff, polite. Polly had been most animated when she told them about her second meeting with Monomark.

"At first he tried to cajole me into accepting," she had said. "Then I asked him about the articles in the *Telegraph.*"

Dallington had raised his eyebrows at that. "What did he say?"

"He turned bright red and asked me if I was certain once and for all that I declined the position. I said I did. He stood up and walked out then—leaving me with the bill for tea, no less."

They had all seen the result of that meeting the next day, when the *Telegraph* had blared a headline: LEMAIRE FOUNDS DETECTIVE AGENCY. Monomark's second choice, evidently, but quicker than

Polly to accept the offer. The article below the headline described precisely the kind of agency that Monomark had offered Polly control of. Indeed, the newspaper baron's fingerprints were all over it. The subheadline read TO BE PREMIER FIRM IN ENGLAND, and a quote from a high official at Scotland Yard, probably one of Monomark's cronies, said, "Certainly LeMaire's will be our first and only choice should we ever require outside assistance in a criminal investigation."

LeMaire's firm was already up and running, with daily advertisements in half a dozen papers, favorable stories in the press, and even fairly positive word of mouth. Within a month, Lenox had privately reckoned, he might well take half of their business. If he did that they might as well shutter the firm.

Fortunately, he did have a plan. What was more, it was Monomark who had given him the idea for it. At their morning meeting, he asked Dallington and Polly—the words were directed at Polly, really, for he knew Dallington would never leave—to draw up the last drops from their reservoirs of faith in him. He would return that evening with news.

He took his carriage then and went to Parliament, where he spent a long, tiring day—but a triumphant one.

At six o'clock that evening, as the Members began to make their way through the hall outside the Commons into the benches for the evening session, Lenox stood, watching them wander in as he had for so many years, until he felt a tap on his shoulder.

He turned and saw his brother. "Edmund!" he said. He felt himself smiling. Throughout the course of the case they hadn't seen each other. Edmund was his closest friend, and it was an unusual length of time for the two of them to have gone without each other's company. This was a happy coincidence.

"Charles, what on earth are you doing here? I could have stood you a late lunch, or an early supper for that matter."

"I was here on business, alas. Do you have time for a quick glass of wine now?"

Edmund checked the large clock on the wall. "Quickly, yes," he said. "But what the devil do you mean, business? They had pheasant with chestnut sauce and cranberries this afternoon, too, your favorite thing."

They went to the Members' Bar, mostly empty now, and after they ordered their drinks they sat, Lenox asking what the subject of the debate that evening would be. Foreign trade, Edmund answered. That was the dullest of subjects Parliament could take up, in his opinion, though one of the most important.

"Better you than me," said Lenox.

"Molly says that Jane is having a dinner party this weekend?" said Edmund.

"Yes, can you come?"

"Molly has bought a new dress already, so I imagine we can. She's down in London so rarely these days that she says she never knows the city fashion until she's walking out the door, dressed in the last season. But since Teddy is ashore for leave, she can't tear herself away from home. Speaking of which, you must come down soon."

Edmund still lived mainly at Lenox House in Sussex, where they had grown up. "We thought of coming in July."

"That would please me inordinately. For one thing, we're going to have a dance, for the county people, you know, and it would dispel the rumors that you yourself are part of a criminal gang if you were to attend."

"Is that what they say?"

"The news gets very garbled on its way south, you know. And I may put it about that we're disappointed in how it all ended for you, of course." Edmund smiled, a spark in his eyes. "Anyhow—business? That's why you're in the building?"

"Yes. It's been an interesting day."

Not long before, Lenox had read an article in *Blackwood's* that mentioned that the word "abracadabra" originally meant "I create what I speak" in the Hebrew language, a magician's word that had migrated into English. This piece of trivia had been running through his mind all day, because so much of what he had done was to create money out of nothing—out of mere speech.

He had taken eighteen short meetings that day, he told Edmund, with eighteen friends and allies from his days in Parliament. (Twenty had been scheduled, but two Members had been detained elsewhere.) What all eighteen had in common was that they were men of business, and to each of them Lenox had proposed the same idea: that their firm pay an annual fee to retain the services of Lenox, Dallington, and Strickland on a permanent basis.

The blunt reaction of the second man he had seen, a steel man-ufacturer named Jordan Lee who had a great rotund belly and a thick mustache, had been typical. "Why on earth would I need to hire a detective agency?"

Lenox had been prepared for the question. "You're familiar with the Holderness case?" he asked.

Lee grimaced. "Of course, the poor bastards."

The year before, a quiet senior manager at Holderness had stayed ten minutes after work one evening, opened the company safe, and walked away with nearly four thousand pounds in European certifi-cates of stock. It emerged that he had also been embezzling from the company for years. The two brothers in command of the firm, Andrew and Joseph Holderness, were living in sharply reduced per-sonal circumstances as they attempted to pay off their debts and set the business back on its feet.

"A stitch in time, you know, Lee," said Lenox. "We have a dedi-cated accountant who will do a quarterly examination of your books for fraud, detectives to do thorough investigations into any person you wish to hire—and of course in the case of any actual crime, theft, or violence, we'll be on the spot immediately."

Lenox saw Lee thinking. It was a good offer in general, he thought—though the accountant was, as yet, pure fiction—but the word that had most intrigued him was one thrown in with careful carelessness, "violence." It was what the industrialists like Lee had most to fear.

"How much are you asking for the service?" he asked.

"Six hundred pounds per annum. We'll keep a record of what we do for you, and charge more or return some of that at the end of the year based on our charges. Our own records are scrupulous, of course. I would be happy to show you a sample."

For a moment the question hung in the balance—but then, perhaps because of his long acquaintance with Lenox, perhaps because six hundred pounds was a substantial but not a shocking sum, Lee nodded and put his hand out. "I think it's a clever idea, now you explain it. We've been losing a mint simply from scrapped steel that's gone missing. Your people could start there."

Not all of Lenox's meetings were so successful, of course. Eight of the men declined outright, two had, rather vexingly, already hired LeMaire to do the same job, and three others said they would think it over, in a hard genial tone that made it clear they wouldn't.

In a way it had been a painful day for Lenox, who was so used to his own pride, so long accustomed to the luxury of financial independence, still adherent to old standards of what a gentleman ought to do. He had been inculcated with a disdain for business, for trade. These men, in fact, were those who looked up to him, to his life with his aristocratic wife, and in some of their faces he saw a subtle sense of reversal, perhaps even reprisal. That had been difficult.

And yet in another way it had been thrilling. Business was a kind of game, and for the first time he saw why men like Monomark chose to play it.

Better still, after he had finished his drink with Edmund, he could return to the offices with his news: that he had found five new clients that day, who would pay a total of seven hundred and fifty pounds into their accounts that very week, their first quarterly payments.

"Three thousand pounds for the year, then?" said Dallington uncertainly.

Polly repeated the words, too, but her voice was entirely free of uncertainty. She was beaming, with a look of pure relief and joy on her face, like a gambler who's put his last shilling on a long shot and seen it run first through the gate. "Three thousand pounds!" she said. "Are you sure? It's a fortune!"

Lenox smiled. "I'm sure."

"Not that I doubt your word—only seven hundred and fifty pounds is already twice as much as every farthing we've brought in till now put together, Charles! My God, I could kiss you!"

CHAPTER FORTY-SIX

The next month was one of frantic activity at Chancery Lane, all three of them putting in many long, grueling days of labor, so that the first weeks of May passed in a haze of early mornings and late nights. It was Polly who took the situation in hand, hiring, the day after Lenox's meetings, an accountant, a new clerk, and a new detective named Atkinson. He was a fifty-year-old man who had recently retired from the Yard in search of a better salary, tall and solid with salt-and-pepper hair. He would be the person who went to the firms for a monthly checkup and interacted directly with the managers.

"They'll prefer that type of fellow," she said confidently after Atkinson had left his interview. "You and Dallington are too refined—and of course I'm a woman, which would never do."

Atkinson was an immediate success, as was the new clerk, King. On the other hand, the accountant arrived at the offices in a state of impressive inebriation on his third morning, and they fired him on the spot, replacing him later that afternoon with a meek chap named Tomkins, who turned out to be splendidly intelligent. In his very first week he found a clerical error that saved Jordan Lee, the steel magnate, nearly seventy pounds.

At the same time, for some half-mysterious reason, the business coming in for Lenox, Dallington, and Polly increased. Small cases, mostly, many to do with minor sums of money, though some genuinely enigmatic ones were mixed in as well. Lenox spent three sleepless days helping a butcher in Hampstead recover a kidnapped child, who turned out, in the end, to have been taken by a local woman who imagined that the butcher had scorned her.

Lenox described the influx of cases to Lady Jane one evening, as they sat out upon the small stone terrace that overlooked the back garden at Hampden Lane, the pleasant call of birds in the air, a light breeze making it cooler than it had been for most of the week. Between them was Sophia. She sat on a small wooden horse and rocked back and forth, murmuring some very important words to herself, lost, as so often, in a private and apparently vivid world. It was one of Lenox's favorite things about his daughter—the intensity and liveliness of her interior life. What on earth was she saying to the horse?

"Why do you think more cases have come in recently?" Lady Jane asked.

"I'm not certain," he said. "Perhaps the establishment of LeMaire's firm has raised awareness that such a thing as a detective agency exists—and that means ours, too. A rising tide, and all that. Or I suppose it may be that after the murders, our names appeared in the papers often enough to be noticed."

"I give Polly the credit, personally."

"Thank you, my dear. It's nice always to have one ally."

Lady Jane laughed. She looked very lovely, a slender champagne flute in her hand, the falling light capturing the soft contours of her face. "No, I give you the credit," she said. "I only meant that she always seems to know exactly what to do."

Polly had been at Hampden Lane fairly often in the past few weeks, as had Dallington, a few small quick meetings at first turning into a series of teas and suppers there, until it became a kind of office away from the office. They had sat in Lenox's study for many hours, and though they had always liked each other, something about this second space, combined perhaps with their revitalized business, had knitted the three of them closer together. Even Dallington and Polly were becoming easier with each other again. Partly that was because of Lady Jane, who always interrupted their meetings to bring them sandwiches, or drinks, or to tell Lenox something—interruptions that made the meetings feel homelike, informal, but also somehow more productive. It all seemed very natural for the first time, this business of running a detective agency.

Lenox reached over and put his hand on Sophia's head, though she pushed it away irritably and kept rocking. He smiled. "Yes, she's splendid. To be honest I don't think we could have done it without her, Dallington and I. We both like the detective work, but she sees the whole picture. Thank goodness for Atkinson, to take just one example."

Despite all of this, the agency was still battling uphill. Though Lenox had taken several additional meetings after that first marathon of a day, they had only produced one more client, and the massive initial infusion of money they had received would have to be carefully apportioned out over the course of the year, would have to pay for the salaries of the new employees, the trips to visit their clients, the offices. Lenox and Dallington also continued, rather guiltily, to take cases for free when the clients couldn't afford to pay. Polly—more practical—showed such softness far more rarely.

Then, at the end of May, something disquieting happened: Le-Maire poached one of their clients, a mill owner named Templeton, the Member for Stratford. His first quarterly payment to them would be his last. "Better rates with Monomark's fellow, Lenox," he said when they saw each other at a party. "He told me all about it at Ascot. Same service. It's the nature of business, you know. I'm sorry to have to leave you."

Dallington was furious. Polly was more philosophical; she recommended that they meet with their clients to be sure that they were happy with the agency. Still, it made for a worrying week, and a few late nights looking at the books and making lists of possible new clients, until, almost as if the universe had decided to rebalance their luck, something fortuitous happened.

It was on a June morning (a rainy one, at last) just a week before Obadiah Smith's trial was to begin. The papers were full of the case again, and the Slavonian Club. The journalists all felt sure that Smith would go to prison for a few years, but that it would be impossible to convict him of the murders of Jenkins and Wakefield, as the crown hoped to do. Lenox had pulled out his notes on the case, studying them a thousandth time, searching for some detail to pin Smith to the crimes. The gun—that would have been their best hope, but it had been wiped clean, and packaged in that parcel from Francis. It was maddening. The butler had been too clever for them.

Pointilleux knocked on the door and came in without waiting for an answer. "You have a visitor."

"Who is it?"

"Someone named Mr. Graham."

"Graham! Push him in."

"I will, I will," said Pointilleux testily. He had been in a bad mood all morning because of dyspepsia caused by the breakfast his landlady had made him. ("The egg in this country are pepper beyond anything reasonable.") "He is wet with rain, unfortunately."

Graham was, indeed, wet with rain, but he smiled and put out a hand as Lenox stood and welcomed him in. "What brings you away from Parliament?" asked Lenox. "Look, you're soaked. Let me ring for tea."

The office had another new employee, a maid named Mrs. Barry, and a few moments after Lenox asked for it she came in with a pot of tea and a plate of biscuits. Graham accepted a cup of tea gratefully, sipping carefully as the steam rose from it.

"Busy at the Commons?" asked Lenox, taking a sip of his own tea.

"There's a vote later today," said Graham. "The foreign trade bill."

"I know. I've seen some of the speeches in the papers. You've taken on a very great role."

"Yes," said Graham, nodding grimly, as if it hadn't been by choice, or altogether to his liking. "The first time I've spoken much."

"I feel very sorry to have missed your maiden speech. If I had known you meant to give it I would have been in the gallery."

"It was a necessity at the last moment, unfortunately. Qualls fell ill and had to bow out."

"And then—the responses."

Graham smiled dryly. "Yes, quite."

When Graham had been Lenox's secretary in Parliament, the other party had spread rumors about his conduct—namely, that he was corrupt. These had seemed plausible perhaps more than they otherwise would have because of Graham's birth, which was low for anyone intimately involved with England's national politics. In the last weeks those rumors—quelled when he ran for Parliament—had resurfaced, with oblique mentions in speeches from the other benches. They implied that certain foreign powers, particularly Russia, had bought Graham's influence.

"Is there something I can do?" asked Lenox. "Someone to whom I can speak?"

"Oh, no, thank you," said Graham. "We can handle them."

Lenox nodded. Graham, more than anyone else he knew, would be able to manage his position in the brutal joust of Parliament. "But then why have you come? Not that I don't wish it were a more frequent occurrence."

"I wonder if you recall that form you filled out when we had lunch several weeks ago?" asked Graham. "The very long one?"

"Yes—the exit interview, as it were. They wanted to know how much port I drink, which I thought intrusive of them. Not that it's very much."

"I'm afraid I deceived you," said Graham. The word "sir" still hovered toward the end of the sentence, without appearing. He reached down into his valise and pulled out a thin sheaf of papers. "It was a questionnaire that the House rules subcommittee wished you to fill out."

Lenox frowned. "The House rules subcommittee?"

"We would like to offer you a new position that has been created only this week. As yet it doesn't have a name, but you would be the official house detectives of the Commons and the Lords."

Lenox's eyes widened, and for a moment he was struck dumb. "Never, really?"

Graham smiled. "Of course, we have army officers and Metropolitan Police stationed around the building."

"I remember them."

"But there are as many small and large crimes in Parliament as in any other concern involving several thousand men, and the Yard is not always as quick as one would like in its response, or indeed its solution of them." Graham paused and then said delicately, "There would be a retainer of nine hundred pounds a year, and of course any additional expenses would be reimbursed."

Lenox looked at his old friend, touched. He could tell even glancing at the papers Graham had passed him that this had been his work—his gesture. "I would be honored to accept," he said. "Thank you. Particularly as it means we might have lunch more often now, too."

For whatever reason, it was at this moment that Lenox finally believed that the agency was going to succeed. It wasn't even the money that gave him the feeling. In the next room Polly was meeting with a new client; Dallington was out upon a case, as were Pointilleux and Atkinson; the scratch of different pens rose from the outer office; and in his chest he had a feeling that at last things had clicked into place. It would be easier from here on out. Of course there would be challenges—but not defeats, he felt sure. They would make it.

CHAPTER FORTY-SEVEN

The morning that Smith's trial was to begin, Lenox and Dallington had breakfast with Nicholson in a small, noisy restaurant near the courthouse. They hadn't seen him in some time. He looked tired and flagged down the waiter several times to ask for more coffee.

"We've been trying desperately to find further evidence against Smith," he said. "The case has been given a very high priority at the Yard, as you can imagine—a police inspector and a marquess. No limit to the budget or the manpower at my disposal. But for all that, we haven't been able to find definite proof. There is Armbruster's word, but even he didn't see the murder directly—and of course he's cooperating with us to avoid punishment himself, which makes him less than an ideal witness. Smith must be a genius, I think, to have come through this foul situation without a mark on him."

"He's been both clever and lucky," said Lenox. "Anyone in the world might have seen the murder on Portland Place."

"Sister Grethe comes to mind as a possible witness," said Dallington dryly.

"Too bad her trial begins today, too," said Nicholson. Gwen Smith was also at the Old Bailey. "I can't imagine she'll escape prison, at least. That's a minor consolation."

"You have him on the Slavonian, too, though?" asked Lenox.

"Oh, there's no question at all about that. Dozens of witnesses, each more eager than the last to point a finger at him. The difficulty is that it won't put him behind bars for more than three or four years. That's the law. What's heartbreaking is that it's probably the precise punishment he would have served if Jenkins and Wakefield had lived. He's saved himself nothing, and cost them a great deal—Jenkins especially, of course."

The waiter set down an extra plate of buttered toast at the center of their table, and Dallington took a piece, tearing it into bites moodily. The clink and clatter of silverware and the din of cheerful voices was all around, a London morning, but the three of them sat silent for some time.

At the courthouse there was a push of journalists standing by the doors, shouting questions at the witnesses and solicitors who entered. Fleet Street would use any excuse it could find to bring the Slavonian Club back into its headlines, the story's lurid mixture of aristocracy, money, and sex selling out editions faster than anything else had in 1876, every tutting curate and bored housemaid desperate to devour each minor new detail that the press could winkle out of the case.

"Mr. Lenox! Will he hang, Mr. Lenox!" cried out one chap, and another at the same moment said, "Nicholson! Inspector Nicholson! Is it true as you were a client as well, and you and Armbruster hushed it all!"

Nicholson flushed and turned. "Don't answer," Dallington advised.

At the door there was a small line, and Lenox found himself waiting behind a thin-shouldered man in an expensive cloak. The man turned as Lenox came up behind him. It was Monomark.

"Lord Monomark," said the detective, smiling faintly. He was surprised. "Are you sitting in the galleries?"

Monomark had brilliant, predatory eyes, in a thin, ascetic face. "Surprised you're here," he said, "after all that our Inspector Jenkins said about you in the papers. Wonderful quotes, those, honest and forthright. A testament to the chap. Though they must have stung, I expect. Dear, dear."

It did sting—and the *Telegraph* had reprinted the quotes that very morning. Lenox only widened his smile and said, "They ask you to come when you solve the case, you see. I'm not surprised LeMaire has yet to learn that, however."

Monomark flushed—he was not a man whose jibes were often answered. "We'll see you out of business within the year. Mark my words."

"Did you hear that we'd been named official investigators for the Houses of Parliament?" Lenox asked mildly. "Mrs. Buchanan is there even now. More work than we know what to do with. Tell LeMaire we're happy to hire him back, when he's out of a job."

In another lifetime, Lenox probably wouldn't have made his words so barbed. Business had changed him, however. Monomark, who no doubt thought of him as part of the soft circle of aristocrats to which he had gained only halting and uneasy entry, seemed to reassess him with those eyes. "Parliament," he said. Lenox could tell he hadn't heard of their hiring. "A pack of fools. Everything you need to know about the House of Lords you can learn from the fact that three is a quorum."

"The house in which you sit, if I'm not mistaken, My Lord."

"I didn't—"

But what Monomark did or didn't do would have to wait, because just then, behind them, there was a piercing cry on the steps. "She's dead!" It was one of the runners, who were able to enter the cells with messages. "Gwen Smith is dead! I saw the note! Story to the highest bidder!"

There was a pause, and then the full pack of journalists sprinted toward the boy. Monomark almost looked as if he wanted to join them, and for an instant Lenox liked the old man, his will still so bent upon success, upon victory. "False, I'm sure," he said.

Behind Lenox, Nicholson pushed his way through. "Let's go in," he said. "Enough of this. Scotland Yard—yes, this is my badge, stare at it if you like, but quickly, quickly."

It was the truth: Obadiah Smith's mother was dead. She had poisoned herself. It would be several hours before the coroner confirmed the cause of death, but he didn't have to bother to convince the detectives—she had left a note.

In it, she confessed to every crime of which her son might have been guilty.

And then I did take the pistol and shoot Inspector Jenkins from short range in the head . . . packaged the pistol in a parcel under the fraudulent seal of an invented person of my own invention, Andrew Francis . . . never informed my son that the port had been poisoned . . . I know he believed the club located at 75 Portland Place to be a wholly legal business . . . I take my own life out of guilt and ask only that he be fully exonerated and allowed to live his life . . .

The note ended with an entreaty, incredible on its face, that the new marquess of Wakefield retain Smith as his butler. *It's only fair, Your Lordship,* said the note.

Nine days later, Obadiah Smith received a sentence of two months' imprisonment in Newgate. He also received a hundred pounds from the *Telegraph* to write a story: INSIDE THE SLAVONIAN CLUB: AN INNOCENT'S TALE. In prison that money, in addition to whatever else he had saved, afforded him a life of luxury, in particular the most sumptuous thing a person in his position could buy— privacy. For a few extra coins, as well, Miss Randall went to visit him each night. Smith was working on a book, from what the guards said. It would expand upon the article, profess his innocence, lament his mother's misdeeds. And—what guaranteed that it would make him a small fortune—it would name the names of the aristocrats who had frequented the club.

The same coroner who had determined that Gwen Smith poisoned herself informed Nicholson, one morning, that she had been in a very advanced stage of illness, with mere months to live, perhaps even weeks. Lenox was a father, and just as he had felt a fleeting tincture of admiration for Monomark, so he did for Gwen Smith. It must have taken mettle to plan and then carry out her own death, all to shield her son.

Of course, he was also distraught. After the trial, he, Dallington, and Nicholson took their carriage to Jenkins's house and sat with Madeleine Jenkins for an hour. They apologized for their failure. To Lenox's surprise she seemed better, however, even, when her children entered the room just before they left, allowing a smile to appear on her face. Perhaps he had underestimated her resilience.

"Did we ever contribute to the fund for the family?" asked Dallington as they left, in a low voice.

"The firm did," said Lenox.

"It's not enough."

"No."

And it wasn't. When they returned to the office in Chancery Lane that afternoon, Lenox fetched a small slate blackboard he had in his office. He went and hung it by the door and carefully wrote two names on it:

William Anson
Obadiah Smith

The two men who had eluded him since he returned to detection. The agency would carry on, obviously, and his own work in the next months might lead him anywhere, to any corner of England or the world—and how thrilling that seemed, how distant from the dry closeted workings of Parliament!—but sooner or later he would repay the debt he owed them.

CHAPTER FORTY-EIGHT

In June the citizens of London's leafy western precincts scattered off toward the country, the sea air of Devon, the rolling downs of Yorkshire, where they found slower days, longer evenings, earlier cocktail hours. But Lenox and Lady Jane remained in London for the first weeks of the month, primarily so that he could go to work every morning, and on the month's first Saturday night they had their friends for supper. Toto was at her father's house with George; McConnell, though, had remained through the weekend, busy doing rounds at the children's hospital in Great Ormond Street, and he came early to sit in Lenox's study and drink a glass of hock.

The windows were open, allowing in a breeze and the noise of voices and footsteps from the street. "Have you seen anything of LeMaire since he started the new firm?" McConnell asked.

"Not a sight. Pointilleux still dines with him every week, and says he's happy with the bargain he struck. I'm sure it's remunerative, at least."

"Are you sure the nephew isn't spying?"

"Very sure. For one thing he's the most literal human I ever met. For another we gave him a raise in pay, and a great deal more responsibility than his uncle is willing to give him. He has a whole pile of newspaper cuttings with the articles in which his name appeared after the Portland Place business. Keeps them in his top drawer, thinks none of the clerks know about it."

"I wish I could have helped more," said McConnell. "Found the source of the lead in the port, for instance."

"He covered his tracks well, Smith."

McConnell hesitated, then said, "Far be it from me to question how to do your work, but I confess I've wondered from time to time whether that twenty pounds in Jenkins's pocket might be the answer."

Lenox grimaced. "Have you? I'd been hoping everyone had forgotten."

The doctor looked at him quizzically. "Why?"

"I don't think it has anything to do with the case, and Jenkins was a good chap."

"What do you think it was, then? You needn't tell me if you don't like, but I'm curious."

Lenox sighed. The truth was that he thought he had a good idea about that twenty pounds; and he suspected that it had come directly from the purse of Lord Monomark.

Monomark's reporters famously paid for information, serious sums when it was good information. Lenox's theory, which he had shared only with Dallington, was that as part of his campaign to discredit their new agency, Monomark had paid Jenkins for his negative words about Lenox.

Several things made him think so: the cash itself, which must have come from somewhere; the unlikeliness that Jenkins, long a friend, would have said something negative about him to a reporter; the gloating look on Monomark's face on the steps of the Old Bailey, and his inability to resist mentioning what Jenkins had told the paper. There was even the timing: the morning after Jenkins had died, there had been new quotes in the *Telegraph*, perhaps indicating that he had met with someone from the paper on the day of his death, which would have explained why he'd had the money with him when he died.

Then there was a final detail—the letters on Jenkins's desk at Scotland Yard from various creditors, demanding payment.

In a way it softened the blow of what Jenkins had said. Family must come first, duty. If the inspector had spoken to the *Telegraph* to pay his bills, so be it. It had been intelligent of Monomark, even. Lenox's long and publicly touted alliance with Jenkins had been one of the things that gave the new agency its legitimacy.

Lenox explained all this to McConnell. "That's terribly unfortunate," said the doctor.

"I suppose it might still be related to the case. But in my heart I think Monomark is the answer."

"What a diabolical fellow!"

"Just so."

Fortunately it was hard to stay very angry on such a mellow pink evening, and as the guests started to arrive, Lenox left his study to greet them, conducting them as they arrived out into the back garden, where Lady Jane and a few of her friends were already sitting. Dallington's mother and father were there, and Molly Lenox, and Jane's cousin Emily Gardner, whose fiancé, George, was expected to arrive shortly, and Emily's dear friend Ellen Daring, who was expecting a child. Lenox took a glass of cold lemonade from a table off to the side and watched his wife from the corner of his eye. The bars were off of their windows now, and the regular patrols outside on Hampden Lane had been reduced to a weekly check from Mr. Clemons himself.

"A good horse eats seventy-two pounds of straw a week, and fifty-six pounds of hay," Dallington's mother was saying. "Not to mention two bushels of oats. I think it's simply disgusting. Mark my words, we'll have carriages with engines in them soon, and the city will be much cleaner for it."

"But what will pull them?" asked Emily.

"Nothing at all. They're inventing them in Germany right now. They pull themselves."

Emily was too well-bred to convey her extreme skepticism at this idea with anything other than a very faint lift of her eyebrow, but she said, "I cannot imagine London without horses."

The duchess, who was not a reticent person, said, "It doesn't matter whether you can imagine it."

Just then a footman appeared leading Dallington, who, despite the warmth of the evening, looked unflushed, his dark hair in place, his acerbic face brightening genuinely with each person he saw.

"Have I interrupted a very dazzling conversation?" he asked.

"Your mother is attempting to clear the horses out of London," said Lady Jane.

"Oh, again? I don't know where they'll go. Birmingham, I suppose. A whole city of horses. Anyway it's nonsense, because they'll never build an engine large enough to pull a carriage."

"I tell you the Germans are doing it."

"They're only Germans, not magicians."

"You don't know whether they're both! I've been to Baden twice, and you've never been at all."

"My apologies. I'm sure you spent the whole time touring their engineering colleges, and none of it at the spa."

Just at that moment two more guests came in at the same time, first Edmund and then Polly, who said she was arriving straight from the office. Unlike Dallington she was flushed, and she accepted a glass of lemonade gratefully. Edmund had just been at Parliament; for his part, he said, having been drawn into the conversation, he did not think the horses of London were in any grave or immediate threat of eviction. If the subject was transportation, he was more curious about how Count Zeppelin's balloons and airships might change the skyline.

Soon they went into dinner, an intimate group of fourteen. Later Lenox would recall it as one of the nicest parties he could remember them having at this house on Hampden Lane—every person there a particular friend, no grudges between any of them, the courses rolling away under the sound of laughter, the night cooling until they were all comfortable. Dallington was on especially good form. He told a long and excellent story about the valiant but unsuccessful attempts of a friend visiting America to go upstate, thwarted continuously by the city of New York's system of public conveyance, that culminated in the fellow staring forlornly at the retreating metropolis as he sailed directly and unintentionally south.

When the supper was finished, the men and the women remained together rather than dividing, by common agreement, and they sat up for another hour or so, drinking brandy or iced wine, sitting in small clusters around Lady Jane's drawing room. At last their energies began to flag. Edmund and Molly went home first, the two brothers making a plan to meet for lunch the next day at the Athenaeum Club, and shortly after them went Emily and George in separate carriages, and after that everyone decided that it was time, alas, for the evening to end.

When the last guests had gone Lenox closed the door behind him. "Are you awake?" he said to Jane, who was standing in the soft light of the front hall

"Just scarcely," she said. She smiled sweetly and gave him a fond kiss on the cheek. "What a wonderful evening, Charles. Thank you."

"No, thank you. Look, is this Dallington's cloak, though? He's forgotten it, the fool. I'll run it out to him."

Lenox opened the door and went onto into the cool evening. He hesitated on his steps, looking up and down across the spaced yellow pools of the gaslight. Then he saw that toward the right of the house two figures were standing very close together, holding hands. One of them laughed, the sound of it ringing in the empty street, and he realized with a shock that it was Dallington and Polly.

After a beat, he smiled, then stepped back into the house with the cloak. It could wait until the next day to find its way again to its owner. He closed the door behind him as quietly as he could—his heart filled with happiness.